About the Author

Mira V Shah is a writer, former City lawyer turned legal editor and the proud owner of three good dogs (and one feral cat). She is the daughter of Indian–African parents and lives in north London with her husband and the pack, merely a few miles from where she grew up, although she often dreams about retiring in Italy should her intermittent lottery entries prove successful.

Follow Mira on Twitter and Instagram: @ShahVMira

Her

Mira V Shah

HODDER

First published in Great Britain in 2023 by Hodder & Stoughton
An Hachette UK company

This paperback edition published in 2023

2

A CIP catalogue record for this title is available from the British Library

Paperback ISBN 978 1 399 70122 8
eBook ISBN 978 1 399 70123 5

Typeset in Sabon MT by Manipal Technologies Limited

Printed and bound in Great Britain by Clays Ltd, Elcograf S.p.A.

Hodder & Stoughton policy is to use papers that are natural, renewable and
recyclable products and made from wood grown in sustainable forests. The logging
and manufacturing processes are expected to conform to the environmental
regulations of the country of origin.

Hodder & Stoughton Ltd
Carmelite House
50 Victoria Embankment
London EC4Y 0DZ

www.hodder.co.uk

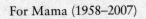

For Mama (1958–2007)

Part One
The Arrival

Three months before

The house draws me in like a magnetic force. Standing tall and proud. Picture perfect. As if every single brick has been immaculately polished, emitting a warm orange glow that fizzes through my fingertips. I take my time walking towards it, easing myself into every step. Listening to the sound of my four-inch heels clicking on the pavement, my long cashmere coat brushing up against my bare legs. I tilt my head to the side, catching the scent of my freshly blow-dried hair, bursting with honeydew and coconut. Asda's finest.

He stands outside in a pressed navy suit stretched tightly over his stocky frame, with slicked-back hair, a touch too wet. He's younger than he sounded on the phone. This must be his first big-ticket sale. I bet he can almost taste that 2.5 per cent commission.

As I edge closer, he looks up, unable to stop himself from raising his eyebrows. I know what he must be thinking: *This can't be her, can it? I expected someone different.* 'Mrs Rhodes?' he asks quickly, before offering me a limp, clammy palm.

'Please, call me Serena. Paul?' I don't recognise my own voice. It seems different somehow, as if squeezed out through pursed lips. My palms start to itch and my cheeks flush red hot. What if he can see right through me? That I don't belong here – looking to buy this house, in this neighbourhood. I'm already five minutes late, and I notice the irritation crinkling his brow. I'm about to apologise, but manage to swallow it down, because that's not what Serena would do. Instead, I pull myself together, standing a little taller.

'Great.' He nods, gesturing towards the building like a showman. 'So, this is it. Number 11. As you might expect, with the kerb appeal, space for three cars in the driveway and close to the sought-after Highgate School, we've had a lot of interest in this one.' He turns towards the house and struts down the pristine mosaic path that I already know so well.

As I follow him, my eyes hover over all three storeys of the stunning orange brick, before resting on the royal-blue front door with the chunky brass knocker.

'Properties like this don't come up that often, even in Highgate.' He continues his spiel, speaking at a hundred miles a minute, piling on the pressure. But I'm prepared for it. 'We had an open day on Saturday. Several offers close to the three-million mark. You're lucky they were all rejected.'

I detect a little frustration in his voice, but he offers up a playful wink, as if he's letting me in on a secret. As if we're in this together.

God. Now I get why people can't stand estate agents.

'How soon can you move? You said you were chain-free?'

My gaze lingers on that royal-blue door, and he clears his throat when I don't immediately respond.

'That's right,' I say quickly, remembering that today I'm Serena – millionaire, power woman, serious house-hunter. 'We're renting a penthouse near London Bridge,' I say deadpan, fiddling with my wedding band. 'Walking distance from the office.'

'Ah, it's *very* nice round there.' He pauses, studying my expression as if suddenly unsure of himself and seeking guidance. 'So, bigger house, quieter neighbourhood – you're looking to start a family, then?' I ignore him, taking in the immaculate driveway, from the twin lollipop-shaped bay trees framing the front door to the wrought-iron gate leading to the two-hundred-foot back garden. 'Well,' he rattles on, as though I've acknowledged his question, 'you're in for a real treat. The sellers have lived here for almost fifteen years, but only did it up last summer. They've been splitting their time between here and Cannes, but decided to settle out there permanently when the children started university. You know how it is,' he says casually, as if everyone flies out to Cannes when their children start university.

I sigh deeply, almost choking on my impatience.

'Sorry I have this tendency to ...' he mumbles, lowering his gaze and clicking his tongue, before pulling out a key from his pocket and inserting it into the keyhole.

The entrance is even more perfect in real life. Natural light pours through the huge bay windows and down the white-washed hallway, bouncing off the Victorian covings. The ceiling is so high you could skydive from it. My eyes widen, and when I catch them in the mirror, I'm terrified that I've exposed myself.

As we continue inside, Paul taps my arm. 'Sorry, Mrs Rhodes. The owners have respectfully asked that we take our shoes off ... if you don't mind.' He shuffles off his own shiny brogues awkwardly. 'The parquet flooring is brand new.'

Reluctantly, I remove my heels, feeling my identity shrinking along with my height.

Paul guides me around every inch of the house's two-thousand-plus square feet, rarely leaving my side, but remaining silent for the most part, letting me take it all in. The spacious living room with a bespoke EcoSmart fireplace. The state-of-the-art kitchen with an enamelled lava countertop, high-spec and showroom-clean. The curved terrazzo staircase leading up to four grand double bedrooms, and a fifth en-suite bedroom in the loft. All dressed in luxurious shearling carpet and 100 per cent organic linen curtains, Paul revels in telling me; and designer light fixtures hang from the lofty ceilings that I'm sure wouldn't look out of place in a Soho gallery. I utter a soft, satisfied groan, picturing Serena living here amongst all this space and grandeur. Imagining her spending a leisurely Sunday morning lying in a grand king-sized bed, a cup of Earl Grey tea warming her palms as she riffles through the weekend papers, or sitting at the kitchen island, gazing out onto her crisp, freshly cut lawn while planning her next adventure.

As we walk back into the hallway, Paul scurries ahead to use the downstairs toilet, and I make the most of these few moments alone. I pluck a single leaf from a giant ficus tree (even the plants are extravagant here) and place it in my pocket. I run my hands over the crystal-clear windows, pausing for a few moments to stare at my barely there fingerprints before wiping them away with the sleeve of my coat.

We reconvene outside, Paul rubbing his hands together, smelling like a meadow – of course, the owners wouldn't think twice about leaving posh hand cream out for house viewings. 'So ... what do you think?' he asks, grinning like a Cheshire cat.

Stay non-committal, Rani. Non-committal. 'I like it,' I say casually, as though I visit houses like this all the time. 'But we have a couple more to see, and of course, my husband needs to visit.' I stress the word 'husband' to convey that he's the key decision-maker, setting up an explanation as to why this viewing won't lead to an offer.

'Are the other places in Highgate as well?'

I shake my head. He probably has the local market imprinted on his brain.

'How well do you know the area?' he asks.

'A colleague moved here recently, but otherwise not very well.' I glance across the road, growing anxious, wondering if anyone will recognise me, dressed in an outfit I would never normally wear.

'Well, let me tell you, you won't find a better neighbourhood. A real village feel, but in Zone 3. People actually speak to each other. See that lady over there,' he says, waving in the direction of the street, 'she's said hello every time I've been here.'

I swivel round, making sure to keep my back to the street, pretending to take in the house one more time.

'Such a friendly place,' he continues, looking me up and down. 'Trust me. You'll fit right in.' But his eyes scamper away, betraying him.

I feel my jaw tighten. 'Right, I'd best shoot off,' I say, looking at my phone as if I have somewhere else to be. 'I'll be in touch.'

He moves to offer his hand again, but quickly decides against it. 'If you like it, you'll have to act fast,' he says. 'A house like this will be snapped up in no time.' Then he turns towards the street, and I do the same, keeping my head down. 'Nice to meet you, Mrs Rhodes,' he says hurriedly, before dashing off towards a lime-green Mini.

I head in the direction of the station, but continue to glance behind me. Paul is already tucking into a meal-deal sandwich his eyes fixed on his phone, scrolling, a smile break-ing across his face. When I'm sure he's not watching, I stop, remaining completely still for a few lingering breaths before turning round and walking briskly back towards the house. But instead of continuing down its tiled front path, I cross the road to the building opposite. It resembles number 11 in style, but the once-identical orange bricks have faded to a dull brown and the paintwork is chipped, spots of rust crusting at the edges.

I pull out a set of keys from my handbag and insert one into the lock, jerking it from side to side until eventually it fits. Then, stepping into the porch, I slam my back against the door and kick off my heels to lightly massage my ankles. It's been so long since I've worn shoes like this. With my spare hand, I pick up the pile of post, then hobble up the three flights of stairs to our top-floor flat. My heart sinks as I see the dirty plates piled high in the sink, the countertop smeared with dried pasta sauce, the laundry basket overflowing with crumpled shirts and school uniforms. I picture the pristine kitchen island at number 11, which now feels like a million miles away.

In our bedroom, I strip off the cashmere, silk and organic cotton I paid for on credit, careful not to rip the tags. I coax the cheap gold-plated band from my finger and toss it into a drawer, before collapsing on the chair by the window.

This is where I have the best view of the house.

Staring out onto the mosaic pathway, I notice that Paul is back. Hands in the air, a smile plastered on his face, going through the motions like a wind-up toy. My gaze flits to the couple next to him. I can only see their behinds, but the woman is tall and slen-der, with smooth golden hair and a classic Chanel bag hanging off her shoulder. The man is dressed all country chic in slim-fit navy jeans and a Barbour hunting jacket. *They* look like they belong here. As Paul leads them towards the house, I can see his smile is wider, his movements more expressive – he already knows that these two are the real deal.

When the front door shuts behind them, I stumble over to the bed, eyes growing heavy, about to close. And as I sink my body into it, curling tightly into a ball, the image of the house across the street follows me into my dreams.

Natalie

'Here we are at last, Mrs Riley. I can't stop saying it,' he purrs at me, rubbing my bare shoulder as we turn into the driveway of our new home, the roof all the way down on his red Maserati, classic jazz bursting from the speakers. Charles always knows how to arrive in style.

I watch the removal men emptying the van of our boxes and furniture, huffing and puffing under the weight of them. I grip the handle, my fingers shaking with nervous excitement, taking in the royal-blue front door with the chunky brass knocker.

'Where do you think you're going, young lady?' His warm breath tickles my ear. I smell whisky and oranges. But before I can say a word, he slides both our seats back, bends over and scoops me out of mine.

'Charles! Stop!' I giggle up at him, squealing with pleasure, lightly kicking my feet and slapping his arms playfully. 'Put me down. Put me down. What will our neighbours think?'

'Who cares! Let them look at you,' he says, swinging me around before stepping triumphantly out of the car and carrying me down the mosaic path. 'My *perfect* wife.'

The removal men stop to stare at us, nudging each other. One of them wolf-whistles loudly, and I feel my cheeks grow hot, but Charles's eyes only widen with pride. 'So, tell me … what do you think? Is it just as you remember from the viewing?' he asks, lowering me onto the smooth parquet flooring.

I allow myself a moment to take it all in. Gasping in wonder at the majestic terrazzo staircase, the whitewashed walls, the bay windows flooding the house with light. I peer up at the ceiling, where shadows shimmer over the original Victorian cornices – and suddenly my body is ice cold as the rounded shapes morph into disfigured faces and the long, thin branches outside resemble witches' fingers. I can't explain how or why, but it feels as real to me as a memory.

It's nothing. Of course, it's nothing. I'm exhausted from work and my mind is playing tricks on me.

Focusing my attention back on Charles's handsome face, I pull him towards me, seeking stability and warmth. 'Thank you,' I whisper as the men pile our boxes up high. But I can still feel my pulse racing. What am I walking into?

We started house-hunting a few months ago, just the other side of Hampstead Heath in Belsize Park. Charles's best friend, Seth, lives there with his wife, Darcy, and their two children, so he knows the area well. But late one evening at work, I started playing around with the location field on Rightmove, just to see what else might be available in our price range, and saw the words that made my heart leap from my chest like an escape artist. *Priory Gardens, Highgate.*

I clicked on the entry and zoomed in on the profile of the house. There were so many features, from the striking orange brick to the mosaic footpath, that moved me in a way quite incomprehensible. It felt like I was looking into the eyes of someone whose face I recognised but was unable to place.

The next day, I left work early to view it on my own. I had no expectations – I just wanted to see where my instinct would lead me. But as I followed the estate agent into the hallway and stared up at the enormous oak tree in the garden, I felt something awaken deep within my bones.

This was no ordinary house. This was my childhood home, a home from a past I'd long forgotten. It was fate – what else could it be? With Charles by my side, I was finally in a good place, loved and secure, and buying this house was a real possibility. My past and my present seemed to be joining full circle, and I felt excited – fuelled by a hopeful sense of belonging that I was ready to explore. Eventually, I would tell Charles the truth about this house; about my life. And I had faith that everything would be okay.

Charles directs the movers into the living room. I hear them laughing and joking around like they're the best of friends. I'm about to join them when I feel my phone buzzing in my trouser pocket. Work, probably. A disgruntled client? A demanding partner? It wouldn't be the first time on my day off.

I quickly answer it, barely looking at the screen. 'Natalie speaking,' I say, on autopilot, preparing myself for the worst, but it's a familiar high-pitched voice that greets me instead.

'Hello, darling. I just thought I would check in to see how moving day is going.'

Mum. Of course, she'd have today marked in her diary. She's been that way since I was a child. There for every match, every competition. Cheering me on from the front row, my greatest champion. She'd *never* forget today.

'Oh, hi, Luella,' I say, as enthusiastically as possible. The last time I called her Mum was before her fiftieth birthday. She went through a bit of a mid-life crisis, hiring a nutritionist, a dermatologist, and a personal trainer, demanding that I call her Luella from then on. She may feel old, but she certainly doesn't look it. Mum is one of those women who seem to bypass time, like a Hollywood sweetheart. A part of me thinks she's going to live forever.

'We've just arrived.' I sigh, walking away from the noise. 'Boxes everywhere. It's absolutely …' I hesitate, remembering who I'm speaking to. 'It's fine. I'm sure we'll be unpacked and settled in a day or two.' Over the years, I've become so used to sugar-coating the truth, especially for her, and the last thing I want is for her to invite herself over. Just hearing her voice makes me realise that I need more time.

'Why don't I come and help anyway? It'll be fun. Where is it you've mov—'

Too late. 'No, no, we'll be okay,' I quickly interrupt her. 'Let's wait until all the furniture has arrived,' I add, raising my voice and pressing the phone against my ear, trying to block out the laughter from the next room.

'If you're sure, darling. Sounds like you have company, anyway.'

'It's just the movers. You know Charles … always the life of the party.'

At the mention of his name, he pokes his head around the door, mouthing, *Who's that?* I see the frown lines creep up his forehead.

'Just a minute,' I say, holding the phone away from my ear. 'It's Luella.'

'Say hello from me.' He smiles, tight-lipped, before clearing his throat. 'Darling, the movers are leaving.' His tone is firm, purposeful.

'Charles says hi. I hope you don't mind, but I think I had better go.'

'Don't worry, sweetie, I've got to crack on with the salmon anyway. Gosh, first a wedding on the Italian Riviera, and now a house in London. Look how far you've come. I'm so proud of you, Natalie.'

I stare up at the ceiling, that same spot that sent my pulse running riot. Soon she'll know: that I haven't come far at all. That I'm merely at the beginning.

Rani

'Steady on, Rani ... save some for the rest of us!' Sasha grins at me with pearl-white teeth. Teasing what's left of the Sicilian lemon gin out of my grasp before turning her back on me to swap corporate law war stories with Joel's old flatmate, Aman.

I slump deeper into my seat, staring at the solitary drink in front of me while listening to the threads of conversation that I'm not part of: rants about slave-driving bosses and measly pay rises; summer holiday plans and the latest restaurant openings in town. Sasha's pashmina snakes off her chair, falling into my lap. I run my fingers over the softness of it, remembering the way that cashmere coat brushed over my legs. How incredible it felt to possess something so luxurious, even with the tag digging into my shoulder blades, even knowing that it wasn't really mine. But this feeling soon passes, crushed by reality – the rejection email I received this morning. *Thank you for your interest in our company, but after careful consideration, we have decided not to progress further.* A polite 'fuck off', just like all the rest. Why do I bother?

Taking one last gulp, I sit up straight and stare hard at Joel across the table. 'Come on. Look at me,' I mutter under my breath. 'I need you.' Just one glance to numb the sting of it. But he doesn't see me. His pensive eyes are glued to Amber's gorgeous face, their voices muffled by the alcohol. I watch them, a little envy creeping up my throat. *They look good together, don't they? Much better matched than you and him.* Amber at the head of her reclaimed-elm dining table, holding court in a tropical-print maxi dress and blood-orange lips. Joel with his floppy dark-blond hair and golden skin. Ricardo the bodybuilder, Amber's current squeeze, sits beside her, curling his burly arm around her waist, dropping kisses on her tanned shoulder, which is turned away from him. I wonder if he notices it too.

Joel scratches the back of his head before adjusting his tortoiseshell-rimmed glasses. He does this when he's nervous. I prick up my ears, trying to catch their conversation. I hear my name just as the alcohol gushes into my bloodstream and my head starts to spin. 'What was that?' I exclaim, louder than I intended.

They all stop and stare at me.

'You just said my name, Joel?'

'Oh, it's nothing, Rani.' Amber giggles, answering for him. 'I was just reminiscing about our university days. I can't believe how much we've all changed!'

Not here. Not now. As if I need another reminder of what a disappointment I've become. Tears prick at my eyes, but I wipe them away with the back of my hand before standing up and throwing myself into the space between Sasha and Aman. 'Don't you just *love* this song? Come on, let's dance! You can talk shop any time.' Grabbing Sasha's hand, I try to hoist her up, but I do it with such force that I lose my balance and stumble into her lap.

'Jeez, Rani. What's got into you?' she chides, flicking her long, thin braids out of her face.

'Don't be so boring, Sash! I can't tell you the last time I was drunk enough to dance. Plus, don't you want to impress what's-her-name?' I nod my head in the direction of the only stranger in the room: a petite flame-haired beauty who is clearly the result of Amber's attempt at playing Cupid. 'She's hot. And just your type,' I mouth.

Sasha breaks into a coy smile, placing a hand loosely over my lips. 'Okay … okay, I'm coming. But only if you keep shtum!'

I lead her out onto Amber's spacious terrace, stumbling over terracotta pots of lemon and olive trees. Sasha collects Amber on the way out, and soon it's just the three of us again, swinging our hips like there's no tomorrow. My shoulders loosen as the memories come flooding back. How they found me lying on the sticky floor of the student union on our first night at Oxford, hoisted me up and stroked my hair as I cried hysterically in their arms. I'd just been told about Mum's diagnosis. The odds weren't great, and I could feel my world crumbling around me. But they supported me every step of the way, to the brutal end. Camping out in my room, feeding me spoonfuls of pesto pasta, washing my hair and singing me to sleep as the grief took hold. How quickly we became the best of friends. Rarely seen without each other.

Wild with bittersweet nostalgia, I shoot them a cheeky smile before opening my mouth wide and howling into the night sky. 'Aaaaaaaaaaaaah-ooooooooooooh!'

'Rani!' Amber's voice is knife-edge sharp as she pulls me towards her, covering my mouth with the palm of her hand, her face dead serious. 'Shh. You're going to piss off my neighbours!'

I catch Sasha sighing loudly. Ignoring her, I nudge and wink at them both. 'Ugh, don't be such party poopers, guys.

Come on! Why can't we have fun, like old times?' I ask, my words slurring out of me.

Sasha scoffs. 'Girl, this isn't you. What's going on?'

I grin, lunging towards her and wagging my finger in her face. 'Oh, I *can* be fun, Sash, if I want to be. Remember that house I told you about?'

'What house? Oh, you mean the one opposite you?' Amber looks at me, curious.

I nod my head to the music. A cool shiver dashes down my spine as I realise that I've caught her attention. 'Well, I didn't tell you at the time, but I went to see it.'

'What? How? Didn't they realise you live in the flat across the road?'

'Nope,' I say confidently. 'I made up a name. Went shopping in Reiss and pretended to be some hot rich chick.' I hold out my hand and fake-pout. '*Serena Rhodes*, pleased to meet you.'

'That's so intense, Rani,' Sasha exclaims, rolling her big Bambi eyes. 'Why didn't you just stalk it on Rightmove like everyone else?'

'Obviously I did that *first*. But it wasn't enough, Sash. I had to see it in person. Walk around it as if it were mine.' I'm beaming, looking at them, searching for understanding, intrigue, companionship in their faces. Something.

Amber's expression turns sour, and I feel my cheeks flush as I realise how she must see me. 'Yeah ... okay,' she says, sounding unconvinced. Her parents bought her this three-bedroom maisonette overlooking Clapham Common as a graduation present, because she couldn't possibly rent somewhere. I can barely imagine what it feels like to have disposable income, let alone a house that is all mine. 'But Reiss?

Rani, can you even afford that? Joel's worried about ...' She stops mid-sentence.

'What did Joel say?'

She grimaces, and I turn around, seeing Joel with my coat in his hands.

'Come on, my Bollywood Cinderella. It's almost midnight. I bet you the babysitter's already watching the clock.'

We say our hasty goodbyes, kissing cheeks and promising to catch up soon. Although with their hectic schedules, who knows when that will be. Joel wanders out of the door without me, towards Clapham Common station, and I sprint to catch up with him. 'Hey! Wait up!'

I follow him onto a waiting train and flop into an empty seat. I start to feel dizzy under the fluorescent lights, so I lean back and close my eyes, willing the carriage to stop spinning around me.

'That bad, is it?' He laughs. 'You're going to be paying for it tomorrow morning.'

'Ugh. Don't ever let me drink again.' I see the almost empty bottle in front of me, and Joel and Amber sitting across the table, whispering softly to each other. 'Hey,' I say, lightly patting his hand. 'Why were you talking about me?'

He turns his face towards mine. I notice faint bags under his hazy eyes. 'Oh, Rani. It was nothing. What Amber said, a passing comment about your uni days. How different you all are now,' he says, scratching the back of his head again.

But I can tell there's more. 'And ...?'

He nods slowly, clearing his throat. 'She's ... we're just worried about you.'

'What?' I snap, more loudly than I intend to. A man dozing opposite suddenly wakes up and glares at us. 'Ugh. Amber's so dramatic.' I don't need their pity. I don't need anyone's pity. 'Look, Joel. Next time you feel the need to talk about me, just come straight to *me*, okay?'

'But Rani, I've tri—'

The man opposite groans angrily, but I don't care. I need Joel to understand. 'And another thing. You don't think it bothers me too that I'm almost thirty and unemployed, that I haven't made something of my life? I made that choice, Joel. You know how much I love our girls, how I'd do anything for them, but having them changed *me*. No one else. Only *I* have to live with that, only *I* have to accept that. I just wish people would stop going on about it.'

His forehead creases as I speak.

'Look, I'm sorry,' I mutter, swallowing the bitter taste in my mouth. I have to stop resenting him for a decision I made. 'I didn't mean to have a go at you. It's been a long week.'

'Rani, I get it,' he says, looking away. There's silence for a second, and all we can hear is the man's snores. 'How's the job hunt going? Any interviews yet?'

But he still doesn't understand. This is about so much more than a stupid job. Mum and Dad left India the day after they got married. They arrived here with nothing; they knew no one. People spat at them in the street, shopkeepers refused to serve them. But they stayed, they hustled, working sixteen-hour days scrubbing dirty toilets in seedy hotels in the hope of giving their children a brighter future.

Then I had to go and ruin it all.

Natalie

He lies next to me, deep in sleep, our luxurious velvet quilt rising and falling to the rhythm of his body. I study his handsome features. Thick chestnut-brown hair you can lose yourself in, a chiselled jaw that takes years off his fast-approaching forty years. But it wasn't his looks that reeled me in. It was an instinct.

From the moment he fixed his piercing green eyes on me, I knew that I belonged to him.

The floor underneath us is a sea of cardboard boxes, filled to the brim, taped firmly shut. It feels strange to be surrounded by chaos. Charles's Bloomsbury penthouse was always pristine, not an item out of place, not a speck of dust in sight. On the night we met, nine months ago in the rooftop bar of the Shard, he invited me back to his for a nightcap. I remember thinking that it must be a bachelor pad he maintained in town for entertaining purposes, while his real home was a country estate somewhere in the sticks, complete with a wife, three children and a subservient hound.

It was supposed to be a fling, a one-night stand, just like all the others. I drank in the explicit flirtation, the warmth of touch on my naked skin; a taste of what it would feel like to be loved, but without the expectation. I could never live up to the expectation. I didn't envisage seeing him again, let alone being the woman he chose to marry. But when he pursued me, promising me a life I'd always dreamed of, I wanted to believe in it. I wanted to believe that I deserved a happy ending.

I sense movement beyond my eyelids, vibrations in the air around me. My eyes are still hazy with sleep, but I force them open, expecting to see Charles's handsome face.

But the first thing I notice is the cornicing encircling the light fitting above my head. It looks so familiar. The indentations remind me of a set of tiny, crooked teeth, locked in a sneer. And then I see her, staring back at me. Little more than a blur, except for deep-set eyes and thin, curved lips.

'Leave me alone!' I yell, suddenly wide awake, my heart thudding in my chest. I push her away from me, burying my head under the pillow to drown it all out. To drown her out.

Why is she here? What does she want?

Footsteps hurry towards me. A firm hand grips my shoulder. 'Natalie?' His voice is soft, concerned. 'What's wrong? Wake up, my love, wake up!' I turn onto my back, lying still to catch my breath as he smooths down my wispy bed hair. 'Did you have a bad dream?'

I nod my head, because I can't find the right words. Because a bad dream is the only explanation.

'It's okay, you're okay now,' he assures me, kissing my forehead and settling down on the bed next to me.

I clutch his arm, still gasping for breath. 'Where did you go?'

But he doesn't respond, just runs his fingers over my silk nightdress, grazing the top of my breasts before winding slowly down towards my stomach.

I gulp down warm acid, mentally preparing to make my excuses and disappear into our en-suite bathroom to tidy myself up. But before I can say a word, he holds me still, fixing his gaze on mine.

'Charles, what's going on?'

He places a firm finger on my lips and whispers, 'Hush. One moment. I know what will make you feel better.' Then, reaching under the bed, he pulls out a wicker basket with a tea towel on top.

'What's this?' I ask, already rummaging inside, taking out a flask of what smells like freshly brewed coffee, a paper bag of soft peaches and a selection of warm pastries.

'Breakfast in bed. From the café opposite the station. I popped over there while you were sleeping.' He leans back on the headboard, watching me, his smile growing wider.

'Oh, how lovely,' I mumble. My appetite is gone, but I don't want to offend him, so I tear off a piece of pastry, forcing the sugary-sweet almond paste down my throat.

'Enjoy every mouthful, darling. I know you'll be sweating it off on a run soon anyway.'

As I take a sip of coffee to wash it down, he pulls back the quilt and takes my free hand in his, stroking my newly polished wedding ring. 'Promise me just one thing, Nati,' he says, catching my gaze. I pause, waiting for him to continue, my heart racing. 'Promise me that we'll always be like this.'

I craft my mouth into a reassuring smile. Then, leaning in, I kiss him longingly, deeply, so he doesn't notice the panic in my eyes.

Rani

'BOO!' Lydia and Leela jump out from behind a tree, falling to the ground in fits of giggles as Joel pretends to run away screaming.

His face is beaming. I can't bear it.

'Mummy, Mummy, we scared Daddy!' Leela tugs on my leggings to get my attention.

'Yes, I saw, sweetheart,' I mumble with feigned enthusiasm, rubbing my eyes and wishing I had brought my sunglasses to hide behind.

We continue around Queen's Wood, on the same route that we always follow. I could walk it blindfolded, but the girls never seem to get bored. There's always something that intrigues their curious little minds: a stream flowing between footpaths after a day of heavy rainfall, a bouquet of fresh flowers left on a memorial bench, bushy-tailed squirrels chasing each other up thick tree trunks. And I envy them their innocence. How hopeful they are about their tiny corner of the world. Yet how little they know of what lies beyond it.

As they hop, skip and jump ahead, Joel hangs back, typing on his phone, his face crumpling with frustration. 'You're not going to believe it. They've taken my Year 11s from me as well! I thought the promotion would be a good thing, but …'

I tune out, distracted by a well-dressed couple walking towards us holding hands. They don't seem much younger than I am, but I feel ancient looking at them. So fresh-faced, and talking intently, as if in their own private bubble. I catch snippets of their conversation, something about taking a sabbatical and travelling around South America.

That could have been me.

'Rani, are you listening?' Joel moves towards me, pupils flickering with disappointment.

I shrug. I know I should say something to console him – if not words, then a smile or a nod – when really all I want to do is scream. What happened to us?

I dragged my feet out of Highgate station, down Shepherds Hill towards Joel's flat. I'd never felt so nervous, my stomach crumbling like molten rock. He knew I was coming, but he had no idea why.

I'd spent the whole train journey down from Oxford in the shaking toilet, in front of the dirty mirror, hating every inch of my ugly dark face. The same words taunting me, over and over. *Remember that night, Joel? How I told you I was on the pill, how I begged you to keep going? Well, I lied. I was just a pathetic little virgin ... and guess what?*

I rang the doorbell.

He sprinted down to let me in, his floppy dark-blond hair bouncing on his smooth forehead. 'Congratulations, chica – or should I say the finest trainee reporter the *Guardian* has ever seen!' He grinned, and my heart sank. 'So ... when do you start? You're going to be running that place soon, I just know it. Oh God, Rani, what's wrong?' His smile faded as he noticed the fear etched on my face.

I'd planned to ease him in gently, but when I saw his kind, sincere face, my fingers grasped the test in my coat pocket, and

I could hold it in no more. 'I'm pregnant, Joel. I'm pregnant!' I cried, before sinking to the floor.

For a second or two he just stared into space. Paralysed. But then, like clouds moving to make way for the sun, he crouched down next to me, wiping my damp face with gentle fingers. '*We're* pregnant.' He smiled, water collecting in the corners of his eyes. Whether they were happy tears or not, I didn't know. I may never know.

'But … but my job … you're …'

'I know. It's a lot,' he said, taking my hand and squeezing it tight. 'But it's you and me, Rani. We'll make it work.'

We head back as the scorching sunbeams penetrate the canopy of trees overhead. Solid in the air like dry desert heat. My body is slowly melting away, and I pause at the exit of the woods to wipe my hand over the sweat collecting on my brow.

Joel pulls off his backpack and the girls crowd around him, their tongues hanging out like thirsty dogs. 'Hang on, chicas,' he says, rummaging inside. 'I think Mummy needs this more than we do!' He pulls out a flask filled with home-made iced tea and pours me a cup.

As I gulp it down, our eyes lock. He reaches into his jeans pocket and teases out a crumpled tissue, leaning towards me as if he is going to wipe the damp space between my nose and lips. I feel nervous. My hands start to shake. It's been so long since we shared a moment like this. Then suddenly I snap out of it. Snatching the tissue from him, and turning and walking down the street towards our flat.

As I reach the driveway, I glance hastily at the house across the road. The cars I glimpsed this morning are still in the driveway. A Toyota Corolla next to what looks like a brand-new Maserati. I'm about to point them out to Joel, who is buried in his phone again, when I catch sight of movement behind the linen curtains in the loft conversion, and a hand pulling them open. My breath quickens in anticipation.

They've arrived at last. The new owners of my dream home.

I watch as a slender woman emerges from the shadows, a pashmina loosely draped over her barely-there nightdress. Is this the same woman I saw from my window that day? She looks younger than I thought, much too young to own a house like this. Joel and I have been saving up for years, but I doubt we could even afford the deposit on our tiny rented flat. I observe her smiling with wide, eager eyes, gesturing at someone not yet in view, and I can't believe that this is her just-got-out-of-bed face. Such smooth, translucent skin, not a blemish in sight, but it's her hair that I can't stop staring at, a thick golden mane that flows down past her shoulders.

At university, it was always Amber who turned heads, but even she has nothing on this woman, whoever she is. She belongs on the French Riviera, sunning herself on a million-aire's yacht – even this five-bedroom house in north London is not worthy of her.

I'm suddenly aware of my own appearance, wishing that I'd made more effort this morning. Dabbed some concealer over my wide-open pores, thrown on something vaguely flat-tering instead of Joel's vintage tee and an ancient pair of leggings. With every year that goes by, I care less about my appearance, I grieve less for my pre-baby figure. It's a form of acceptance that this is who I am now. Cellulite perme-ates my darkened skin like snake in the desert; stomach fat ripples over my C-section scar. My war wounds. A constant reminder of what my body went through to bring these two little people into the world.

I begin to turn away, realising I've been staring at her for longer than is socially acceptable. But then an older man appears behind her, wrapping his arms around her, planting kisses all over her slender neck. I think back to the woods, Joel and I locking eyes, and how quickly I pulled away.

I can't remember the last time we touched each other like that, and my mind runs away from me, piecing together the details of their lives. The intricacies of their body language ooze love and devotion, but there's something unnatural about her manner that intrigues me, almost as if she's putting on a show. I smile to myself, imagining him as a ludicrously wealthy banker and she as his ravishing trophy wife.

Feeling my cheeks grow warm, I fight my desire to stay with them. But it's a fruitless task. They have me, locked inside their intimate embrace. Almost as if it was meant for three.

Natalie

We're just about to leave the house when I hear my phone ringing in my Chanel handbag, a wedding gift from Charles. Luella. I hold it up to him and shrug.

'Your mother? Again?' he exclaims, tutting under his breath. 'Just let it ring out.'

'I can't. She's probably lonely.'

'Fine. But she's going to have to let go at some point.' He bends down and slides his feet into a pair of suede Tod's loafers. 'Besides, she's not alone. She has Gerald,' he mutters under his breath, barely convincing himself.

'Morning!' I sing down the phone, as chirpy as possible. 'We're just heading out to grab a bite to eat. Charles is here too.'

'Oh, how lovely. Why don't you pop me on speakerphone?'

'Umm …' I motion to Charles, smiling apologetically. He raises his eyebrows, mouthing, *Really?*

'Oh, Charlie, Charlie, Charlie. How I miss that handsome face.'

'Hello, Luella,' he says, eyebrows still raised.

'How are my favourite newly weds? And what glorious weather for your first full day in your new home. Speaking of which, I'm still waiting for my invitation …'

'Ha ha.' He glances at me, shaking his head. 'You know we'd love for you to visit. Just give us some time to make it homely first.'

I squeeze his hand gratefully as we cross the main road, the cars zooming past us. 'We have decorators coming next week,' I tell her, 'and most of the furniture won't be arriving until next month.'

There's a long pause at the other end. 'It's just ... well, you're all I've got. What's that, Gerald? Oh, shut up, you know what I mean.'

Poor Gerald. He's a nice man, worships the ground she walks on. He's always ferrying her around, from gym class to hair appointment, like her own personal chauffeur. But he'll never be enough for her. I don't think anyone will.

'Hi, Gerald!' I shout, feeling a little sorry for him. 'Look, why don't we arrange a date for us to visit you instead? Just until we get the house in order. Imagine you coming all this way for us to serve lunch on the floor!'

Charles shoots me a look, mouthing a firm *No*. I don't blame him. Mum can be a lot sometimes. At our wedding breakfast last month, she had one too many glasses of fizz and too few canapés under the blazing Italian sun. Just as Charles stood up to speak, she grabbed the mic off him and gave an impromptu speech of her own. 'Ladies and gentlemen, thank you all for coming. I'm the mother of the bride – I know, I know, you don't believe it. Most people think we're sisters. A few have even got us confused. I know Charles has made that mistake once or twice.'

His face turned bright red when she winked at him, but other than that, he took it well, laughing along with all our guests.

I mouth back, *Don't worry*, feeling confident that it won't happen. Our diaries are always jam-packed – when we're not at work, we're travelling, hosting dinner parties or attending one of the many black-tie events that we never seem able to get out of. Before we got married, I'd join Priya and Hannah from my office for the occasional after-work drink. There were a few friends from university too, who I'd meet for a pre-Christmas catch-up, but now I don't seem to have a moment free.

'That would be fabulous, wouldn't it, Gerald?' Luella's shrill voice bursts out of the phone, making me jump. I see Charles grimacing from the corner of my eye.

We cross Stanhope Road and turn left onto Hurst Avenue, which takes us all the way to Crouch End Broadway. The high street is swarming with people, all with the same idea of making the most of this wonderful spring weather, and as I weave in and out of the crowds, trying to keep close to Charles, Mum continues nattering away.

'Did I tell you I saw my old colleagues from the library last week? I showed them your wedding photos and we ended up going through the whole lot over lunch. I'm thinking of making an album,' she says proudly. 'There's a particularly stunning one of the two of you. You know the one I mean, Natalie? Just as the sun was setting over the palm trees. Roberta said it could have made the front cover of *Harper's Bazaar*!'

My skin tingles as her words wash over me. 'I'm sure she was just being nice,' I say quickly. 'Anyway, we're just outside the café now, so we're going to have to love you and leave you.'

'Of course. But before you go, I don't think you've actually told me where you've moved—' I quickly hang up the phone before she has a chance to finish, my heart beating double time.

Charles observes me curiously. 'Haven't you told her where we live?'

'No, not yet. And I'm in no hurry to do so – imagine her showing up on our doorstep with a family-sized suitcase!' I rub his shoulder affectionately, laughing the lie into the air around us, when really I feel my body growing tense just thinking about how she'll react when she finds out.

Rani

Freya's smooth, sun-kissed face beams at us from the laptop screen as she comically teaches the girls how to lunge and squat. 'Yep, that's right. Bend that knee. Now the other one.'

She's changed so much since she moved to Australia at the start of the year. Back on her feet, working as a fitness instructor at Barry's Bootcamp. I can picture her yelling motivational mantras at yummy mummies desperate to shed their unwanted pounds.

'You've got it, girlies! That's great!' She cheers, fist-pumping the air.

She was only sixteen when Mum died. Dad was an absolute mess, barely able to keep his head above water. Freya would text me late at night: *Dad's out again, Rani. I have no idea where he is. He's worn the same clothes every day this week. I don't think he's even showered.* Eventually he'd return, all bloodshot eyes and stinking of booze. I tried my best to check in with them, but if I'm honest, I was knee-deep in survival mode. As they lived out their every day in this house of death, Dad even sleeping in the same bed where Mum had drawn her final breath, I remained at Oxford in bittersweet denial. Throwing myself into university life, keeping myself busy from the moment I woke up with lectures, tutorials, clubs and socials. Anything to distract myself from the harrowing memories, the cruel ravages of cancer.

As the girls continue lunging, Freya sits cross-legged on the floor of her beach-view apartment. I can just about make out the greenish-blue sea through the window behind her. 'You would not believe how freaking *delicious* this man is! He's like a new breed. I could just bite into his—'

'Shh!' I whisper, pointing to the girls. She's talking about the new guy in her life, Will. From the glint in her tired eyes, I know they slept together last night. 'But I'm really happy for you. You seem different ... free.' She looks so much like Mum now, before she fell ill. Her wavy jet-black hair that never seemed to thin out, her warm cappuccino skin, with pockets of freckles around her delicate button nose. I try to fight the relentless grief, but one solitary tear escapes, trickling down my face.

'What's wrong?'

'It's nothing,' I mumble, a sob threatening to reveal itself. I rub my eyes and glance back at the girls, but they're still happily exercising. 'I've been struggling, Freya. I miss her ... I miss Mum' – I gulp – 'so much. I feel lost without her. My life ... it's nothing like I thought it would be. I thought I'd have it all figured out by now. I mean, I'm going to be thirty this year. Thirty!'

'Oh Rani,' she says softly, nodding her head. 'I understand. You know, I miss her too.' She leans towards the screen, almost touching it with her hand. 'I'm worried about you. Are you sure there's nothing else going on?'

I sigh, aware of the distance between us. 'It's everything, Freya. I love being a mum, of course I do, but I feel so pathetic. I spend every day at home, moping around, while everyone around me – Joel, Sasha, Amber, you – you're all out there living life. I mean, what kind of example am I setting for them?' I ask, nodding at the girls.

'God. I'm so sorry, I had no idea you were feeling like this. I've been so preoccupied with the move. But listen, Rani, you're incredible! When Mum died, you just kept going … and when you fell pregnant, you took it all in your stride again.'

I know she's trying to comfort me, but her words only make me feel worse, and the seal over my heart starts to melt away. Tears are flowing in abundance, and Leela immediately stops what she's doing and looks at me, her tiny forehead creasing with worry. 'Mummy, Mummy, are you okay? Do you need a hug?'

'Oh, I'm fine, darling. Happy tears,' I assure her, squeezing out a half-smile. I turn back to Freya. 'I'm sure it's just the crazy hormones talking.'

'Okay. But if you need someone to speak to, just call me. Any time.' She stares intently at me. 'And find something new that excites you, makes you feel alive. Remember how rubbish I was at sport? Well, look at me now. Honestly, it saved my life. Whatever it is, Rani, just do it.'

As we say our goodbyes, she promises to visit us next year. But we both know there's no likelihood of that, not unless one of us wins the lottery. Closing the laptop screen, I watch Lydia and Leela playing so happily together. My heart should be bursting with pride right now, but instead I just feel empty, like I've been bled dry.

Heading into the bedroom to put my laptop away, I spot our elderly neighbour, Jemima, in her front garden opposite, a pair of secateurs in one hand, the other resting on her lower back as she takes a break from trimming her prize-winning rose bushes. I nod at her, and she waves back at me before wiping her brow. I'm just about to turn away when I see two figures in the distance walking hand in hand. My heart leaps as I recognise their faces.

Without thinking, I grab a half-empty rubbish sack from the kitchen and sprint down the stairs. When I reach the drive, I open the dustbin in slow motion, one eye watching them gliding down the pavement towards me, heads held high, shoulders relaxed, bodies moving in unison, like models posing for a magazine. I'm so utterly transfixed that for a moment I forget how to breathe. I forget that my mouth is wide open.

As they move closer, a special kind of sweetness fills the air. Whiffs of Aesop soap and hand cream – Amber is obsessed with this brand. The initial rush I felt morphs into intense self-doubt as I imagine how they must see me. Greasy hair piled on top of my head. Gigantic panda eyes. I'm tempted to duck back inside, but it's now or never. They look like the type of people who lead busy lives.

The woman opens her mouth as if to speak, but decides against it just as her companion steps towards me. 'Hello, I'm Charles,' he utters in a plummy voice, before pulling her into a side hug. 'And this is my wife, Natalie. We've just bought the house across the road.'

'I saw you from the window this morning with your family,' Natalie pipes up, as light as a feather. She's dressed elegantly in slim blue jeans, ballet pumps and a timeless Chanel bag that probably cost more than everything in my wardrobe put together. Her face is glowing.

'Lovely to meet you both,' I gush, aware of how my accent has sweetened to match theirs. 'I'm Rani. I live in the top-floor flat with my partner, Joel, and our two girls. You know, it's so nice to see other young people moving here. We've struggled to make friends, apart from the ones we've met through NCT. Joel teaches at the local comprehensive, and I think he's sick of being asked to secure their kids a place. Anyway ...'

I realise that I'm babbling. Some people get tongue-tied when they're nervous, whereas I blurt out words like I'm playing a game of *Pictionary*. I feel mortified, replaying what I've just said. Friends? Why would they want to be friends with someone like me?

'We'd never actually been to Highgate until Natalie stumbled across her dream home here. It looks like such a lovely area, so different to the City.' Charles pauses. 'Listen, we don't want to keep you, and we've heaps of boxes to unpack.'

'Of course.' I nod, imagining an abundance of designer items.

Charles starts to turn, his hand placed firmly on Natalie's back.

'We must have you over for dinner one day!' she blurts out, unexpectedly, before eyeing Charles.

He freezes momentarily, a poker-straight face. 'Why yes, of course ... once we've settled in. Natalie's learning to cook and could do with the practice.' Then he laughs mockingly, his hand sliding towards her shoulder, giving it a squeeze.

Natalie smiles back, nodding her head, but her cheeks blush rose pink.

Up close, Charles commands a large presence. I knew men like him back at Oxford – white, public-school-educated, trust-fund babies. We called them 'the Unattainables'. Only a select few ordinary mortals crossed the line into their heavenly realm, and unsurprisingly, I, with my immigrant parents and Primark wardrobe, did not make the cut.

'That would be great!' I say, a touch too eagerly, already thinking about us gathered around that state-of-the-art kitchen island, sipping on rosé and tucking into olives and cheese from the local deli.

They're all smiles as they turn to cross the road. 'And if you have any questions at all about the area, you know where to find me,' I add to their backs, laughing nervously.

As I watch them heading up the tiled footpath to their front door, my whole body feels lighter, like a weight has been lifted off my shoulders. Natalie and Charles aren't that different from Amber, Sasha and the rest of the gang. Successful. Loaded. Child-free. But unlike my friends, they know absolutely nothing about me; they have zero expectations. This is my chance to have a taste of the life I've always dreamed of, to become the person I've always aspired to be. And that thought is nothing short of liberating.

Natalie

I'm in the cab on the way home from work, drifting off to the soft hum of the engine. It's so cosy in here, like a warm cashmere blanket wrapped around my shoulders. Just as I'm about to enter the world of dreams, we come to an abrupt stop.

'Don't get too comfortable back there, luv. You're home now.'

'Thanks, John,' I murmur, yawning. 'Can you charge it to the client account again?'

'Of course, I know the drill,' he chuckles, holding the door open for me.

As I stumble outside, the cool night air hits me, and I realise that he's parked across the road, outside the building where Rani lives. It been a few days since we met. I've spent most of that time in the office on a marathon disclosure exercise – head pounding, eyes twitching, reviewing document after document. I haven't had a high-profile case like this for months. Our legal team even made it into the national papers. I know this because Mum sent me a screenshot from *The Times* with my name highlighted in bright yellow. She'd cut and pasted the excerpt into a precious notebook that never leaves her side. *Our little book of achievements*. But still, Rani's troubled face, her sad, expressive eyes, have found their way into my mind. She intrigues me. How open she is with her emotions, how at ease she seems in spite of them, and I wonder what her secret is; I wonder how she can be so real.

Opening the front door, I tiptoe upstairs and into our bedroom, hovering over Charles's resting body, waiting for his semi-conscious grunt. Then, slipping out of my work clothes, I pull my phone out of my handbag and lay it on the bedside table. The screen lights up and I quickly cover it so as not to wake him completely.

It's 3.09 a.m. In just under four hours' time, the alarm will go off. I'll smear make-up on to a face I no longer recognise and drag myself back to the office to do it all over again. The Natalie before Charles wouldn't have bothered leaving the office at all. She would have spent those hours head-down on the desk, using the mouse pad for a pillow, or lying on one of the sleeping pods in the basement. She'd have done anything to avoid having to return to an empty flat, curling up under the duvet clutching a chilled bottle of vodka like a comfort blanket.

But now I have him, this generous, loving man who wants to give me everything, and I'm terrified. What if it was a mistake buying this house; if it's too much too soon? With work being all-consuming, and flickers of memories haunting me like a bad omen, I can feel my tightly wound composure slipping, darkness seeping through the cracks in my mind.

What if Charles starts to see the real me? What if I lose him?

I pull on my nightdress and slide down under the covers, nestling into the warmth of his semi-naked body. My head feels heavy and I'm looking forward to a few hours' rest after a long day. But just as I sink into sleep, I'm jerked awake by the sound of crying somewhere in the distance. Desperate and tortured, like an injured animal in the wild.

I glance at Charles, but he's sleeping peacefully. So I quietly slip out of bed and peer through the curtains, thinking that it might be a fox or a badger. But the street is deserted. There's nothing in sight.

Crawling back into bed, I lie still with my eyes closed, willing the sound to stop. I bury myself under the duvet, hoping to drown it out. But on it goes, through the night, faint yet relentless, like a dull ringing in my ears. And it dawns on me that maybe it's not coming from outside the house at all, but from inside my head.

Part Two
The Friendship

Rani

Thank you for your interest in our proofreader position. But after careful consideration, we regret to inform you that we won't be taking your application further on this occasion.

'Ugh. Not again,' I mutter, frustrated, slamming my laptop screen shut. Not that anyone can hear me.

It's the third rejection I've had this week with the same generic wording. For a job I didn't even want. Sometimes I feel like giving up, accepting defeat, but I need something to make the hours pass quicker between drop-off and pick-up. I need my own income instead of feeling like a teenager with a weekly allowance.

Pressing my hands over my eyes, I run them down my face, pulling at the skin. I breathe deeply in and out, before taking a long sip of sugary chai and jumping to my feet, psyching myself up for the school gates, for the cliques and the petty gossiping. I don't fit in anywhere amongst the uber-glam yummy mummies dressed head to toe in skin-tight Sweaty Betty, the career bitches who stride past me in their LK Bennett court shoes, tapping away at their phones, always in a hurry, and the huddle of pubescent French nannies who wouldn't look out of place walking the runway at London Fashion Week. I'm still that short, ugly brown kid who no one wants to be friends with.

It's a two-minute bus ride to the girls' primary school in Crouch End, but I always walk, even when it's raining. It's not like I'm ever in a hurry.

Pausing for a moment on our driveway, I fiddle with my phone, choosing a podcast to listen to. Something funny, I think, to drown out my thoughts. As I click play on a new Adam Buxton episode, I steal a look at number 11 in all its grandeur. I wonder what the owners might have in store for this evening – an art gallery opening in Soho, or perhaps a long weekend in the Cotswolds, while I'll be sharing last night's left-overs with Joel in front of an episode of *Seinfeld*.

As I set off down Shepherds Hill, Adam moaning in my ears about another first-world problem, I hear a voice behind me, calling my name.

'Rani!'

I turn swiftly around and see Natalie jogging towards me, wearing a tight-fitting sports bra and a pair of sheer black leggings. Her long golden hair has been tied into a high ponytail, accentuating her cheekbones. I sigh, noting my own oversized denim overalls and the same top I've worn all week.

'I thought it was you,' she says.

As she comes closer, I can tell there's something different about her today. Her complexion is glowing, but her eyes seem smaller, distant.

'Oh, hey.' I try to sound casual, when really, now that the initial surprise has ebbed away, I'm left with pure intrigue. 'Out for a run?' I ask, wondering why she's at home so early on a Friday afternoon.

When she reaches me, she stops to catch her breath. 'Yes … work has been full on this week, so I took the afternoon off to relax. What about you?'

I smile sympathetically, while thinking how naturally she associates running with relaxing when I can barely run for the bus. 'School run – the only running I do these days!' I laugh, blushing. *Was that even funny?* 'Sorry to hear about work. What is it you do?'

'I'm a lawyer ... for a US firm.'

Of course she is. How else could she afford a house like this? 'Oh, my friend Sasha is a lawyer. Corporate,' I add, wanting to contribute, pretend like I'm already in her world.

'Yes, there are a lot of us around.' She smiles, showcasing twin dimples to their full effect. 'Charles thinks I work too hard, but I love it. The fast pace, the pressure ... and the salary doesn't hurt! But it's become so difficult juggling everything lately. I've barely had any fun all week. Actually ...' Her eyes sparkle. 'We promised you dinner, didn't we! I know it's last minute ... you probably have plans, but if not, why don't you and Joel pop by?'

A rush of adrenaline shoots through me, and I pause, picturing that magnificent open-plan kitchen and the giant Crittall doors overlooking the two-hundred-foot lawn.

'Umm ... I think we're free, but honestly, I totally under-stand if you and Charles want some alone time.'

'No, it'll be fun,' she says, with a decisive flick of her ponytail. 'Oh, and bring the girls if it's too short notice for a babysitter. Charles adores children.'

The rejection email suddenly feels light years away.

'Shall we say seven-ish? And it's totally casual. Just come as you are.' She looks at her watch. 'Gosh, is that the time already? I'd better get going. See you tonight!' she exclaims, jogging past me.

I glance at my phone and realise I'm also running late, and quickly head to the bus stop just as the W7 pulls in.

'Do we have to go?' Joel grumbles, hanging up his blazer and suit trousers. 'I was really looking forward to vegging out on the sofa tonight.'

That's what we do every night, I groan in my head, teasing a brush through my tangled hair and rummaging in a drawer for concealer. 'She invited us, Joel. How could I say no? It'll be nice to have some local friends, don't you think?'

He grimaces at me before pulling on a plain black polo shirt and light-blue jeans – his signature weekend uniform. 'I guess … but Rani, have you *seen* their house? Just imagine what it's like inside.' I stay quiet, pretending to concentrate in front of the mirror. 'I mean, what if Lydia or Leela break something?'

'They're kids, Joel, not animals!'

We head downstairs, the girls skipping with excitement. As we cross the road towards number 11, Lydia stares at the house and then up at Joel.

She nudges him. 'Daddy, Daddy, why don't *we* live in a house like this?'

Hearing her words makes my heart sink. I know we've outgrown our tiny flat, but we can't afford to rent a bigger place with just one income.

'Maybe one day you will.' He grins at her. 'And then we can all move in with you!'

I lead them up the mosaic path, feeling the guilt take over as I recall the viewing with Paul the estate agent. What would Joel think of me if he knew? *But you're not Serena,* I quickly remind myself. *You are Rani, invited inside this house for the very first time.*

'So, it's Natalie, right? And … Charles?' Joel asks, jerking me back into real time.

I nod, worrying about what we'll say to each other, whether we'll have anything in common. 'She's a lawyer. I have no idea what he does. Something very well paid, I expect.'

Joel sighs. He had offers coming out of his ears after university, but he's a public-sector man, just like his father was. 'Better be a wine drinker,' he grunts, nodding at the bottle of red in my hands that we can't really afford.

I ring the bell. Almost immediately there's movement at the door, and it swings wide open. Natalie is on the other side, looking as radiant as ever in an emerald mini dress, her golden hair cascading over her delicate shoulders like garlands of flowers. If this is casual, I can't imagine what her dressy looks like.

Before she has a chance to welcome us in, the girls run past her, catapulting into the space around them like they finally have room to breathe. While Leela wanders down the hall in a world of her own, Lydia stops in her tracks as it dawns on her that she is somewhere unfamiliar. She turns back to face Natalie, staring at her in admiration. 'Hi, Mummy's friend. Thanks sooo much for inviting us.' Her eyes widen. 'Wow. You're sooo pretty. I hope I get to be just like you when I'm old.'

Natalie laughs as she bends down to Lydia's height, placing a finger on her button nose. 'I'm sure you'll be much prettier, but it's more important to be happy and loved.' She looks up at me and winks, before straightening up to introduce herself to Joel.

She really does have it all.

I start to take off my trainers, thinking about last time I was here.

'Oh, don't worry about that, we're getting this parquet floor removed soon. Charles thinks it's tacky,' she says casually, shimmying down the well-lit hallway into the open-plan kitchen. Jazz floods out of the surround-sound speakers, and there's a delicious aroma of spices in the air. 'Sorry about the mess. We haven't got around to unpacking everything yet.'

Joel and I steal a glance at each other, confused. There are several piles of boxes neatly stacked against the wall, but apart from that, it's spotless. 'Are you kidding? It's like a showroom in here,' he laughs. 'You should see our place. Toys everywhere. Dishes piled up high in the sink.'

I feel a punch to the gut.

'Oh, I can't take any credit. Magda, our cleaner, is a god-send.' She hesitates, as if a little uncomfortable. 'So, I've decided to go Moroccan this evening.' She spots the bottle of wine in my hands. 'Ooh, and this Rioja will go perfectly. Thank you. I'm not a big drinker, but Charles will love it. He's due back from work any moment now.'

As I help the girls onto the high stools at the breakfast bar and take out their colouring books, Joel wanders around the kitchen, observing the expensive-looking appliances and gadgets. 'Your house ... it's really something. My God, tell me that's not a Sub-Zero refrigerator? These things cost an arm and a leg!'

I shoot him a look, but Natalie smiles back at him. 'I have no idea; that's Charles's area of expertise. But I've cooked tonight, so you'll have to eat at your own risk!'

I'm surprised by how confident she seems now. When we first met, she barely said a word. 'It smells amazing, Natalie. And I love how you've made this place your own. Scandi chic.' I gulp, realising what I've just said.

'Oh, were you friends with the previous owners?'

Joel looks at me, confused.

'No.' I shake my head, hoping my expression doesn't give me away. 'We barely knew them. I just dropped round with some post one time.'

A key sounds in the door. 'There's Charles,' she says, rushing out of the room. 'Help yourself to the hors d'oeuvres. Oh, and there are some crisps for the girls. I won't be a moment.'

While Joel continues to explore, I quietly tuck into the assortment of breads, hummus and olives, straining my ears to listen to their conversation.

'Hi, darling. How was your day?'

'Fine. Long. Come here.' I imagine him caressing her face, planting kisses on her soft cheeks. 'Ah, you smell so good.' I hear the shuffling of shoes on the wooden floor. 'Oh, do we have company?'

'Didn't you get my message? I bumped into Rani … you know, from across the road? They've just popped in.'

'Oh. Right.' His voice drops and he clears his throat. I'm struggling to hear the rest over Leela and Lydia's crunching, and Joel's gasp as he examines yet another kitchen gadget. 'That's a shame … looking forward … two of us. You know …'

There's more rustling. Bodies colliding. 'Stop, Charles,' she squeaks, before softening it a little. 'Please stop, their children are here.'

'Well, I suppose … good practice for later …'

I hear muffled laughter, but after a minute or two, she's back in the room with us, her hair a little tousled and her cheeks flushed pink. He follows close behind her, a smug expression on his face.

After a round of greetings, we all sit at the kitchen island – apparently the Italian marble dining table is being hand-crafted as we speak. 'So, what's everyone drinking?' Charles asks, rubbing his hands together. 'Joel, you look like a wine man.'

'Actually, darling, they've brought a lovely bottle of Rioja.'

'Ah,' he says. 'Why don't we save that for another day? I've got just the thing for tonight.' He rummages in a cupboard and pulls out a wooden case. 'A vintage Château Cheval Blanc. Trust me, once you've tried this, you won't be able to drink anything else.'

I make a mental note to google how much it costs.

'None for me, thanks, I've got to catch up on some work tomorrow,' Natalie says, helping herself to a glass of elderflower pressé with a sprig of rosemary.

'My wife, she never stops. You'd think she was married to the job.' Charles winks at Joel as he pours the wine. It occurs to me that he forgot to ask what I wanted to drink. 'What is it *you* do, Rani?' he asks, handing me a half-full glass.

I feel my throat clamming up, my cheeks growing warm. The dreaded question that I knew was coming. 'I … I …'

'She's interviewing, aren't you, Rani? Now that the girls are both at school.' Joel smiles at me in a way I know is intended to be supportive but only ends up making me feel worse.

'Yeah. Something like that,' I mumble, taking a sip of the wine, thinking it tastes no different to the cheap stuff we drink.

There's an awkward pause, and I rack my brains for something to say. But I have nothing interesting to offer.

Charles sits down. 'Come on, let's not fill up on the hors d'oeuvres,' he says, looking only at me. Natalie has barely touched them. 'Who's ready for dinner? What's on the menu, Natalie?'

'Lamb tagine with apricots. It's your mother's recipe.' She smiles adoringly at him.

Joel eyes me. I start to feel a little sick. 'Umm …' I say. 'We're actually vegetarians.'

'What? All of you? Surely not.' Charles says. 'No one in their right …' He stops himself. 'Is it a religious thing?'

I'm used to people making this assumption. 'No. Just a personal choice. I've never eaten meat.'

'Oh well, never mind.' He pauses, swirling the glass of red in his hand, then looks up again. 'So you've not even been tempted to try it? A nice crisp pork belly or a juicy rump of lamb?' He smacks his lips together. 'You're missing out, I tell you. I'd rather die of starvation than give up meat! But then I'm a country boy at heart,' he adds, patting his stomach. 'Eat what you kill!'

There's a bitter taste in my mouth as warm acid shoots up my throat. I don't know what to say. I glance over at Joel, and he's lost for words too. His lips are tightly sealed, and I tell he's gritting his teeth.

'Oh God, how stupid of me!' Natalie exclaims, breaking the silence. She hits her forehead with the palm of her hand. 'I can't believe I just assumed like that, without even asking.'

'No, it's my fault,' I assure her, wishing I had said something before. But I was so surprised by her invitation, it didn't even cross my mind. 'Anyway, I'm pretty full up from the bread and hummus. You guys eat, though, we don't want the lamb going to waste.'

Leela stops colouring a butterfly pattern and nudges me. 'Did you say lamb, Mummy? You want to eat a baby sheep?' Before I have a chance to reply, to reassure her, she jumps out of her seat and bursts into uncontrollable wails.

'Leela, calm down. It's okay.' I laugh nervously before crouching down to her level and rubbing her tiny shoulders. 'It's not the same lamb we saw at the farm.'

'Of course it is, Mummy. *She* killed it,' she chokes out amidst her cries, pointing at Natalie, who has turned pale.

I don't know what to do. Stay and try to calm Leela down, or make our excuses and leave? The wails continue, and I'm just about to apologise when Natalie jumps out of her seat. 'Please stop, please stop,' she begs, head down, hands over her ears. 'It's too much.' Her voice is trembling.

I'm shocked at her outburst, but as I observe her, it's clear that there's something more to this. I don't think it's about Leela at all.

Charles rolls his eyes, like he'd rather be anywhere else. He looks like he's about to say something, but we don't give him the chance, picking up the girls and hurrying out of the house as quickly as we can, mumbling apologies under our breath.

It's over, I think, my heart deflating like a lead balloon. My chance to get close to her, to be part of her world. Before it even began.

Rani

'Get in my mouth,' I growl to a thick chunk of ricotta doused in red pesto that I've just spooned onto my plate.

'It's like you haven't eaten all week!' Sasha scoffs. I notice she's piled her long braids into a high bun, and wonder if that's her corporate look.

'Come back to me when you're living with two little people, okay? We only have bags of grated Cheddar in the fridge these days. Or Babybel. Ugh. Amber, hand me your plate. You're eating, right?'

'Duh. Give me *all* the cheese. Everyone at work seems to be on some ridiculous gluten-free, dairy-free, meat-free diet. Fun-free, if you ask me. I'm having to drink celery juice for lunch just to fit in when all I'm craving is a big juicy hamburger.'

Sasha and I eye each other. But then Natalie's face suddenly pops into my mind. Frozen in panic after Leela's wild accusation. I've been hoping to catch her on the street to apologise, but I've not seen her at all. It's like she's vanished into thin air. I really need to speak to Sasha and Amber about it tonight; get their perspective.

'Oh, sorry, Sash, you know I don't mean you. You're doing it for the animals. They're doing it to be trendy. It's completely different.'

'True. It does look tempting, though. Vegan cheese just doesn't cut it. Although I did have a great faux feta made from cashews the other day. Eight pounds a pot!'

'It's not like you can't afford it,' I mumble, my mouth full of cheese and bread – all the good stuff. She says nothing in response, and my heart sinks – I didn't mean it as a dig, but I do resent her success a little bit. The thought tugs on my chest, and I hurriedly change the subject. 'Anyway, thanks for coming to my neck of the woods tonight. I know Crouch End is a ball-ache to get to, and this place isn't exactly fancy, not like the restaurants you're used to in the City.'

Sasha brushes my arm. 'Nonsense, it's super-cute. I like the whole Italian deli vibe. And the wine is delish.' She takes a large gulp, as if proving her point. 'So, what's the latest on the job hunt. Found anything interesting?' She plucks a handful of cherry tomatoes off the vine and tears off a piece of focaccia to dunk into a pool of balsamic vinegar and olive oil.

I lower my eyes, chewing to buy myself some time. 'Ask me anything, literally anything, except that.'

'That bad, is it?' Amber glances at me sympathetically. 'Look, I know we must sound like a broken record, but we're worried about you.'

So we're back to this again, are we?

'It's *your* time now, Rani. To find your feet, start living for yourself.' She leans in, pointing at me affectionately. 'I know you're still in there somewhere.'

'I get it, Amber, okay? I'm trying!' I exclaim, feeling deeply patronised. I take a swig of the fruity red wine, letting it wash over the lump in my throat. 'Look, if you must know, I've been applying ... for jobs I could do in my sleep. But literally the next morning, I wake up to these shitty one-line rejection emails. I doubt they even read my application – probably take one look at the date I finished uni and hit delete. You have no idea how soul destroying it is!'

Amber touches my hand. 'Oh that sucks, Rani. I'm sorry. I didn't realise. But we've all been there. I had my fair share of rejections when we graduated. You just have to brush it off and try again.'

I bite my bottom lip. Why does she always have to make it about her? And anyway, it's hardly the same. She got a job with her PR mogul uncle after graduating with a third. I don't think she even had to interview. 'Anyway, what's the latest with you guys?' I ask, desperate to change the subject again. 'How's Ric, Amber?'

'Ohhhh,' she groans, her smooth forehead wrinkling a little. 'Your guess is as good as mine. The sex is so good, but I get the feeling that's all he wants me for. And I don't blame him. I mean, I was like that too once. But I'm not young any more. I want something more. I mean, hello? Body clock?'

Sasha's eyes light up. 'Wait. Hang on a second. Stop right there, pretty lady. Don't tell me Amber Rossi might finally be thinking about settling down!'

'Well … maybe. I mean, how gorgeous are Lydia and Leela? If I could just have one of them. Here's one Rani made earlier. Ha ha! Don't you think, Sash?'

'Me? Well, considering I'm not into men, I'm single, and this is the first Friday night in months I haven't had to work, I think babies are a long way off for me. I wouldn't mind coming home to a cute dog every night, though. But congrats, Amber. You're finally getting old.' Sasha winks playfully, her grin as wide as her face.

'Oi. Watch it, you!'

I hear them laughing and joking, but my mind drifts away towards Natalie. She has everything I've ever wanted – a successful career, a dream home, and, from what I overheard at the dinner party, she and Charles are thinking about starting a family. She's done it the right way round.

Sasha senses I'm not paying attention. 'Who are we kidding, Amber? Look who Lydia and Leela have as their parents. Honestly, Rani, you and Joel are amazing for creating those two. The dream team!'

I smile tersely, not sure what to say in response. 'Sure. We make it look so easy.' I shrug, my voice sharp, sarcastic, before taking another gulp of wine. 'Oh. Did I tell you I met the neighbours? You know, in that huge house. We went round for dinner,' I add.

Sasha's ears prick up. 'So … what are they like?'

'I mean, they have it *all*, and then some.'

'I'm not surprised, with a house like that.'

'Yeah. The woman, Natalie, seems lovely. Her husband, Charles, he's quite a bit older, I think. Super-posh … bit of a snob, actually,' I say, thinking of that bottle of red he pulled out as if it was nothing. I googled it when we got home, and it retails at over £500. 'He reminds me of that group at uni who basically walked around like they owned the place.'

'What did we used to call them again?' Sasha asks.

'The Unattainables.'

'Yeah. That's right. I remember one was all over Amber until he realised she was half Italian and not a purebred.' She laughs, punching Amber's shoulder jovially. 'You do know, though, they practically *did* own the place. Their families donated shit-loads to the colleges.'

'No way?!' Amber snorts, wine spraying out of her nostrils. She still looks amazing, though.

'But listen.' I raise my voice over theirs, eager to offload. 'It was mortifying, guys. Natalie made this lamb tagine and Leela started screaming – you know how she's animal-obsessed at the moment. Anyway, she practically accused the woman of murder!'

'Oh my God, Rani, that sounds like the dinner party from hell. I doubt they'll be inviting you around again in a hurry ... probably for the best, by the sounds of it,' Sasha says dismissively.

My face drops. I can't hide my disappointment, and take a long sip of wine to compose myself, just as the door to the restaurant opens and a light breeze fills the room. I notice Amber and Sasha glance at each other with wide eyes as they look behind me. Sasha lowers her voice a little. 'Speaking of posh white men, check out the one who just walked in.'

I turn around and quickly jolt back to face them. I can feel my cheeks burning. 'Guys, that's him,' I say in a hushed voice.

'Who?' they both ask at the same time.

'My neighbour. Charles.' I bury my face in my hands.

'Oh God.' Amber shakes her head, grinning. 'What are the chances! Well, why don't you go say hi, test the water? Maybe it wasn't as bad as you remember.'

'I can't, Amber. I'm so embarrassed.'

'Stop obsessing. It wasn't your fault, Rani. Leela's just a kid.' Sasha winks. 'I mean, you could just ignore him ... it's not like they live opposite you or anything!'

They both laugh, shaking their heads. I'm annoyed that they're not taking this more seriously, but Sasha's right, we're neighbours. It would be rude if I didn't pop over to say hello and, at the very least, find out how Natalie's doing.

I take a swig of my wine – Dutch courage – and turn around as if I'm about to call the waitress over. 'Charles!' I shout, leaning over the back of my wooden chair. 'It's Rani, from across the road. Do you fancy joining us?'

As he spots me, a hint of frustration pervades his features, but almost immediately he softens them, like a skilled artist painting over a blemish. 'Oh, that's kind of you, but I'm in a bit of a hurry, I'm afraid.' He utters quickly before turning away to talk to the woman at the counter, pointing at various items. Bread, cheese, olives, hummus. I study his body language, looking for clues. He seems distant, his movements stiffer than before, but I'm struggling to see his face properly and find myself standing up and walking over to him.

'That's okay, another time maybe. Anyway, I've been meaning to pop by the house to apologise for last Friday. Are you and Natalie about later this evening?' I'm at his elbow now. 'How is she?' *I've been worried about her*, I continue in my head.

His shoulders tense at my mention of her name. I catch him exhaling, short and sharp out of his nostrils.

The woman hands him a brown paper bag with a bottle of champagne and a loaf of ciabatta peeking out of it. He stays silent, tight-lipped, focused on touching his phone to the payment device. Then, just as he's about to leave, he turns to face me, his green eyes darkening ever so slightly.

'She's fine,' he says. 'Look, I really must go. Enjoy your evening, Rani.' Then he lifts his gaze up and over my head to Sasha and Amber, who are grinning behind me, and smiles softly back at them.

Natalie

The Northern Line rush hour is just about bearable on a Friday evening, free of the full spectrum of social butterflies, from the *just one* drinkers to those who intend to make a night of it. But the carriage still feels hot and stuffy, lacking in proper ventilation. I shake off my trench coat and collapse onto a seat that has just become available, opposite two young women in matching cream silk blouses, nattering away with wide, toothy grins on their faces. I pause, observing their closeness, their ease in each other's company, and a false sense of nostalgia creeps up on me, a longing for the female friendships I never had, the girlie weekends away that I never went on and probably never will.

I was so close, I think, frustration clawing at me. Rani is someone I could see myself confiding in, about who I am underneath it all. I'd imagined us hanging out after a long week, putting the world to rights, or heading to the spa for a day of pampering. Last Friday could have gone so differently, if only I hadn't ruined it with my childish antics. I don't know what came over me. Why Leela's cries pierced my eardrums. I felt like I'd been possessed by someone else entirely.

Drowning in tiredness from yet another long working week, I close my eyes and tip my head back against the window. But as my body starts to let go, the exhaustion only expands inside me. Settling beneath my heavy eyelids, scratching away at my sore temples. I feel like I could sleep for days, but the thought of going back to that house fills me with fear. A whole weekend with Charles was the one thing I used to look forward to. Now, all I can think about are the nightmares that await me. First the shadows on the ceiling, then the incessant crying in my head. It's as if the house is tugging on my soul, and I'm starting to unravel.

When I exit the station at Highgate, a message pops up on my phone.

Welcome back to the land of the living, darling. I can't wait to see you x

I feel guilty, and try to psych myself up, rapidly tapping my cheeks with the palms of my hands, willing warm blood to flow into them. Charles has seen enough already. He doesn't deserve this.

Me too! I text back. *Just walking back from the station x*

But my hand flaps like a lost bird as I turn the key in the lock, and I curl it into a tight fist to steady my nerves. I'm expecting to see Charles smiling at me from the hallway, but it's just cold, hard silence that greets me instead, penetrating the pit of my stomach and swallowing everything in sight until my body feels empty. Jumbled memories like scattered jigsaw pieces flashing through my mind. A door slammed shut. Tiny fists banging on a window. Crockery smashing on a tiled floor. And darkness, so much darkness. I try and grasp at them to form complete images, but nothing makes sense apart from this inexplicable urge to leave, and get as far away from the house as I can.

I'm just about to step back and slam the door shut when I hear noises coming from the living room. 'Hello? Charles ... is that you?' My voice echoes back at me. I don't recognise it. It sounds fragile, like a young child's. But there's no answer. I take my phone out of my handbag to call him, but it rings out. Holding my keys firmly in my hand, ready to attack, I cautiously push open the living room door with my foot to find out what lurks on the other side. My heart is beating out of my chest, double, triple time, and as the door opens, I hear myself gasp in sheer disbelief.

The room is brighter than bright, like a golden palace. I glance around, searching for the source, and see rows of candles framing the floor, flickering in unison, sparks of light bouncing off the walls and ceiling. I gaze, mesmerised, and only then do I notice the *pièce de résistance*: Charles, sitting on a blanket in the middle of the room, holding a bottle of champagne that he's about to pop open, surrounded by a grand feast: cheese and crackers, frittata, Padrón peppers, olives and bread.

'I bet you're wondering where all the boxes have gone?'

'Yes. How did you ...?' I ask as the panic drains from my body, distorted images fading to dust. *It's your overactive mind, Natalie; it never quietens.* My mum's voice echoes inside my head. She's right, of course. That and the incessant tiredness. It's just Charles here. No one else.

'I took the day off work ... Oh, wait, before you sit down, you might want to check the bedroom ...'

I head up two flights of stairs to find a grand triple wardrobe bringing the bare walls of our bedroom to life with a pop of sea green. It's the same wardrobe I've been lusting over for weeks, but I couldn't justify the cost. I wonder how he knew. 'Charles, you're too good to me,' I shout down to him. 'It's perfect.'

Pulling open the doors, I notice that my clothes have been hung up on the rails and neatly folded away in the drawers. It's the colour coordination that gives him away. I can't believe his thoughtfulness: an investment director who's used to flying around the world in business class, taking the time to arrange my silk blouses and dresses. I scan the rails, looking for something to change into. I have in mind my lucky little black dress that I wore when Charles and I first met, but I can't seem to find it, and there are several others missing, too – all figure-hugging mini dresses from high-street shops in similar dark shades. In their place are a collection of flowy bright maxi dresses that I haven't seen before, in luxurious fabrics with crisp designer tags – Missoni, Zimmermann, Erdem – pieces I would never have been able to afford for myself.

'So, what do you think?' My heart jumps; I didn't even hear him come up the stairs. He stands behind me, curling his arms around my waist.

'You did this ... for me?' I ask, still stunned.

'Of course, my darling. My company has a personal shopping service. I sent them a photo of you, along with your dress size, and they delivered them this morning. I can't wait to see you in that one.' He points to a high-necked Alexander McQueen piece while rocking me gently from side to side.

'Thank you,' I murmur under my breath, the guilt rising from my stomach. 'You really shouldn't have, Charles. They must have cost you a fortune.' I turn to face him.

'Don't be silly, darling. Worth every penny. No one will be able to take their eyes off you.'

I smile self-consciously, but I don't want to ruin the mood. 'Which one shall I wear tonight?'

His warm breath vibrates over my neck, his lips tickle my skin. 'Well, actually, I was thinking … none of them,' he whispers into my ear. 'I want you. I want *this*.' He cups his hand over my belly.

I turn away, pulling out one of the new dresses and holding it in front of me. 'Are you sure you don't want me to try it on?' I ask coyly. But I'm stalling. After this, after everything he has given me, I can't find the words to tell him no. I can't deal with seeing the disappointment on his face. I've just turned twenty-six. I'm not ready to be a mother. And I don't know if I ever will be.

'As you wish … but only if you let me take it off.' He winks at me. I can see him growing hard through his trousers; I can feel the sparks flying off him.

'Give me two minutes, my love,' I say, blowing him kisses before shimmying off into our en suite, the dress in my hand.

I shut the door, pausing to study my reflection in the mirror, my deceit burning through the raw cracks on my lips. It's ugly. *I'm* ugly. I throw my head back in disgust, shaking off my work clothes and sliding the dress over my head before smoothing down the coloured silk with the palms of my hands. I'm doing the right thing, I assure myself. People like me shouldn't have children.

'Are you okay, darling? Need help putting it on?'

'No thank you. I won't be a moment,' I sing, before reaching down into the tiny inside pocket of my washbag for a single white tablet, popping it onto my tongue and letting it dissolve in my mouth.

Rani

The front door bangs shut, causing the whole flat to shake. 'Every time,' I mutter under my breath.

'Rani, where are you?'

'In here,' I shout back, scrubbing my turmeric-stained fingertips under the tap.

Joel walks into the kitchen, stretching his arms over his head and groaning with pleasure. His face is gleaming, tiny beads of sweat dripping off it onto his Nike T-shirt.

'Good game, I take it?' I ask.

He nods. 'Mmm, smells good. What are you making?'

'Lydia's favourite, masala sandwiches.'

'That reminds me.' He grins. 'It's seven years today.'

'What is? What are you talking about?' I say, frustrated, wishing he'd just get to the point.

'Us. It's been seven years since our first proper date. Seven years since you told me you were pregnant with Lydia.'

'Oh.' I dry my hands and turn my attention to the sandwich toaster, switching it on and waiting for it to heat up.

'Well, don't you think we should …'

'What, Joel?' I ask, hand positioned on my hip. I'm exhausted after dropping the girls off at a free community dance class at the local church, then rushing home to tidy the flat and make lunch.

'I just thought it might be nice if we did something,' he says, scratching his head.

'Oh,' I say again, this time with surprise.

'It's been seven years, Rani. You get less for murder!'

'That's not technically true.'

'You know what I mean.' He winces. 'Anyway, do you fancy it? Just something local. Maybe we could head to the pub down the road?'

I'm torn. I want to say yes, but a part of me is curious, wondering where this has come from.

'Well?' he asks, eyebrows raised in anticipation.

I sigh quietly under my breath, feeling my jaw clenching. Then I turn away for a moment, carefully inserting a masala sandwich into the toaster and clicking the lid shut. 'That sounds … nice, but Joel, you've never remembered our anniversary before, let alone wanted to celebrate it. Why now?'

'I know, I know.' He shakes his head. 'We've always had the girls, though, haven't we? But now that they're getting older, I thought we could finally spend some time together, just the two of us.'

'Yeah,' I say, clicking my tongue against the roof of my mouth. It feels strange just thinking about it, but I can't tell him that. 'Why not?' I shrug, feeling my body gripped by nervous tension.

'Great.' He smiles, but it falls short of his eyes. 'Maybe the girls can go across the road to Jemima's?

'Hmmm. I'll ask. Can you keep an eye on the toaster while I give her a call?'

I breathe a sigh of relief almost as soon as I leave the room. I'm grateful for a moment to myself, to process what just happened. This isn't us. We don't do things like this, Joel and me. We barely celebrate our own birthdays. He despises romantic gestures; always has. What was it he used to say? *They're just tricks of the mind, Rani. What men do to distract their partners from who they really are.* You see, Joel believes that true romance is found in the simplest of moments. During those testing periods in life where love is all you have to hold on to. I witnessed this with Dad, how dedicated he became when Mum fell ill. How every action, every thought, every decision revolved around her. So when those words came out of Joel's mouth, I swallowed them whole. I thought I'd finally found a man with more substance than frivolous passion.

I don't know what to make of this sudden change of heart. Has Joel done a complete one-eighty, or is there something else going on, something he's not telling me?

Heading into the bedroom, I root around my messy desk, looking for my phone. I steal a look at the house across the street, noticing that both cars are parked in the driveway, and I wonder what Charles and Natalie are doing right now. The curtains in their bedroom are closed, so they could be still in bed, enjoying a weekend lie-in.

But as my fingers graze the hard edges of my iPhone, underneath a pile of Leela's handwriting homework, I catch a glimpse of movement on the street outside and jerk my head up just in time to see Natalie, dressed in leggings and a white tank top, jogging down the street towards the woods, her lips pressed together in deep concentration – or something else. My stomach turns somersaults. I haven't seen her since the dinner party. All I can think about is Charles's curt response at the deli. *She's fine.* But she wasn't fine that evening. Far from it.

With barely another thought, I dash into the hallway and pull on some battered trainers. Then, shouting to Joel that I have an errand to run and telling him to pick up Lydia and Leela from the church, I head straight out of the door.

Natalie

I wake to the smell of freshly ground coffee beans luring me out of bed. The maxi dress lies crumpled on the floor, as if the person inside it has vanished into thin air. I trace my gaze over its garish print, shining even brighter in the yellowy morning light. I remember how uncomfortable I felt wearing it, like I was trapped inside someone else's empty shell. But this is the world I live in now – and the dress is a small sacrifice to pay for fitting in.

My forehead starts to throb, shots of pain firing into my skull, as though a tiny person is tapping inside my head in a repeating rhythm – *vod-ka, vod-ka, vod-ka*. I wrap a long cashmere cardigan over my silk nightdress, before dashing into the en suite to freshen up. Then head downstairs to start the coffee machine – an altogether different vice, but it's enough to pacify my craving, until the next time.

Charles is in the garden, trimming overgrown hedges as he makes small talk with our neighbour over the fence. I remember how reluctant the estate agent was to mention her, knowing that many young couples would be put off by a widow in her seventies. But all I could think about was how perfect this was. Someone who might have lived on this street for decades; someone who could piece together the fragments of my memories.

As I pull open the patio door, Charles turns to face me, beaming. I'm glad I dabbed on some CC cream after brushing my teeth. 'Good morning, my love,' he says peeling off his gardening gloves. 'How are you feeling?'

I wander across the lawn, smiling through my nerves.

He pulls me towards him, planting kisses on my forehead. 'Natalie, meet Jemima. Jemima, my darling wife.'

A woman with wispy grey hair pokes her head over the fence. 'Hello there.' She holds out a sturdy yet wrinkled hand. 'My goodness, aren't you something.' Her eyes flutter for a moment or two. 'Wait a second. Have we met before? You look so familiar.'

I study her snow-white skin, her rosy cheeks, hoping for any sort of recollection. But I feel nothing. I open my mouth to respond, but Charles answers instead. 'I don't think so. Unless you saw us viewing the property?'

'No, that's not it. It's just Natalie I remember.' She scratches her head. 'Never mind … it must be my age. Every young person looks the same these days!'

I glance over at Charles, taking in the sweat collecting on his brow and the curious expression written on his face. Then I catch sight of the gigantic oak tree behind him at the bottom of the garden, and feel a strong sense of dread.

Come on, Natalie, snap out of it. Now is not the time.

'Maybe I have a doppelgänger wandering around London!' I almost choke on fake laughter. 'Anyway, I'd better go and get changed. I'm dying to head out for a run before it gets too warm.'

'That must be it! It was lovely to meet you, Natalie.'

'You too,' I shout, already halfway up the lawn so they don't notice my face burning red.

Closing the front door, I jog on the spot for a few minutes to warm up my muscles before easing myself down the hill towards Queen's Wood. I can tell by the sounds vibrating through my AirPods that it's busy here. This seems to be the place to let your kids run wild – climbing trees and diving into the soft beds of leaves.

As I roam off-piste, the crowds fade into the distance. All I can hear are birds singing in the canopy above my head, and the sound of my feet smacking the ground. My steps take me further into the wild depths of the woods. I leap over dense foliage and gnarled roots; I cast my eyes over little streams, water bubbling as tiny frogs hop out onto fallen tree logs and squirrels stop to quench their thirst.

As I run, I think about Jemima's words. I picture Charles's curious expression and feel a pang of guilt about how much I've kept from him. My vision becomes so cloudy with tears that I can hardly see where I'm going. Suddenly, there's a sharp snap beneath me. The pain that follows is excruciating, and I fall in slow motion, screaming in agony. As I hit the floor, my hands clasp my ankle, the source of the pain. I jerk my head around in desperation to see if anyone is about to help me, but it's a wasted effort. I'm all alone.

Instinctively, I grasp at my pocket for my phone, but I realise I haven't brought it with me. An old habit, back from when no one but Mum used to call. All I have is my bank card and house keys; both useless. Thinking quickly, I tear the scrunchy out of my hair and use it to compress my ankle before elevating it high in the air above me. My head drops to the ground; my hands curl through the soil, searching for something to grasp for support. It feels rough against my smooth skin. The pain seems to be dulling, but walking is out of the question. I have no idea where in the woods I am, or how long I've been running for. I have no other option but to sit tight and wait for someone to find me.

I'm lying on my back, listening to the calming sounds of the birds above my head, when I hear a voice.

'Natalie, is that you?'

I twist my head in the direction of the voice. It sounds familiar, but I can't quite place it.

'Natalie, it's Rani. Are you okay?'

I strain my eyes to make out her features, my head still fuzzy from the shock of the fall. 'Oh … Rani, hey,' I mutter, blushing as I recall my outburst at the dinner party. But I manage a smile to let her know that I'm all right.

'Do you need some help getting up?'

I nod my head. 'Yes please. Thank God you found me! What are you doing out here?'

'Running, like you.'

'Oh. I've never seen you here before,' I say, glancing at her sweatpants and long stripy tee.

She blushes. 'It's my first time actually … in these woods. I normally stick to the streets.'

Then I suddenly remember what she said when we bumped into each other on Shepherds Hill. *School run – the only running I do these days.* And I wonder what she's really doing here.

Rani

With an effort, I help her to her feet.

'Can you believe I didn't bring my phone out with me? It's lucky you ran this way,' she says, testing her ankle gingerly.

I wonder what she'd think if she knew the truth. Now that I'm here, I realise how crazy it sounds, following someone I've only just met. I've never done this kind of thing before. But still, somehow I don't regret it.

'I could help you walk home if you want ... or if that feels like too much, we're not far from Muswell Hill.' I hesitate. 'We could head to a café and you could call Charles from my phone.'

'That sounds perfect. Thank you. But are you sure you don't have anywhere else to be?'

'Not unless you count two energetic kids bouncing around in a tiny flat. I'll let Joel handle them on his own for a change.'

She grips my shoulder to steady herself, and together we move as one. From behind, we must look like an amateur comedy duo, her winning the genetic lottery at around five foot seven, me scrapping the barrel at five two. But we make it work, and after a few pauses for her to rest, we reach Gail's café on Muswell Hill Broadway.

Natalie sinks into a free chair and manoeuvres the one opposite to elevate her foot. Once she's settled, she waves her bank card at me. I politely decline, but then realise I left in such a rush that I forgot to grab my purse. Holding the sleek gold

Amex in my hand, I run the edge across my palm, then examine the front. It reads *Miss Natalie Sabian.*

When I reach the front of the queue, I order us mugs of frothy coffee and carry them to the table. We sip them in silence, smiling awkwardly at each other. A few customers look over at us – well, at Natalie really. Even make-up-free and pale from the fall, she's extraordinary. I wonder what it must feel like to be her, to move through the world never going unnoticed. Life must be so much easier when you don't have to shout to be heard.

The silence between us starts to feel a little tense. I want to bring up the dinner party, to apologise for what Leela said, but I don't want to make things more awkward between us.

'Do you need to ring Charles?' I blurt, unable to bear it any longer.

'Let's finish our coffee first,' she says decisively. 'We're expecting a delivery this morning that I don't want him to miss. I'm getting tired of sitting on garden furniture.' As she takes a sip of her drink, frothy milk coats her upper lip, and I watch her wipe it away with the back of her hand. 'So, the dinner party ...' She smiles sheepishly. 'I've been meaning to pop round to apologise, but work has been so busy.'

'What?' I shake my head, edging my hand closer to hers. 'You've got nothing to apologise for. Leela – she's only five years old and already an animal activist!' I laugh, trying to break the ice.

'You don't know how relieved I am to hear you say that. I've been so embarrassed all week. Gosh, five ...' She pauses, staring into the distance pensively. 'I can't remember what that was like ... You must have been so young when you had them.'

I nod, sighing into my chest. Then, before I can stop myself, I start to explain, as though I need to prove I wasn't always like this. Drifting through life without anything to show for it. 'When I fell pregnant with Lydia, I'd just finished a master's at Oxford. I had a job lined up at the *Guardian* but had to turn it down.'

'I can't imagine giving up on your dreams like that.' But there's a slight hesitation in her voice, as if somehow she understands.

'Yes. It was … is hard. I love my children and don't regret having them for a second, but I wish I hadn't had to give up so much in the process.'

'And now? Joel said they're both at school, right?'

'Yeah. I thought that would make a difference too. I've applied for so many jobs I've lost count, but' – I shrug, thinking of Natalie in her elegant work clothes, getting out of a cab after a long day at work – 'nothing. Not one interview. And these are *admin* jobs. I've given up on journalism. I mean, what national newspaper is going to hire someone who has to be home by three o'clock to pick up her kids from school?' A knot forms in my throat, and I know how pathetic I must sound.

Natalie looks at me keenly, as if thinking carefully about what to say next. 'What about doing a course? Or maybe you could even volunteer for the local newspaper?' Her eyes light up and it pains me to see it. Hope when I know there is none.

I take a moment, allowing myself a few precious seconds to get lost in her flawless beauty. 'I've toyed with that, but we can't afford it,' I say, the knot in my throat tightening. 'I see how hard Joel works, how much he puts up with, and I feel guilty that I can't do my bit; I feel guilty spending his money. But at the same time, I resent him. It's not *his* life that has been on hold.' I reach for my lukewarm coffee and take a gulp, trying to steady myself, realising that I'm probably boring her. 'Anyway, enough about me! What about you? How are you finding Highgate?'

'Oh,' she says abruptly, briefly looking away, 'it's lovely here. We got so lucky with the house.' She smiles, but I catch a flash of something else in her expression. Apprehension, or even fear.

'How long have you lived in London? Did you grow up here?' I ask quickly.

She looks nervous again, as if she's out of her comfort zone, and I'm annoyed with myself for being so nosy. 'No, but not far away. In Kent, mostly. It was always just Mum and me – Dad left when I was young. I hardly remember him.'

'Oh, I'm sorry.' My heart aches for her. I know what absence feels like, but at least I grew up with two loving parents. 'How about siblings?'

She shakes her head. 'I'm so jealous of people who have them. My childhood was quite lonely really. I don't remember much, but …' Her voice drops to a low hush. I can barely hear it amongst all the background noises. People chatting, plates clattering, coffee machine gurgling. 'I did have this one imaginary friend.' She tries to laugh it off, but her smile slowly fades at the edges, and her expression becomes strained, as if she's fighting a hidden emotion.

I wait, curious as to why she has brought it up, where it's leading, but she seems to have drifted off, a million miles away. I clear my throat, and she snaps out of it. 'Oh gosh. I've never told anyone that before.'

'Ha ha, don't worry, your secret is safe with me.' I laugh, tucking my hair behind my ears, hoping to gloss over the awkwardness. 'How's work? It sounds tough.'

'It really is. Doesn't leave much room for anything else.' She pauses. 'Charles and I have only been together a year, but I've spent so much of it in the office. I need a better work–life balance.'

A year together and they're already married and trying for a family? She can't be more than twenty-five. Though I can hardly judge, can I?

'Well,' I quip, 'make the most of your time together, because I can assure you, having children is a real passion-killer!' We both laugh, and her dimples appear again, but I get a sense that she's still holding back. I can see it in her eyes, now cold and distant.

'Here,' I say quickly, picking up my phone. 'Do you want to ring Charles? I'm sure he'll be wondering where you are.' As I hand it to her, she stares intently at the screen, as if she's reading a message.

'Is everything okay?'

'I'm just looking at your screen saver. They look so beautiful here, so innocent.'

'Thanks,' I say, my voice flat, thinking of Leela's screams at the dinner party. 'It's wonderful seeing them grow into such different people. Lydia's the charmer – you could probably tell. Always gets glowing reports from teachers, all the party invitations … Whereas Leela's much more introspective. She spends a lot of time on her own. She hasn't mentioned having an imaginary friend like you, though!'

'Oh God, please let's not mention that again – so embarrassing. I don't even know why I said it!' She buries her face in her hands. When she looks up again, she's beaming. But I catch sight of a solitary tear clinging to her lashes and I take that as my cue to pop to the toilet, leaving her my phone so she can call Charles in private.

When I return, just minutes later, I'm surprised to see that he has already arrived, the back of his neck glowing bright red. I wonder how he got here so quickly. Perhaps I was in the bathroom longer than I thought.

I watch as he folds his arms around her, like she's a young child, and as she mouths the word *sorry* again and again. It seems like such a strange reaction, but maybe that's what it's like to care so deeply for one another.

He senses me approaching and turns to face me, a wide smile splashed across his charming face. 'Rani. So kind of you to spend your Saturday morning looking after my wife,' he says, planting a kiss on both of my cheeks.

'Oh, it's nothing. I'm just glad I was around when it happened.'

'Yes. How fortunate.' He raises his eyebrows, as if mocking me, and I feel myself blush. *Did he see me chasing after her?* 'Anyway,' he continues, eyes on his shiny Rolex, 'we'd better head off. Would you like a lift back?'

I contemplate a ride in the Maserati. Gliding in style down familiar roads, catching the envious glances of passers-by … but I should give them some space. 'Thanks, but I think I'm going to stretch my legs and run home,' I reply, lying through my teeth. 'I hope you feel better soon, Natalie. I owe you a coffee sometime.'

'That would be lovely. But honestly, you don't owe me a—'

He cuts her off. 'Not to worry, Rani. I'll take over now.'

She hobbles out of the coffee shop, leaning on Charles for support. As they step outside, he picks her up and carries her like a baby to the car. Everyone stops and stares at them, thinking, *There goes a couple in love.*

Rani

My stomach grinds with nerves as the girls and I play dressing-up in the bedroom. It's been so long since Joel and I have been on a date; it feels like we're doing it for the very first time. While Leela goofs around, drawing on a Charlie Chaplin moustache with my eye pencil, Lydia poses in front of the mirror, one hand on her hip, the other behind her head, her lips painted a delicious shade of cherry red. I don't know where she's learnt to move her body like that. Her confidence terrifies me. I think of Natalie in the coffee shop this morning, elegant and poised even after her fall, and I wonder if she was this way as a young girl, aware of her beauty and the power she holds over those around her.

Lydia turns to look at me. I'm wearing a cream denim skirt and a skin-tight black bodysuit – both items from my pre-baby days. Part of me feels ridiculous, choosing an outfit for a guy who has seen me give birth – twice. But I can't help but glow inside. Could Joel be right? Is this all we need to feel whole again, a little bit of excitement? 'Mama, you look so pretty,' She says, handing me the lipstick, like I'm finally worthy of make-up.

'Thank you, darling. Now why don't you and Leela find some earrings for me to wear?'

Hearing them chatting behind me, I take a minute in front of the mirror, homing in on every curve, every line, every flaw. She's right, I do look quite pretty, but I don't want to look just pretty, I want to look desirable. I want heads to turn the way they always do with Amber. I want Joel to see me and for his jaw to drop, just like it did the first time we met.

I remember that day so vividly. I was sitting at the window in a wine bar in town, waiting for Amber and Sasha to join me after their final exams. It wasn't our typical watering hole, being upmarket and rarely frequented by students. But it was a juicy carrot dangling on a stick to get us through the long study days and nights.

'Ladies. Get in! I have the best idea,' Amber had shrieked as we'd left the library late one night, huddled together to keep warm.

'What? Run away to gay Paree? Join a cult? Shag that tutor you're obsessed with?' Sasha had giggled.

'Don't tempt me. I might have to if I'm gonna pass these damn exams ... But seriously, I'm going to be your favourite person ever.'

'You'll always be our favourite person.'

'Aw, Rani. But listen, what's the one thing you want to do after we finish? It can be anything – well, as long as we're not going to end up in prison or dead!'

'Hmm. I really want to go to Pride in Brighton,' Sasha had whispered, still uncertain. She'd only come out to us the month before and wasn't yet ready to tell the world.

'Done. Brighton here we come.' Amber had smiled, hugging her closer. 'I don't know about you, but I'm sick of living in these gross sweatpants. Let's go shopping! My treat, of course. Rani?'

'Well … there's this posh wine bar opposite college. Have you seen it? Apparently it's the place where all the freelance journalists hang out.'

'Ha ha, trust you to make it about your career. But if there's wine, you know I'm in!'

So there I sat, massively overdressed in a stunning turquoise midi dress that Amber had bought for me. Avoiding the unwelcome stares from much older men and wondering what the hell was taking the girls so long (later I found out that Amber had walked out of her exam and Sasha was consoling her). After forty-five minutes of nursing a solitary white wine spritzer, I was about to leave when I felt a tap on my shoulder.

I turned around, ready to tell them off for standing me up, but was surprised to see a young man with dark-blond hair, an oversized denim jacket and hipster glasses. 'Please don't take this the wrong way,' he said nervously, twiddling his thumbs. 'I've never done this sort of thing before. But since you came in, I've been sitting over there desperately trying to work up the courage to come over and speak to you. Can I buy you another drink?'

My heart pounded through my chest. I'd never been singled out like this before, especially by someone like him. By *him*, I mean a middle-class white man. At school, I was known as the hairy, brown kid who mispronounced words and stank of curry. The boys ignored me, except when they tried to bribe me into doing their homework.

By the time I went to university, I'd discovered contact lenses and waxing, but it wasn't the blessing I thought it would be. Student nights were filled with pubescent white men let loose in the crowds, eyeing up my smooth tanned legs, my dark soulful eyes. Some of them ventured closer, high on coke and

MDMA, leering over me to catch a glimpse of my pert, round breasts. But when they whispered in my ear words like *exotic* and *Bollywood*, I knew what they were after. They would never be serious about someone like me. It was just a game, an ego thing. To be the first out of their group of friends to bang a brown girl. And when they'd succeeded, they'd return swiftly to the familiar. The fair-skinned women they would take home to their parents, the well-bred women who would carry their children.

But Joel seemed different. Mature, worldly. So I thought, what the hell, one drink wouldn't hurt until the stragglers arrived. But one drink swiftly turned into two, two became three, and before we knew it, the bar staff were starting to close up for the night.

We covered everything, from our impressions of Oxford to what it felt like to be one parent away from being an orphan. He'd left university the year I started, so our paths had never crossed; travelled the world after the sudden death of his father, and was now training to be a history teacher in London. He told me that when he first set eyes on me sitting at the window, he'd felt an immediate connection, beyond what could be described as chemistry or lust. And when I slipped into conversation that my mum had died, he realised why: 'Such is the power of grief that it can transcend minds.'

I was in awe of his spirituality, his openness. How he'd maintained so much positivity in his life in spite of his loss, a place I hadn't yet reached with my own. Back then, there was nothing we couldn't say to each other. But now, we never seem able to find the right words.

Natalie

Swallowing down the tiny pink tablets with a large gulp of cold water, I sink my head back onto the plumped-up pillows, stretching my legs flat out on the bed. I try to wiggle my toes, draw tiny circles with my injured ankle, but it's now swollen to almost twice its usual size and feels so tender, the pain firing up my calf muscles, causing me to cry out in agony. Charles clears his throat downstairs, and I quickly cover my mouth with my hand. I don't want him to see me this way. Lying here so vulnerable and weak, my hair forming damp, tangled clumps, make-up melting off my face. This isn't the woman he fell in love with.

Grinding my teeth in frustration, I turn my attention to my surroundings. Anything to distract myself until the painkillers dissolve into my bloodstream. I stare up at the ceiling, focusing hard on the cornices that encircle our new Eichholtz Bernardi ceiling lamp – a housewarming gift from Charles's best friend Seth. Just harmless shapes and patterns, I remind myself. That's all. Everything else is inside my head.

This house cannot touch me.

My eyes start to close. I try to fight them. Tracing the lines and corners of the walls, running down towards the shearling carpet, the intricate panelling painted an elegant pearly cream. A beam of light streams in through the window, catching the centre panel, shimmering around its edges, and all at once it hits me. I gasp in disbelief, goosebumps shooting up my bare arms and legs.

This isn't just a wall. There's a door hidden within it.

It's pitch black. There are voices, footsteps somewhere in the distance. Growing louder, deeper, until I feel their echoes on me. Piercing my body in short, sharp attacks.

I hear a door slam shut.

Plates and glasses shattering on the ground. A loud crescendo of yelling and screaming, one voice high-pitched, the other much deeper, slurring through their words.

I hear a name uttered with a chilling hoarseness, the tone laced with anger and disdain, vibrations ricocheting through the walls.

My body trembles as I shrink further into the dark. Out of sight. Hardly making a sound.

This is the only place I feel safe. Where I know they won't find me.

Suddenly the footsteps return. Climbing the creaking steps one by one. Edging towards me. The voices follow, calling my name, drawing out every syllable. I feel my heart thrashing in my chest, but I'm too scared to breathe. I close my eyes, willing myself to be somewhere else. Anywhere but here.

The door opens. Bright light streams through behind my eyelids.

A hand clutches my shoulder, causing me to jump, and I throw it off with all the strength I can muster, kicking hard and fast, screaming through the pain, 'LET GO OF ME! LEAVE ME ALONE!'

'Natalie? Wake up. It's me, Charles.'

I jerk my eyes open, looking up at him in relief, but also confusion. My body still trembling.

'What are you doing in here, Natalie? What is this place?'

'Huh?'

I take in my surroundings. A musty, damp smell shoots up my nostrils, and there's a slight chill lingering in the air. Where am I?

'Come,' he says. I hear frustration in his voice as he helps me out and carries me back to the bed. 'You need to rest. I'll make you a cup of tea.' Then he turns and walks out of the bedroom, shutting the door behind him.

I sit back up, observing the door within the wall panelling, now left slightly ajar. The last thing I remember is lying on the bed, tracing the edges, long-lost memories returning. What happened after that?

What is happening to me?

He carries a cup of milky, sugary tea on a tray, placing it on the bed next to me before pulling open my wardrobe and taking out a long emerald-coloured gown. It's a brand-new Givenchy; I recognise it from the tag as one of the dresses he slotted onto the rail last week. I watch him hang it proudly on the back of the door in front of me, his way of saying, *You'd look beautiful in this*.

'How are you feeling?' he asks, turning to face me.

'Much better, thanks,' I say, forcing out a smile. 'The painkillers seem to be kicking in nicely.' I need him to forget what happened.

Tonight, we're heading to a dinner party at Seth's house in Belsize Park. The date has been in the diary for months, the first of Seth's fortieth birthday celebrations. Charles is off to

Miami tomorrow for part two. He kindly offered to delay his flight until I'm back on my feet, but I immediately convinced him not to. I need time alone to process what is happening. I don't know whether it's being back here in this house or something else, but I can feel myself letting go. Slipping away.

And Charles has seen too much already.

I need time to get myself back on track before it's too late.

Sitting upright, I lean forward to pick up the mug of tea, and take a long sip, savouring the sweetness, enjoying the warmth flowing down my throat. As I put it back down on the tray, I smile at him again, but this time it feels almost real.

He moves towards the bed, perching on the edge. 'I'm glad,' he says, his features mellowing. 'Listen, I know it's the last thing you should be thinking about, but your work phone has been going off all afternoon.'

'Ugh. Sorry. I'll switch it off.'

He hands it to me, and I scroll through my inbox, skim-reading a couple of emails from junior associates that say nothing of significance beyond *look at me, working on a weekend*. My junk folder has a new addition as well, which is strange because our antivirus system is bulletproof. I decide against opening it, making a mental note to flag it to the IT guys next week. Then I hold down the power button and place the phone on the floor.

When I'm upright again, I notice that Charles has edged a little closer. He pats my thigh to get my attention. 'Listen, Natalie. I've been meaning to talk to you about something. I was going to save it for when we'd settled in, but after last few weeks, and what happened to you this morning, I feel I need to say it.' He takes my hand.

'You know it's coming up to a year since we met? Well, I've been thinking a lot about that night and how I felt from our very first conversation. I could picture our lives together and I felt sure that I could make you happy, that I could give you everything you'd ever wanted …' He bows his head ever so slightly. 'But lately, it feels like that things are changing between us. We've fallen out of sync. It's this job of yours, Natalie. It's never-ending.'

I feel a rush of uneasiness.

'So look, I've had a chat with my financial adviser, and we're in a pretty robust position. My salary can more than cover all our outgoings.' He nods proudly at the emerald gown hanging on the door. 'Your mother's, too. So yeah. I just wanted to reassure you. There's no need for you to work any more. You'll soon have more than enough to keep you busy.' He winks at me, gesturing at my belly.

My heart stops. I can't seem to find the words. Again. My career is everything to me. Not just my safety net – and Luella's – but the one thing I'm proud of. He can't possibly think I'd want to throw it all away.

We were curled up under a blanket on the terrace of our Florentine apartment, gazing at the flaming sunset crawling over the Ponte Vecchio. His lips vibrated over my neck, the tantalising smell of our dinner still lingering on his breath. Fragrant slow-roasted tomatoes and garlic-infused mozzarella. I'd never tasted food so good. *It was worth it*, I assured myself, thinking guiltily of those extra few mouthfuls I couldn't resist. And Charles hadn't even batted an eyelid.

I reached behind me to touch his cheek, enjoying the light bristles brushing up against my skin. 'You make me so happy,'

I whispered, wishing we could stay in this moment for ever. 'I have everything I've ever wanted.'

He squeezed his arms tighter around me, kissing the back of my neck. 'Were you always this beautiful? Even as a child?'

My cheeks flushed red hot.

'I mean it, Natalie. I wish I'd known you back then, so I can love every version of you.'

I felt my heart sinking, knowing that our bubble was about to burst. Then I turned to face him, tight-lipped.

'Is everything okay?' He looked concerned.

'Charles, I need to tell you something. I just don't know how.'

'What? Why?'

'I'm scared it will be the end.'

'Don't be silly, darling. Nothing you can tell me will make me love you any less,' he assured me, squeezing my hand.

I took a deep breath, knowing that he'd find out sooner or later. 'I don't know how to say this … I'm not like you, Charles. I didn't grow up like you did.'

'Sure you did. Look at you!' He laughed flippantly.

'No.' I shook my head. 'I didn't have two loving parents like you did, an idyllic childhood. I don't remember my father at all. He left when I was young. It was just Mum and me, struggling for years to make ends meet.' I continued, repeating what Luella had always reminded me of. 'It was so hard for her, Charles, without an education. She did the odd job here and there, but some days we barely had enough food for the two of us.'

He caressed my face affectionately. 'My God, Natalie. I never would have guessed. Just look at you now, a high-flying lawyer. But listen,' he says, staring deep into my eyes, 'it doesn't change a thing. I promise you I will take care of you. You'll never have to want for anything again.'

He frowns at me quizzically, tensing, waiting for me to speak. I know I should be grateful, that other women would jump at such a kind gesture. 'Charles,' I say lovingly, entangling my fingers in his, 'I've never had anyone care for me the way you do. What you're offering me is wonderful. Truly. But you know how much this job means to me.' I straighten up a little. 'Do you remember what I told you on our first night in Florence … about my childhood?'

He nods, still frowning, the lines creasing his face.

'Mum used to call me her golden child; pinning all her hopes and dreams on me. I was the one who was going to turn our luck around, the one who would heal her broken heart. Can you imagine what that was like? The pressure I felt … that I sometimes still feel.' Tears gather in my eyes just talking about it. 'Charles, I worry …' I hesitate, choosing my words carefully. 'I hope this never happens, but if it at some point it doesn't work out between us, I want to be sure that I'll be okay, that I'll never end up like her.'

He jerks his head back, stunned. 'I can't believe you're saying this, Natalie. It doesn't make sense. How can you think about us breaking up? We've only been married a month.'

'No. No. That's not what I mean …'

'You don't know hard it's been for *me* these last few weeks. Watching you suffer with all the nightmares and the constant exhaustion, barely able to keep your eyes open. Every day I come home to an empty house, I fall asleep in an empty bed, when all I want to do is be with you, to hold you, to take care of you. I feel like I'm married to a ghost.'

'Oh, Charles,' I cry. It pains me to hear that he's been feeling like this. 'I'm sorry, I really am, but I don't know what else I can do. We have our weekends, don't we? We always make the most of them. And our trips away? Isn't that enough?'

He lets go of my hand and edges away from me, his body language cooling. 'But what about when we have a baby? Surely you won't be going back to work after that, not with all the hours you put in.'

This, again. The guilt claws away at me. I take a deep breath, knowing that I have to tell him the truth – not the whole truth, but part of it, enough to reach some sort of compromise, I hope. 'Charles, I'm only twenty-six. There's so much I want to do first. We could live abroad for a few years. I could work from the New York office. We have so much time.' I lean forward, reaching out for him, but he jolts up, sighing deeply and shaking his head.

'Don't you think you should have told me this before our wedding? And what about what *I* want?' he asks, bending over me, a fist pressed solidly into his chest. 'Or is that irrelevant? I'm going to be forty next month. Forty. You knew that when you married me.'

I can feel my cheeks burning, sweat prickling down the back of my neck. But it's *my* body, I want to say, *my* life that's going to change.

'Where is this coming from?' he asks. 'Have you been talking to someone … someone from work? Oh, wait – don't tell me it's that woman from across the street. Don't you remember her unruly child? I wouldn't go taking parenting advice from the likes of her.'

'No. No.' I shake my head. 'I haven't been talking to anyone. This is me, Charles. All me. Please, sit down, let's talk about this properly.' I reach for his hand again, but he snatches it away. 'Charles, listen to me. What you're asking of me, it's too much. You have to understand.'

I can tell from his heavy breathing that he desperately wants to react. To say something, do something. But instead he throws his hands up in the air and storms out of the bedroom, slamming the door behind him. I hear noises in the room below as he moves boxes, rifles through them. I hear the wheels of a suitcase on the wooden floor and his muffled voice speaking to someone on the phone. My name is mentioned a couple of times, but the conversation is too faint to grasp.

A few minutes later, he stomps down the stairs, dragging the suitcase behind him, and my insides shiver as anxiety takes hold. But there's not a tear in sight. Instead, I remain focused on the door handle. Because any minute now, he'll bound back up the stairs and swing the door wide open, and I'll run into his arms, apologising.

I wait. But nothing.

All I hear is the front door being slammed shut, the car starting, and the noise of him driving out of my life. Just like my father.

And yet the emerald dress remains swinging on the hanger in front of me, taunting me with its vile perfection.

Rani

I sit perched on the edge of the sofa. My nails are painted a warm shade of red, and for the first time in ages, I'm wearing lipstick. Lipstick, for God's sake. I glance nervously at my phone. It's way too early. Joel's gone to a training session at the school and won't be back for ages yet. Trust me to be sitting here all dolled up when he's the one who suggested this date. I sigh deeply through flared nostrils; I bet it hasn't even crossed his mind.

I'm just about to loosen the button on my denim skirt when my phone rings. Jemima. I really hope she's not calling to cancel.

'Hi. Is everything okay?'

'Rani. Hello. Yes, fine. I know the girls aren't due here until later, but I was wondering if you fancied bringing them over now instead. There's something I wanted to speak to you about.' Her voice quavers a little. Maybe she's feeling lonely and fancies some adult company. I look at the clock – let's face it, I've got time to kill.

'Yes, of course. I can make that work.'

I help the girls pack their matching unicorn rucksacks with all the sleepover essentials, then we head down the stairs, across the road and through the gate into Jemima's front garden. It's usually bursting with colour this time of year, sunshine daffodils next to rows of bright pink hyacinths. But today I barely notice them. My eyes are glued to the house next door, with its royal-blue front door and twin lollipop bay trees, hoping to see a flicker of movement behind the curtains. But it sits completely still.

I ring the bell, and within seconds Jemima unlocks the door and peers her head around. As does Scruff, her ancient miniature schnauzer, who utters one solitary yelp before hobbling towards us wagging his tail. His fur is mostly grey now, with small patches of blistering red mange.

Jemima breaks into a smile. I notice that her thinning hair has been chopped into a chic grey bob and she's spritzed on a familiar floral scent – the one she wore when her husband, Michael, was around. She looks almost like she used to do before he passed, and I smile, remembering what he used to call her. *My very own Dolly Parton.*

'There you are, my little cherubs. Oh, how I've missed you both!'

Lydia leaves my side and glides straight into Jemima's arms. It takes Leela a second or two to overcome her shyness, but she soon joins her sister. I watch Jemima squeeze them tightly, kissing their soft cheeks. But her right eye starts twitching a little, and I get the sense that she's holding something back. 'Come in, come in, all of you. Gosh, don't you look lovely, Rani.'

We follow her into the lounge, the girls still clinging to her legs.

'Thanks! Thought I'd make an effort for a change. Lydia. Leela. Be gentle, please. Let Auntie Jemima sit down.' I hover over the sofa. Scruff jumps up, just inches from my face, his fine whiskers almost touching my skin. I feel my nose wrinkle and my throat start to close.

'Are you okay, Rani?'

'I'm fine. It's just my asthma. Seems to be playing up at the moment. Don't worry. I have my inhaler at home if it gets worse.'

'Down, Scruff, down,' she orders sternly, and he immediately follows her command.

'He's such a good dog,' I say. 'Anyway, thanks so much for having the girls. We really appreciate it.'

'It's nothing. They make me feel young again. Speaking of good little girls, can either of you smell anything baking in the oven?' She winks at me as they shout in unison.

'CHOCOLATE CHIP COOKIES!'

'Oh Jemima, you didn't have to go to all that trouble. What do you say, girls?'

'THANK YOU, AUNTIE JEMIMA.'

I glance at my phone to check the time, and feel butterflies in my stomach again. Maybe I should change into something more comfortable? Will Joel even notice the effort I've made? 'So ... was there something else?' I ask, eager to distract myself.

'Oh. Yes. Have you met our new neighbours yet?'

'I have, yeah, a couple of times. I bumped into Natalie earlier actually. Have you?'

She nods her head. 'Charles and I spoke over the fence this morning. Such a charming young man. He has a touch of my Michael about him. Natalie joined us too, for a little while. She seemed so familiar, but I guess all young people look the same when you get to my age!' Her rosy cheeks blush crimson.

I smile sympathetically, fidgeting with the house keys in my hand. I want to continue chatting to her, and any other day I would, but I really need some time alone to compose myself before Joel gets home.

'Sorry, Rani, I know I'm keeping you. Look, it's probably nothing, but I could hear shouting through the walls when I rang you earlier, and other noises too, as though something was being thrown. I didn't know what to do.'

My mouth opens in surprise, but I try to remain calm. Couples argue all the time, so maybe it was harmless. But what if it wasn't? 'Have the noises stopped now?' I ask, straining my ears.

'Yes. Just before you arrived.'

'Okay.' I pause to take a breath. 'That's good. I can understand why you were worried, Jemima, but it was probably nothing.' I swallow my concern before forcing out a half-smile.

'Yes, I expect you're right ... Anyway, I'll let you get on, Rani. And pick the girls up any time tomorrow, there's no hurry. You're only young once!' she says, combing her fingers through her grey bob.

'That's great, thanks ... Right, well I'll head off then.' I bend down and kiss Lydia and Leela on the tops of their little heads, silky soft beneath my lips. 'Enjoy yourselves, chicas, and not too many cookies before bed, please!'

Closing Jemima's front gate behind me, I walk towards number 11. But as I reach the driveway, a car reverses abruptly onto the pavement, braking just in time, mere inches away from me.

I jump back, my heart pounding.

The driver turns round. Charles. I take in his tight mouth, his raging eyes, and a cold shiver creeps down my spine as I remember what Jemima just told me.

When he sees me, he quickly rolls down his window and pokes his head out. 'Oh God, I'm sorry. I didn't see you there,' he says, his voice light and jovial, his face already morphing into an apologetic smile.

I'm still shaken up, struggling to form complete sentences in my mind. But before I have a chance to reply, he swerves around me and zooms off into the distance with a squeal of tyres.

When I get back to the flat, Joel is in the hall with his shoes on. He must have just walked in. I'm dying to fill him in on what just happened, but I'm worried it might ruin the mood.

Hearing me behind him, he turns, a solemn expression on his face.

'You're back already?' I ask.

'Yeah. We finished early.' He avoids looking directly at me.

'Okay, well, the girls are already at Jemima's. So if you want, we can head out now and get some drinks in before dinner.'

'Great,' he says, but it's as if he's trying to convince himself. 'Just give me a few minutes to freshen up.'

It's an awkward start to our first proper date in a long time, but we're soon strolling down Shepherds Hill to our local pub. I glide my hand into his. It feels strange yet familiar. Our eyes meet, and I watch him with interest, trying to tap into his mind. But I'm struggling to read him, as if a part of him is somewhere else.

When we reach the pub, Joel pushes the door, holding it open for me. 'My lady.' He grins, with a nod. He seems to have relaxed a little, and I let out a silent exhale.

'God, look at this place. It's as if we've gone back in time,' I say, stepping inside, marvelling at the antique furniture and the quirky paintings on the wall. 'It hasn't changed a bit … even if we have.' I laugh nervously.

But Joel's already at the bar. I catch him resting his phone on the counter, tapping away. He turns around. 'So, let me guess … a white wine spritzer?'

I nod, walking towards him. 'I'm starving – do you mind if we order food now as well?'

'Yeah, sure, order what you want. I'm just gonna get something light,' he says sheepishly, lowering his gaze. 'I had some snacks at school.'

'Oh. So that's where the budget's going?' I ask in jest, trying to lighten the mood, but he's already turned away again, looking through the menu.

Our plates have just been cleared and I'm now several glasses in. My mind is a little hazy, but my belly is warm and content. It feels a bit like the old days, evenings buzzing with excitement and opportunity, and I find myself hopeful for the night ahead.

Joel, on the other hand, is still nursing his one and only pint – stone-cold sober. It's not like him at all. He seems distracted again, his eyes intermittently flicking to the phone resting on his lap and frustration creeps up on me. This was his idea. So why does it feel like I'm the only one making an effort?

I shrug it off, polishing off the rest of my drink and nodding at the barman to make me another one. Then I begin to tell Joel about my day, my encounter with Natalie and Charles this morning and what Jemima said earlier.

'It's weird, because they seemed so in love. Typical newly-weds.' I laugh. 'I can't imagine them fighting.'

'Why do you care?' he asks bluntly, taking a large gulp of the foamy dregs of his beer, running a hand over his mouth. 'And anyway, they could just have a healthy sex life.'

I shrug, unconvinced and wondering if that's a dig at us. 'I dunno … I'd like to think I'm friends with Natalie now,' I say, cupping my hand around the drink the barman has just brought to the table, before taking a long, reassuring sip.

'Ha. You can't be serious, Rani?' Joel's hazel eyes look greener in the pub lighting. It changes his face somehow, hardens it. 'After that horrendous dinner party?'

'What's that supposed to mean?'

'Nothing, forget I said anything.' But then his hand grazes the back of his head, and I know he's not finished.

'Go on … I can tell you want to say something.'

He sighs. 'Well, she's not really your sort of person, is she?'

'What? Beautiful? Successful?' I ask sarcastically.

'You know that's not what I meant … Look, it's getting late. Let's just get the bill and head back.'

I want to press him further, but now is not the time. I'm on a high, and I don't want anything to bring me down. And as I gulp down the remains of my drink, an idea pops into my head.

When we reach home, I open the front door and race up the stairs to put on some Motown. The alcohol fires up my body and I feel fearless.

As Joel enters the flat, I remember what he said at the pub. *He wants this*, I tell myself. *He wants you*. Grabbing his hand, I pull him towards me, thrusting my body against his. Then I push him onto the couch and step back, slowly undoing the buttons on my bodysuit while swinging my hips to the rhythm of the music.

'What's going on?' he asks, yawning. 'I'm tired, Rani.'

He's fighting this. He's been fighting something all night, but I don't care any more. I just want to feel desired, in control. 'Shh,' I whisper, sliding down my skirt. 'You don't have to do anything.'

Crouching in front of him, I take his face in my hands, close my eyes and lean in.

'Rani, please.' He brushes me off.

But I'm determined. I won't take no for an answer. 'Who's Rani?' I ask coyly. 'I'm Serena,' I whisper in my sexiest voice. 'High-flying lawyer by day, tantalising seductress by night.'

'Huh? What are you talking about?'

'Shh.' I unbutton his jeans and start to peel them off. My heart is racing. I feel so alive.

But then he rolls sharply away to one side, causing me to flop down onto the floor. 'Rani, stop. I can't take this any more. We need to talk.'

Natalie

'Na-ta-lie. Na-ta-lie. Wake up,' a voice sings somewhere in the distance. I can't make out where it's coming from. 'Na-ta-lie ...'

I blink my eyes open and gasp, panic jolting into my chest like an electric shock, vibrating over every inch of my body. 'Luella! What ... what are you doing here?' I'm not ready. I need more time.

I watch her plump lips curve into a deep half-moon, her long lashes flutter over sea-blue eyes. 'Don't be silly, darling. I live here. And it's *Mum* to you.' She winks.

It's then that I really take her in, noticing how different she looks, as if her whole face has been rolled flat like dough.

She leans towards me and brushes my hand with hers. It feels cold and rubbery. 'Come, darling, come. Let's go down-stairs. There's something I want to show you.'

I close my eyes, hoping this is just a dream and that I'll soon wake up alone in my bedroom. But when I open them again, she's still here – all painted red lips and a giant oval face like one of those inflatable dolls. I open my mouth to scream, but nothing comes out.

I follow her downstairs, observing my surroundings. I don't recognise anything here. My bright and airy living room is now dark and dingy, the walls plastered with William Morris wall-paper, the backdrop to a traditional fireplace.

I look at Not-Luella for an explanation. 'Where are we?'

Her rubbery fingers curl through my hair, over the contours of my face. She does this with affection, but her expression is blank, emotionless. 'Shh, child. Come. Follow me.'

We move out of the living room and back into the hallway. I sigh, feeling slightly comforted by this space that resembles my own – high ceilings and tall windows letting in the light. As we walk towards the kitchen, I hear voices – one sounds like a woman, but the other is too faint to make out. I stop at the doorway, unsure whether I should continue. It seems wrong somehow, and a strong sense of uneasiness knots inside my stomach.

'Come,' Not-Luella says firmly.

I don't think I have a choice.

They're standing with their backs to me, in front of the stove. A woman in a long-sleeved floral dress, a white apron tied around her waist, and next to her, a young girl perched on a chair, a wooden spoon in her tiny hand. She can't be more than three or four. I watch them as they hum a tune together while preparing a dessert of some kind, the sweet scent of spices filling the air – cinnamon, ginger and something else I can't quite make out.

Not-Luella rolls her gaze towards them, as if to say: *Look at them*, *observe them*, and I realise suddenly that the woman is my mother, and the child, I think, is me. 'No!' I cry out. 'It can't be. What's going on?' I step towards them, but before I reach them, my head knocks hard against something. 'Ouch,' I exclaim, rubbing my forehead. I try again, but the same thing happens. It's like an invisible wall separating us.

Mum turns around, as if she can hear me. Her face is a picture. I'd forgotten how beautiful she used to be. The girl turns too, grinning, a tiny gap between her two front teeth, her eyes sparkling like firecrackers. It *is* me. Young Natalie.

'Mum,' I shout, my voice laced with fear. 'It's me. Natalie.'

Her ears prick up for a moment, but then she turns away. Young Natalie does the same, and together they laugh, as if lost in each other's love and affection.

I feel a deep stab of pain, as if someone is scraping at my insides with a blunt spoon. I turn to Not-Luella. 'I don't understand?' I say, like a question. But she just smiles in a deliriously terrifying way that makes me want to crawl into the darkness forever.

Suddenly, my surroundings change before my eyes. Swirls of colours and shapes move around me like I'm travelling through a kaleidoscope. When they finally settle, I realise that I'm outside in the garden, still in my nightdress, biting wind and sharp droplets of rain tearing at my bare skin.

Panicked, I run up to the patio doors. My mother and Young Natalie are still there, dancing around the kitchen, feeding each other home-made muffins straight out of the oven. I can almost taste the sugary sweetness on my lips. 'Hello? Mum? Can you hear me?' They continue dancing, lips dotted with crumbs, eyes wide, barely blinking, as I tap on the glass. The gusts of wind become stronger, wilder, and my nightdress blows out, feeding ice-cold air over my bare body. Not-Luella just stands there, still as a statue.

'MUM. WHY CAN'T YOU HEAR ME?' I yell, banging on the glass, tears streaming down my face. 'I'M SCARED. PLEASE!'

My eyes flicker. My heart beats rapidly and I press my hand to my chest to try to steady it, feeling my skin sticky with sweat.

I'm disorientated, as if lost in time and space. It takes me a few seconds to fully regain consciousness, to assimilate back into the present. When I do, I realise that I'm lying on the patio, in what looks like low evening light. I must have fallen asleep after Charles left. But how long have I been out here like this?

I can smell a barbecue a few doors down, and hear children squealing with excitement somewhere in the distance. A dark shadow suddenly appears on the patio, and I freeze, sensing that I'm being watched. Is it Charles? No. He must be at Seth and Darcy's by now, the party in full swing. I slowly turn my head. But there's no one there. I'm alone.

I have no memory of how I got here from the bedroom. But I remember the nightmare almost as if it was real.

Rani

'I can't do this any more. This ... pretending,' he says, sliding his jeans up his slim legs before sitting back down on the sofa, drawing away from me. 'Do I actually make you happy, Rani? Or are you only with me because you have no other option?'

I hear the bluntness of his words, but I can't make sense of them. I open my mouth, but it's like I've forgotten how to speak. Staring down at my hands, it occurs to me that I'm half-naked on the living room floor while Joel, my partner of seven years, the father of my children, is about to end our relationship to the tune of the Supremes' 'Where Did Our Love Go'. I feel exposed and reach my arms out, clutching my skirt and top like a life raft, pulling them over my body to stop myself from shivering. Joel leans over and offers me a blanket. I remember a time when he wouldn't have hesitated to wrap it around my shoulders.

'I'm sorry. I didn't want it to out come out like this. You deserve so much better. It's just that ... it's never felt like the right time to bring it up.'

'I'm so humiliated, Joel,' I whisper through tears. 'I dressed up for you. I threw myself at you. Couldn't you have just fucked me like you meant it, or am I really that disgusting?'

He's suddenly behind me. I feel his fingers graze my bare skin, stroking my hair. 'No. No. No. Don't say that. You're beautiful, Rani. I just can't *live* like this any more.'

I jerk my body away, but then slowly turn towards him, knowing the question I have to ask. 'Is there someone else?'

He shakes his head, bowing it in shame.

'There is, isn't there? For God's sake, just tell me. Who is she?' I look around for his phone. 'You were texting her earlier at the pub, weren't you? I knew it. I knew something wasn't right.'

'Oh, Rani.' He takes a deep breath that seems to go on for ever. 'Nothing has happened.'

'Who is it, Joel?' I glare at him, my eyes burning from fighting back tears.

'It's no one,' he says, scratching the back of his head. His soft features sharpen with tension. 'It's … I've … I've been talking to Amber.'

My stomach contracts with shock and rage. 'What? *My* Amber?' I feel a sudden tightness grip my chest. 'You've got to be kidding me!' I stand up tall and start pacing around the flat, energised by anger. I can't bear to look at him.

'Why her? Out of all the women in the world, you had to pick her?!'

He follows me into our bedroom and hovers behind me as I sort through a pile of laundry, folding through my frustration. I have to do something; I have to keep my hands busy. My mind keeps rushing to visions of them together at Amber's dinner party, locked in conversation. Of course it's Amber.

'Listen to me, Rani. Nothing happened. We're just friends.' He clasps my arm.

I pull away, trying to concentrate on matching socks and folding my M&S knickers, but I can't let this go. 'Why then … why say it?' I ask, throwing a pair of socks onto the bed. 'Why even mention her name?'

He sits down and looks up at me, trying to catch my eye. 'I met up with her last week, that night I said I was seeing people from work. And again today.'

'No. No.' I shake my head, flopping down on the other side of the bed as the lies multiply, curling myself into a ball. I can pretend no more. 'No. No, I don't believe it. You wouldn't do that to me. She's not even your type.' I realise how pathetic I sound.

'I asked to meet her, Rani. To talk about us. Me and you.'

My mind is a blur. I can't seem to grasp at the right words. So I just stare vacantly up at the ceiling.

'I needed someone to speak to, someone who knows us both.' He moves around the bed to face me. 'You've been slipping away from me, Rani. I didn't know what to do. I didn't know if you'd ever return.'

I choke, disbelief lodged in my throat. 'I don't understand. Why her? Why not come to me first? I'm sure I told you to do that.'

'I've tried, Rani. I've tried so many times.'

'When?' I ask, through gritted teeth.

'Every time we have a conversation, it feels like you're somewhere else. You're always somewhere else.' He sighs.

I sit up again, anger stirring. 'So come on, then. What happened? What advice did *Amber* give you?'

He kneels down on the floor and stares up at me with raw, sad eyes. 'You know what?' His voice is calm, his gaze fixed on me. 'It felt good to be heard, to smile and laugh. When was the last time we laughed together? I mean *really* laughed, just the two of us?'

'Do you like her?' I sound croaky, like I'm someone else entirely. 'Do you ... want to be with her?'

'No. Not like that. I don't. We don't.' He swoops his hair off his face. 'I promise you, nothing happened. Nothing is *ever* going to happen. But it could have … if we'd let it.'

'Why are you telling me this then? What do you want from me, Joel? What do you want me to say?'

'I want you to be honest. About us.'

We sit in silence, staring at nothing. Neither of us knowing whether to stay or go.

Minutes pass before I find the courage to speak again. 'Okay. I'll give you honest,' I whisper, a single tear rolling down my face. 'I don't know if there is an *us* any more.'

The room is completely still, as if it is any other day. That blissful silence before the girls run in, leaping onto our bed, smothering us in cuddles and kisses. I roll over, instinctively seeking the warmth from Joel's body, but his side of the bed is empty, as if he's been gone for days rather than hours, and the torment of earlier this morning comes hurtling towards me at full speed.

'No. No,' he had pleaded with wide, panicked eyes. 'Think of the girls, Rani. This can't be it. Tell me what I need to do to fix us.'

'I … I don't have the answers. I don't know anything any more. I'm just so tired.' I massage my pounding forehead. 'Please, Joel, let me sleep. Oh, and I think you should take the girls to your mum's this weekend. I need time to think.'

Isn't that what you're supposed to ask for? Space. Time. Those two magic words that are supposed to make it all okay. But I didn't really mean it – surely he knew that? I'd been bruised, my ego battered. I felt hurt and rejected.

He stared at me, mouth slightly open, as if in quiet expectation.

My pulse was racing. I was waiting for a sign, a gesture. I was waiting for him to show me that I was worth fighting for.

I heard him clear his throat, as if about to say something, but then head bowed, he turned away, and walked in silence out of the room.

I pick up my phone from my bedside table, expecting to see an array of messages begging for forgiveness, but there's only one name on the screen. A name that makes me want to hurl the phone across the bedroom and feel the satisfaction of it smashing into a million tiny pieces.

I don't have the energy to deal with her right now. What I need is to leave, escape these four walls. I pull on the first clothes I find, grab my keys and purse from the kitchen counter and shut the door on the remains of last night.

The bright light of the morning sun clouds my vision. It takes me a few moments to acclimatise. Everything looks as it has always done. The birds are still singing, the trees are still swaying softly in the breeze. I felt the same way the first time my world came crashing down. When Mum died. I remember pushing my way through the huddle of aunties and uncles, people I barely recognised from India, with their forced words of comfort and lazy platitudes. Gasping for breath as soon I made it out of the front door. Out there in the open air, I could almost convince myself that everything was the same. A weird sense of juxtaposition between the turmoil in my mind and the order of the world.

Reaching the top of Shepherds Hill, I continue up the steep hill of Jacksons Lane towards Highgate Village, stopping off at a café for a double-shot latte. Staring at the happy families crowded around tables with bowls of porridge and plates piled high with pancakes. When I enter Hampstead Heath, I see an empty bench just across from the Ladies' Pond and sit down for a while, watching the immense green space fill with people. Couples walking their dogs. Groups of friends gathering on picnic blankets.

A pair of middle-aged women in their swimwear stand at the edge of the pond, staring down at the water, plucking up the courage to dive in. It must be freezing, even at this time of year. Within seconds, there's a splash, followed by a loud scream. After rapidly treading water for a few minutes, they're out again, frantically drying themselves with towels. I hear one of them say, through chattering teeth, 'I can't believe we did that. I feel so alive. Fancy going in again?'

Observing these two women would normally put a smile on my face, as I think of my two best friends and how we might one day grow old together. But my mind won't go there. It feels like a barren wasteland, the emotions draining out of me. Grief. Anger. Joy. Yet somehow, amongst all that emptiness an image comes to mind, blurry at first and then crystal clear. Flawless face. Sparkling eyes, with a hint of darkness. I'm not alone. There's still a drop left. A glimmer of hope.

After aimlessly circling the pond, the exhaustion starts to hit me. My head feels heavy; my eyes are like slits about to close. I leave the Heath and start my descent from the mansions and townhouses towards the pocket of Highgate I call home. When I reach Priory Gardens, I wander down it, hands in pockets, head hanging loose. I feel disconnected from the shiny front doors, the blooming trees and the cars parked in driveways, all sights that should be familiar to me, should ground me. But as I cross the road towards our building, something stops me in my tracks. Not a feeling or a sensation, but a force. That same magnetic force taking over.

I think of what Jemima overheard yesterday afternoon, and Charles's raging expression as he almost drove into me. And I find myself compelled to turn back and walk up the tiled path to the royal-blue front door of number 11.

Natalie

The doorbell goes and I jump out of my skin, spilling coffee all over the kitchen island. It's past midday, and I'm already exhausted. With Charles away, I spent most of the night shuffling, crawling, dragging my feet around the house. Eyes wide. Senses heightened. Running my fingers over the fine cracks in the walls, crouching inside the hidden cupboard in the loft, looking for clues, anything to spark more memories.

I may have moved here for a reason, but I never imagined this, this fear that now resides inside me. And I know that I have to make a choice. To let the past haunt me and swallow me whole, or to seek it out on my own terms.

I run a cloth under warm water to soak up the coffee before hobbling upstairs to change, peeling off my leggings, which cling to me like skin, and sliding into a flowing cream maxi dress. My mother's voice echoes in my ears.

Focus, Natalie, focus.

It doesn't matter how you feel inside. What's important is how the world sees you.

The bell rings again, spurring me into action. 'Just a minute, please,' I call from the landing, my voice still shaky, before stumbling into our en suite, dousing myself in Penhaligon's Halfeti and massaging Chanel tinted moisturiser and blusher into my lacklustre skin. I stare at my reflection, watching the transformation take place. That's better. Much better.

Clutching the banister for support, I make my way downstairs. A night on my feet hasn't done my ankle any favours, so I scurry back into the kitchen to drop a couple of painkillers down my throat.

Then, pausing for one final look in the hallway mirror, I cautiously peek through the spyhole on the front door. Charles installed a home security camera a few days ago, knowing that I'd be home alone when he went to Miami. He has an app on his phone so you can see who's outside, but I haven't got round to downloading it yet.

'Rani, hi!' I say, opening the door. I'm surprised to see her. Pleasantly so. 'So sorry for keeping you waiting.'

She looks me up and down, as if trying to read me. 'That's okay. I can come back another time if—'

'No, it's just my ankle,' I say quickly, frustrated with myself for not being more welcoming. 'I'm not used to hobbling around.'

'Oh.' She smiles sympathetically. 'How are you feeling?'

I can sense that something isn't right. She's happy to see me, but her smile doesn't quite make it to her eyes. 'Okay. The swelling has gone down a little, but I think it's starting to bruise.' I instinctively tug at my dress to cover it. 'Do you fancy coming in for a bit?'

'I don't want to impose.'

'Nonsense. Charles is in Miami with some friends. I could do with the company.' I heard from him this morning – a cold one-liner letting me know that they were about to board. I know he's waiting for me to apologise, to make things right again. My actions must have seemed so out of character. Until yesterday, we'd never had an argument. I beckon her in.

'Sorry. It's a bit of a mess at the mo. Magda's unwell. Some sort of flu, I think. And with my ankle, I can barely walk, let alone manage a hoover.' I know I'm gabbling, and hope she doesn't pick up on my nervous energy. I've forgotten what it's like to have company without Charles by my side.

'Don't be silly. It's immaculate,' she says, her eyes circling the hallway. 'As usual. Our flat always looks like a building site!'

'The joys of having kids, I suppose. Do you fancy a drink? We've got wine, I think.' Maybe I could join her. Just one glass won't hurt, to steady my nerves.

'Actually, I don't suppose you have something non-alcoholic? I have a bit of a headache.'

'Yes, of course,' I say, disappointed. 'Will elderflower cordial do?'

'Sounds great.' She follows me into the kitchen, her fingertips grazing the countertop. 'God, I love this house.'

My throat starts to close as I see Not-Luella in the room with us. Her thick red lips and giant oval face staring right at me. With one blink, she's gone. She was never here. It's the insomnia, I remind myself. Playing tricks on my mind. I quickly turn away, busying myself pouring cordial into two glasses, throwing in ice cubes and a sprig of rosemary. It's been my lifesaver since I moved in with Charles. It doesn't have the same kick as a vodka lemonade, but it's all about tricking the mind.

We head out into the garden, sitting side by side on the rattan sofa. I stretch my legs out on the corner section to elevate my ankle, enjoying the intimacy between us while trying to forget where I woke up this morning. The sun is out in full force, and

I watch as beads of sweat collect in the space between Rani's nose and lips. 'Is everything okay?' I ask her.

She takes a small sip of the cordial and nods as the sugary sweet liquid runs down her throat. 'Well. No. I've had a bit of a rough night.'

'Oh, I'm sorry. Do you want to talk about it?'

'I want to … But I'm ashamed. Charles clearly adores you. Anyone can see that.' She turns away. 'It's what I used to think about Joel. But then …' She pauses, as if waiting for me to say something.

'Yes?' I ask, offering a little encouragement.

'Our chat at the coffee shop, it sort of spurred something in me. We've been in this rut for years, and I thought that if I tried to remind him of a time before we had kids, it might change something between us. We might start opening up again, letting go of the years of resentment.'

I nod as she continues, in admiration of her openness, her trust in me.

'We went to the local pub, you know, the one down Shepherds Hill – it was Joel's idea. I thought we were on the same page. But I could tell that something wasn't right. He seemed distracted the whole time, like he'd rather be anywhere else.'

'Oh,' I murmur, not knowing what else to say.

'It was so awkward,' she continues, grimacing. 'I must have had about five white wine spritzers, so by the time we got home, I was wasted. I wasn't thinking straight. But I dunno …' She pauses to take a breath. 'I guess I just wanted to take control for once, find something to connect us. So, yeah … I tried to seduce him.' Her face crumples with shame. 'But he pushed me away. He told me that he'd grown close to someone else. My friend … my best friend.' Her voice is trembling.

'My God,' I exclaim. 'I'm so sorry. I don't know what to say.'

'It's okay,' she says, shaking her head. 'I just feel empty now – like I've gone through all the stages of grief in under twelve hours. There's nothing you can say that I haven't felt already.'

I smile in sympathy, when all I want to do is tell her that I understand this state of nothingness better than anyone.

'What would you do if you were me?' she asks.

I'm struggling for words. I've never thought about what it must be like to be in that position, to be the victim of a betrayal of trust. The men I used to meet for sex were often married, but it never occurred to me how their wives would feel. I was addicted to the overt seduction, their honeyed words, while comforted by the fact that it would always be fleeting, that they would ask nothing more from me in return. Just one night of pleasure. That was all I was worth. All I had to offer. 'What does Joel want?' I swallow. 'Does he want to be with her?'

She shrugs. 'He says there's nothing between them but friendship, but who knows?'

'Okay … but what about you, Rani?' I hear myself ask. 'Do you still love him?'

'Yes, I think so … though I don't know if that's enough any more. I don't know if I can trust him. But then, what about the girls? If we were to split up, how would I look after them on my own? What kind of mother would I be? I don't have a job, savings, family to depend on.' Her eyelids drop mournfully. This all sounds way too familiar. 'But what if there's nothing left worth fighting for? I'm not the same person he fell in love with; I haven't been for years. How can I expect him to love who I am now if I can't even love myself?' She takes another gulp of her drink. 'Anyway, thanks for listening; it means so much just having someone to talk to. How's everything with you?'

I know it's my turn to share. That's how a heart-to-heart works, isn't it? I want to, I need to, but I can feel my body fighting it, scrunching up into a tight ball. I'm anxious that if I open that door, I won't be able to close it again.

Almost as if she can sense my inner turmoil, she reaches over to hold my hand. It takes me by surprise, but her touch is gentle, unassuming. There's something so liberating about skin-to-skin contact that asks for nothing in return, and I can feel myself loosening up, the words rising to the tip of my tongue.

'Charles and I had a fight.' I throw them into the air, as if panting for breath.

'Oh Natalie, I'm sorry.' Her voice is warm, filled with concern but not surprise. 'What happened?'

'Well, it was about my job, mostly. I understand what he was saying. It takes a lot out of me. But to just give it up …'

'What? He's asked you to quit?' She leans closer, her eyes widening with alarm.

I nod. 'The thing is … I don't need to work. We can manage perfectly fine on his salary alone. And Charles is quite traditional. He grew up on a country estate with a mother who was always around. That's what he's used to. That's what he wants for his children.'

'Yeah, okay, but times have changed. You've worked so hard. Not everyone can say they're a high-flying lawyer! I mean, don't people hire nannies these days, anyway?'

I shrug. 'I guess so. No, you're right. I have worked hard to get where I am. And my mother, she'd be so disappointed. She's always been there, supporting me, guiding me. Even after what I put her through …' I stop myself.

'You know, my mum was the same. I gave her such a hard time when I was growing up, but she never stopped believing in me. She sacrificed so much for me. Thank God she's not around to see me fuck it all up.' Her eyes flick away and I hear her gulp, as if fighting her emotions.

'I'm so sorry, Rani,' I manage to say. I can't imagine what it must be like to lose a parent. I barely remember my father, but this, losing love, is so much worse than not knowing it in the first place. 'I had no idea. Come. I'll show you where the bathroom is.'

Rani

I'm in the downstairs toilet, wiping away my tears. The remnants of last night's mascara run over my cheeks and down the bridge of my nose. I look terrifyingly out of place, like I've stumbled into someone else's world. This is exactly why people like me don't live in houses like this.

The room is a sanctuary, oozing calm and serenity. It reminds me of a spa that Amber and Sasha once treated me to at one of the posh hotels in town. An informal baby shower before Lydia was born. The same whitewashed walls, fresh spring scent, and that final touch, an Aesop handwash and hand cream duo. Two products that only smother the hands of wealthy people. I push down the levers on both bottles, watching the perfumed liquid seep out and run down the plughole, enjoying the satisfaction.

It's been years since we've done anything like that spa day. Coordinating a trip away is out of the question, what with Sasha's working hours, Amber's jet-setter lifestyle and my two little dictators. It's a logistical nightmare even meeting at the weekends. The two of them were supposed to be my best friends – the people I could always rely on, who I'd turn to first. But this huge thing is happening in my life and I'm going through it alone. No wonder I've confided in Natalie, a woman I barely know.

Turning on the tap to clean up the mess, I catch sight in the mirror of a trio of photographs behind me, held in place by striking art deco frames. On closer inspection, two of the photographs look dated in comparison to the vibrant pixels of the third. In this one, the sun is setting over the majestic Tuscan hills, and it's clear from the intimacy of Charles and Natalie's expressions as they stare lovingly at each other that it was taken on their wedding day. The second one features a pretty blond boy with piercing green eyes and a huge grin on his face. Undeniably a young Charles. I spot his parents in the background, standing tall and proud in front of their country estate. Just as Natalie described.

But it's the final photograph that is the most interesting. It looks incomplete, off-centre like part of it has been sliced off with a guillotine. I peer a little closer, observing a long-limbed beauty sitting on a blanket in front of a lake, blonde hair down to her waist and dressed in well-worn brown slacks and a creased white shirt. She's the spitting image of Natalie in face and figure, but without her expensive clothes and natural elegance. This must be her mum. A young child lies next to her. Her face is hidden, buried in a book, but I recognise her as Natalie from her thick golden hair. The woman's hand rests firmly on Natalie's knee, as if protecting her, but her eyes seem to be focused on something or someone to the left of them. A subtle brush of discomfort on her face.

I remember what Natalie told me at the coffee shop, and wonder if the photo was taken before her father left. The illusion of calm before that earth-shattering moment.

Natalie

I walk back into the kitchen and catch sight of my phone on the island, glowing bright. There's a long list of missed calls from Mum, and an array of text messages. I imagine her growing more panicked as each call goes unanswered, wondering what I must be doing on a Sunday afternoon.

She picks up on the first ring, and I swoop in there before she has a chance to say anything. 'Sorry. I was just in the garden watering the plants.'

'Oh.' She breathes emphatically down the phone. 'But you never miss my calls, Natalie. I thought … I thought something had happened to you.'

'No, I was just—' I start to say, but she doesn't let me finish.

'Please, Natalie! My heart. It won't take it,' she pleads, as if in anguish. 'Especially after the fall you just had. It's too much. I can't bear it.'

'I'm really sorry. It won't happen again, I promise.'

Rani returns from the toilet. 'Your bathroom smells like a spa.' I gesture to the garden, mouthing, *I'll be out in a second*.

'Oh,' Luella says. 'You have company?'

'It's only our neighbour. She's popped over for a drink.'

'So you're happy to invite a stranger around, but you can't make time for your own mother?'

I feel terrible. I know she must be lonely. Gerald is all she has for company these days, and it's obvious how irritated she gets with him. 'It's not like that,' I reassure her. 'She's going through a tough time and needed someone to talk to. Listen …' The words pour out before I can stop them. 'Why don't you and Gerald come over next Sunday? We're having a little housewarming. It's meant to be lovely weather. We'll make an afternoon of it.'

There's a long pause. 'Well, I suppose I could be there,' she says, non-committal, but I can picture her lips curving into a smile. 'Anyway, that's not why I called. Poor Charlie rang me earlier from the airport. He's worried about you, Natalie. That job of yours, it's just not worth it. You have *him* to take care of you now. Why are you still putting yourself through it?'

'But—'

She continues over me. 'I've never had anyone who wants to look after me, who wants to give me everything. Your father was utterly useless, as you know. I gave him my heart and look how he treated me. And Gerald, with his PTSD or whatever, I spend more time looking after *him*.' She bursts into floods of tears, her voice quivering. 'Can you imagine how difficult this is for me, Natalie? To watch you take it all for granted? If you can't do this one thing for me, after everything I've done for you, honestly, I don't know how I'll cope.'

The pressure claws at my temples. What she's saying, it doesn't make sense. 'Mum, it's okay. Don't worry, please don't worry. I'm sorry, I just thought this was what you've always wanted for me. To be independent and successful in my own right. And now it feels like you're happy for me to give it all up for a man. I … I don't understand.'

'Oh, perhaps you misunderstood me, darling,' she says, her voice suddenly restored, calm. 'All I've ever wanted is for you to have the life I never got to have. And now here it is, practically served to you on a platter. And you're telling me you don't want it? If you really love him, Natalie, if you really love *me*, you'll know what to do.'

Rani pops her head around the Crittall doors. I feel my face explode with heat, my hands shaking uncontrollably. 'I'm sorry Mum, I don't know if I can …' I hang up abruptly, so she doesn't hear my voice crumble. The room spins around me like a distorted merry-go-round, her words playing over and over in my head.

If you can't do this one thing for me …

If you really love me, you'll know what to do.

I stare up at the ceiling, at the blue skies beyond the skylight and the soft white clouds, wishing I could disappear into them. And a memory passes over me, like a flash of lightning. This same room. This same view. A chorus of laughter flooding my ears and the sweet smell of apples cooking on the stove, leaving a bitter taste in my mouth. I remember the nightmare I had last night, and that same sense of dread pounds my stomach as the laughter continues.

I cover my ears with my hands and squeeze my eyes shut, blocking out the noise. I feel faint, weak, like I'm losing control, and without warning, my body plummets to the ground.

Rani

'Are you sure you'll be okay? I'm happy to stay.'

Natalie shakes her head, her face still ghostly white. 'Honestly, I'll be fine. I must have been out in the sun too long.' She moves down the hall towards the front door and I follow close behind her, in case it happens again. 'I'll probably just run a bath and head straight to bed.'

I'm not sure I believe her. Watching her on the phone, I could tell how stressed she was, and the conversation sounded intense, but I don't push it – I don't want to upset her just as we're getting to know each other. She needs someone to talk to. I do, too.

'I hope everything works out with Joel,' she adds. 'I'm here if you need me.'

Crossing the road back to mine, I decide to treat myself to a hot bath as well, and maybe an episode of *Friends*. I want to feel something beyond this emptiness. But when I reach the drive, I see someone sitting on the steps leading up to the front door.

'What the hell are you doing here?'

She looks confused. Her face is puffy, dark circles forming under her serene blue eyes. 'Didn't you get my messages?'

I pull my phone out of my handbag and see a monologue of texts, like a series of footsteps tracing her thought process and bringing her here, to my doorstep. 'No, I've been out. Why? Did you expect me to be home all day, drowning my sorrows?

I'm only going to ask you one more time before I go inside,' I hiss, trying to step around her. 'What *are* you doing here?'

'I didn't mean it like that. Come on, you know I didn't.' She stands up. 'I just want to talk to you. Face to face. I wasn't sure if you'd pick up my calls. And I couldn't wait any longer.'

I give her my best fake-sympathetic smile, when really I feel tormented. I hate what happened, but when I look at her, my best friend, a part of me longs for us to go back to the way we were. 'Poor you. That must have been really hard.' I push past her and climb the steps, turning so I'm looking down at her. 'But maybe you should have thought about that before you tried to steal my partner and the father of my children!'

'Please Rani. Just hear me out. I'm not going anywhere. I'll camp out here all night if I need to.'

This whole charade is typical of Amber. Making herself the centre of everyone else's sorrow. Thinking that she can twist people's arms with her damsel-in-distress act. But now that she's here, I'm curious about what she has to say. 'Okay, fine. Five minutes.'

She throws herself into a speech like it's a monologue she's been rehearsing for weeks. Her tone is sincere, heartfelt. If my life wasn't the casualty of this affair, I might even be moved by her words. 'It was only ever meant to be about the two of you. I swear to you, Rani. I really wanted to help him. Help you both. I know how much you mean to each other … how much you have to lose.' She tilts her head down, just a fraction. 'But then we began to talk about other things and connected in a way that was missing in both our lives. I've never experienced that before with a guy.' Tears run down her face as she speaks.

'The men who want me, who confess their love for me; it's all bullshit. It's not me they really want, it's the chase. And when I give in, let them take me out on a date, they lose interest. It's like they realise there's nothing worth sticking around for.'

'You were meant to be *my* best friend, Amber.' I feel tears collecting in my eyes, too, but I fight them hard. The last thing I need is her pity. 'Yes, things aren't great between Joel and me, but he wasn't yours to take; he wasn't yours to feel something for. And what about Lydia and Leela? Your god-daughters? Didn't you think about them at all?'

'Rani, please, I'm sorry. Nothing happened!'

'That's not the point. It *could* have, and you put yourself in that position.'

We stare at each other, both breathing fast.

'Now please, just go,' I say firmly, opening the front door and stepping inside. 'Leave me alone. I don't want to look at you any more.' And before she has a chance to say another word, I shut the door in her face.

Rani

'Mummy, Mummy! We're home!'

I'm jolted awake by their voices and the scurry of little foot-steps. My body tenses up, absorbing the sounds, and as I blink my eyes open, daylight streams through our flimsy curtains, blinding me.

I bury my face back in the pillow, groaning. It feels like I've been asleep for years, not hours. 'Hey, chicas,' I mumble, yawning through my words. 'How was Grandma's?' They leap onto the bed, smothering me in kisses. As I tilt my head back to look at them, I spot Joel's dark-blond hair in the doorway and grimace, picturing him and Amber together.

'Hey,' he says, hesitant, as if he's asking a question. 'Jemima said she could take the girls to school this morning. I don't need to be in until eleven.' He moves cautiously into the bed-room, looking like he hasn't slept in days. I almost feel sorry for him. 'I thought we could talk … is now a good time?'

'Not with the girls here,' I say, my voice flat. 'Can you take them across the road while I get dressed?'

He nods, and my heart skips as I see hope light up his tired eyes. 'Joel,' I call out. He stops. 'You know Amber came round here yesterday?'

'What? Oh, I'm sorry. I told her not to.'

'Well, she was here, so …' I sigh, frustrated. They're still talking, I think as he looks down at his feet, turns and leaves the bedroom.

I roll out of bed, stepping straight into the pile of clothes on the floor, and scrape a brush through my hair, going through the motions yet still feeling nothing inside.

When he's back from Jemima's, I slide onto a breakfast stool at the kitchen counter, awkwardly twiddling my thumbs as he makes us coffee. He takes the seat next to me, elbow on the table, chin balanced on the palm of his hand, and we begin, dissecting the broken fragments of our relationship.

'Have you had a chance to think? About what you want to do?'

I shrug. 'A little. But if I'm honest, I'm no closer. I'm still in shock, Joel, and confused. If nothing happened, then why the hell did you tell me? Did you want to hurt me or something?' I visualise the two of them laughing and joking, making a fool out of me.

'No. Of course not!' he exclaims. 'I love you, Rani. I just didn't want to hide anything from you.' His hand tiptoes across the counter towards mine. I move it quickly into my lap. I hate that he's still the good guy, even when it feels like a betrayal. 'I can keep telling you that I'm sorry, but I know it won't mean anything. I need time to make it up to you. We need time to find each other again.' He pauses, scratching the back of his head. 'What if … I dunno, we went to see someone?'

'Huh?' I have flashbacks of sitting in a cold, clinical room. A middle-aged woman in a crisp white shirt and shiny loafers, prodding, picking apart what had happened to my mum, when all I wanted to do was forget. 'No,' I state bluntly. Then, realising I might have been too dismissive, I add, 'I don't know, Joel. I don't know if I'm ready for that.'

He nods, inching closer. I notice a few strands of grey hair on his head that I haven't seen before. 'Rani, the thought of losing you after everything we've been through together … it's unbearable. But I don't think we can do this on our own.'

'You should have thought of that before you broke us.' I take a sip of coffee to distract myself.

He pauses, contemplating, before staring into my eyes. 'We've been broken a long time.'

I say nothing, listening to the voice inside my head. *You're not good enough for him.*

'Look, we don't have to decide anything now, but for the sake of the children, I think it's best that everything remains the same,' he says.

'What? You want us to play happy families? After what you did?'

Why are you pushing him away? Do you really think the girls are better off without him? Wow. World's best mother, you are.

'Like I have a choice,' I mutter under my breath.

'What was that?'

'Nothing,' I whisper, looking down at the floor. Part of me thinks I should suck it up and be grateful. I have two beautiful girls, a partner who can provide for us, somewhere warm to rest my head at night. That would be enough for some people. It's all Mum had, and I think she was happy. But is it enough for me?

What happened between Joel and Amber has made me realise just how vulnerable I am. What if he had decided to run off with her? Where would that have left me? A single mum with no job, no money, no family I can rely on. I'm tired of feeling this way. I'm tired of putting my life on hold. I want to be someone my girls can be proud of. I want to show them that they can do anything.

Natalie

My phone beeps somewhere on our brand-new dining table. I follow the vibrations, peering under wads of legal documents and case files, careful not to tip over the countless mugs of cold coffee. I catch the familiar fluorescent glow and pull my phone out. *Took an earlier flight. I'll be home in an hour.* My heart sinks to my stomach. It's only Wednesday. Charles wasn't supposed to be back until tomorrow afternoon. I'd thought I'd have more time to tidy up. I need him in a good mood from the moment he arrives home. Because I'm going to tell him that I'm not leaving my job.

Firing up the coffee machine, I gulp down a triple-shot macchiato. Then I get to work, throwing files and paperwork into drawers, dirty mugs and plates into the dishwasher, scrubbing at surfaces until they are sparkling clean. I try to remain focused, but everywhere I turn, I see flashes of Luella giggling at the stove and Not-Luella hysterically mocking me. A cool shiver slithers down my body as I remember waking up outside on the patio, disorientated, the pain burning a hole in my chest. I thought I could handle the nightmares if it meant getting closer to the truth. But I was wrong. I'm too weak; I'm not ready for this. I should have listened to my mother; let sleeping dogs lie. My hands start to shake, and I feel terrified. How much longer can I keep this from Charles? How much longer before he sees the darkness within me?

Pull yourself together, Natalie, I chide. *You've been through much worse and survived. This house will not destroy you.* I coat chicken breasts in lemon and herbs before popping them in the oven, then I head upstairs, sliding off my jogging pants and discoloured white tee, folding them deep within my wardrobe, out of sight. Then I lay my new sunflower-yellow maxi dress on the bed, ready to slip into just before Charles arrives.

But as I turn on the bath taps, my phone beeps with a message.

Remember what I said, Natalie. You have everything you've ever wanted, please don't throw it away. Looking forward to seeing your new house. L x

A lump swells in my throat. I felt so sure before. But now, reading my mother's words, I'm torn. With the housewarming this coming weekend, there's no way I can tell him. There's no way I can face it all. Charles. Luella. This house. Three high-speed trains hurtling towards me. I have no choice but to stay quiet.

My stomach heaves, and I almost choke on a rush of brown liquid that shoots out of my mouth before washing away down the plughole.

Natalie

'Darling! We're over here!' Mum waves at me from the entrance of the station, looking effortlessly chic in a pink gingham sundress and a floppy straw hat. But then her face starts to expand like a balloon pumped with helium, her prominent cheekbones sinking like quicksand. Blinking wildly, I force my attention to Gerald, who remains unchanged in his usual brown cords and a creased grey sweater, then back to Luella again. I sigh with relief. It's just my mind up to its usual tricks. *Stay focused, Natalie*, I tell myself. *It's only one afternoon. You can get through this.*

We greet each other, touching cheeks. Gerald is characteristically warm, like a big, cuddly teddy bear. 'Natalie, my dear. You gave your mother such a scare with the fall.' He ruffles my hair. 'But it's lovely to see you in tip-top form again.'

'Oh stop it, Gerald,' Mum snaps at him. 'That's old news now.' She seems happy to see me, but something isn't right with her body language. Her eyes are twitching, her hands fidgeting by her sides. As she catches me looking, she quickly stands up tall and folds my arm in hers. 'Darling. What a wonderful area. So elegant. So you.'

On the way to the house, Gerald walks awkwardly behind us, like a bodyguard. Mum does her best not to include him in our conversation. When we arrive, I notice Jemima out in her front garden, muttering to herself as she furiously pulls up weeds.

My stomach bounces up and down with nerves. I don't know if I'm ready for this, the two of them face to face.

Jemima, meet Luella, my mother.

Luella, meet Jemima, your old neighbour.

I take a deep breath and clear my throat. 'Jemima, hi. I haven't seen you out and about for a while.' I look down at my ankle. 'I've been working from home this week – it's done me the world of good. How are you? Oh, and this is my mother, and her partner, Gerald.'

Jemima stands up to greet us. I watch her insert her right index finger into her mouth to tease the glove off her hand. 'Hello, Natalie. Nice to see you back on your feet again.' Then she blinks, looking from me to Mum. 'Goodness me, Natalie, aren't you the spitting image of her! Lovely to meet you,' she says, eyebrows raised and her thin lips quivering in excitement as she offers Mum her now bare hand.

I watch Mum's body tense up as their palms meet. But a second is all she can manage before she briskly pulls away, threading her arm through mine again. She looks so uncomfortable that I almost want to apologise for her rudeness.

Does she recognise Jemima?

Is she worried that Jemima recognises her too?

I force myself to break the tension. 'We're having a little housewarming with some friends this afternoon. Rani and Joel from across the road will be swinging by as well. You're welcome to pop along if you fancy it.'

'Oh gosh, I couldn't. I'm sure you don't want an old bag like me cramping your style! I've got these weeds to wrestle with, anyway. Kind of you to ask, though.' Jemima looks at Mum again and smiles nervously. 'You know, this might seem a little strange, but you remind me so much of someone who used to live here. Right next door, in fact.'

Mum untangles her arm from mine. I watch her jaw start to quiver and her left hand reach down, gripping the brick wall to steady herself. It's just a small, subtle change. Barely noticeable. Then suddenly, she's back to normal again, laughing out loud. 'How funny,' she says. 'I wish it *was* me. You know, I get this a lot. I have one of those faces. Gerald will tell you.'

We hear an obedient grunt behind us.

'Sadly, I've never lived anywhere quite so lovely. But,' she adds as she puts her arm around my waist and pulls me close, 'at least I have my beautiful daughter to experience it all for me.'

'Sorry about that. I could have sworn it was you, but I'm not as young as I used to be.' Jemima glances down at her gardening gloves, flustered. 'Now, you must get on. I'm sure your guests will be arriving soon.'

'It was a pleasure meeting you, Jemima.' Mum pulls me away, her jaw still trembling ever so slightly. 'Come on, Natalie, before we're unfashionably late. So which house is yours?'

'It's this one. Just next door.'

I wait with bated breath as she turns towards it, taking it all in. From the mosaic tiled path to the polished brass handle on the royal-blue front door. Her face is expressionless, a blank canvas, giving nothing away. *She thinks I don't remember.*

But there's her hand again, hovering in mid-air, searching frantically for somewhere to rest.

Rani

'You're here!' Natalie opens the door, smiling, as we walk up the path. She's wearing a brightly coloured long-sleeve maxi dress in an ikat print – it looks insanely expensive. She could pull off anything, but I can't help but notice the way it hangs loosely off her slender frame, muting her natural curves, so different to the skintight mini dress she wore with confidence at the dinner party.

Lydia skips straight inside and down the hall into the kitchen, already at home here. But Leela hangs back, hiding behind me. I nudge her forward. 'What do you want to say to Auntie Natalie?'

She looks up, blinking. 'I'm really sorry,' she murmurs, before pulling a crumpled dandelion necklace out of her dungarees pocket. 'For you. I made it myself.'

'Oh my goodness, Leela,' Natalie gushes, popping it around her neck. 'It's beautiful, thank you. And no need to apologise, it's all forgotten. Now, come in, come in!' She welcomes us through, enveloping me in a hug. But her body feels rigid against mine. Is it Charles? I wonder. Did something else happen between them?

Joel stands next to me; he's so awkward it's unbearable. Barely brushing her cheeks as he greets her, avoiding her gaze when she speaks to him. I know he's thinking of me after what happened with Amber, but I feel like screaming at him: *IS THIS WHAT IT'S GOING TO BE LIKE FROM NOW ON?*

As we follow Lydia into the kitchen, my chest is all butterflies seeing the ghost of Natalie's past – the spot where she fainted after the phone call with her mother, and her fight with Charles. I catch sight of him in the garden, surrounded by a group of women, and I watch as he makes them laugh while topping up their wine glasses – the perfect host.

He turns his gaze towards us and a wave of something unreadable passes over him. I can't make it out. But then he's strolling up the garden path, a welcoming smile lighting up his face. 'Rani, Joel, I didn't think you were coming! Lovely to see you both again. Crikey, don't you scrub up well!' He offers me his cheek, and as it brushes against mine, he whispers softly into my ear, 'I see you, Rani.'

'Huh?' I ask as he grazes my other cheek.

'You'll be asking for a set of keys next,' he continues. I notice that his usually warm eyes are now stone cold, and feel shivers down my spine, but within seconds he's back, smiling, shaking Joel's hand. 'Now, let me guess. You've come for more of that Château Cheval Blanc. Well, you're in luck, my man,' he says, slapping Joel's back in a hearty manner. Joel answers for both of us, and after pouring two large glasses, Charles leads him away towards the barbecue. I watch their backs for a moment, before taking a deep breath to steady myself.

The girls are already in the garden with the other children. Their new playmates are a young boy with a toothy grin and a sweet-looking chubby girl with long brown hair – both dressed like they're going to the races. I watch Leela drift away from the group, tiptoeing barefoot on the grass, smelling the flowers and chasing butterflies. Lydia seems to be getting on well with them, though, so I make the most of my alone time with Natalie.

'How have things been with …?' I tilt my head in Charles's direction.

She takes a sip of her drink. Elderflower cordial again. Could she be pregnant already? Maybe that's why she's so tense. 'Good. The time apart has helped … he hasn't brought the work thing up again. I think he gets how difficult it would be for me to leave my job,' she says with a rigid, almost forced smile, her voice barely louder than a whisper.

I'm about to express my doubts when I hear a high-pitched voice summoning us outside. Natalie glances at me, her lips contorting. She mouths, *That's Mum*, and takes my hand.

We join a group of expertly manicured women hovering in wedged espadrilles, a rainbow of maxi dresses just like Natalie's. I can feel myself starting to panic, searching for a way out. I stare down at my own feet before forcing my head back up and tuning in from the sidelines. The women all seem to be listening attentively to one of their number, and I realise that this must be Luella.

'Yes, Natalie was always this beautiful,' she says, proudly. There's a glint in her eye as she takes in my arrival, but she doesn't stop for a second to welcome me into the fold. 'I'd take her for walks in her pram, and I can't tell you the number of times we'd get stopped. Men, women, boys and girls. All eager to catch a glimpse of her. I felt for sure she would follow in my footsteps and take up modelling, but then I discovered just how *smart* she was as well.' She lets out an unexpected cackle. 'Goodness knows where she got *those* genes from!'

I glance over at Natalie. She looks calm, admirably so. Like she's been rehearsing this scene her entire life. I watch as she laughs along with the group, reassuring us that her mother is widely known for her tendency to exaggerate. There's a thick coat of warmth between them. The kind typically found in a secure mother–daughter relationship. It makes me long for my own, but then I realise that something isn't quite right.

It's a superficial warmth, not enough to shelter them from the storm. I've seen Natalie one on one, relaxed at home in her natural habitat, and this isn't it. It's the small hints of body language that give her away. The clench of her jaw. The tightness of a shoulder. Details most people would overlook.

There's a short break in conversation, and Natalie glances over to me, deciding to take this opportunity to introduce me to the group. Suddenly I'm surrounded by glossy hair, golden tans, and several pairs of eyes looking down on me. I feel like a circus clown, and if that's the case, Luella is for sure the ringmaster.

She's Natalie in face and figure.

Well, Natalie plus twenty-five years and a few rounds of Botox.

'So *you're* the famous Rani. I hear that you've been taking up Natalie's precious time on Sunday afternoons.' She loops a slender arm around me to let us know that she's making a joke, but that does nothing to reassure me. 'She's in demand, my Natalie. Always has been. But she can afford to be picky,' she says, fixed on me, measuring my flaws. Then, looking mildly unimpressed, she flicks her gaze over my head. 'Are those two over there your girls?'

Lydia seems engrossed in a game with her new friends, so I beckon Leela over, curling my fingers through the tangles visible in her hair. But she's already distracted, mesmerised by a butterfly fluttering around her. 'Yes. Both mine. Over there is

Lydia, and this is Leela. She's my little wild child. Never happier than when outside in nature.'

Luella smiles at us both, but her eyes betray her, pupils dilating and darkening. It's that same intense look that Natalie had back at the café while staring at the photograph of the girls on my phone.

A stick-thin woman drowning in designer clothes pipes up to fill the awkward silence. She reminds me of a young Victoria Beckham. I think she said her name was Darcy. 'They're gorgeous, Rani. So different, but both little treasures. You're so lucky to have two girls. I have one of each, but I'm still hoping for another girl. Though my husband will have a heart attack if I confess that to him!'

We all giggle in unison, and that niggling uncertainty inside me subsides. I feel sure that the rest of the afternoon will pass without any hiccups.

'Ladies and gentlemen, lunch is served,' Charles announces with authority. Our huddle breaks up, and I glance at Joel. He's talking to someone by the barbecue, but his eyes keep darting from side to side as if he wants to leave. I observe the man's sunburnt face and ginger hair, balding slightly on top – he's nothing special to look at, but his polished loafers and crisp white shirt give him away as a friend of Charles. An older-looking gentleman teeters around them, waiting patiently for scraps of conversation. That must be Luella's partner.

I scan the garden, searching for Natalie. She emerges from the kitchen looking pale and withdrawn, and I try to get her attention, but she's distracted, flitting nervously between Charles and her mother as if waiting for something to happen.

'Now, I can't take all the credit,' Charles is saying. 'All I've done is turn some burgers on the grill. This feast was all Natalie's idea, to christen our new home. Please help yourself to the delicious salads she's rustled up.'

I line up with Darcy, scooping Ottolenghi-inspired salads onto my plate. Orange and rocket with sticky Medjool dates. Caramelised figs and warm feta.

'He never changes,' Darcy whispers, picking at wilting salad leaves.

I can't figure out what she means. 'Have you known him long?'

'Charles? Why, yes. In fact it was his ex-wife, Joanne, who introduced me to Seth. My husband.' She nods to the man Joel was talking to. 'They were university friends.' She pauses, her expression obscure. 'We don't see her any more.'

'Oh?'

But she shakes her head, as if she has been sworn to secrecy. 'I'm so happy that he's found Natalie. I don't think anyone one else would—'

We're interrupted by a ceremonious pop from the kitchen, and a few minutes later, Charles walks out into the garden carrying a tray of champagne flutes. He gestures to us all to take one, before heading towards Natalie, folding her hand into his as if to say, *Don't go anywhere.*

I watch him massage her fingers and my stomach fills with dread.

'Before we kick off, I have a little announcement to make,' he says, waiting for everyone's attention to land on him – it's clear he's used to the limelight, that he commands it. 'I'd like to start by showing my appreciation for this incredible woman.

You all know how hard Natalie works. How much time she has given to Birdie & Smith over the years.'

I hear a *whoop whoop* from a few women who must be her colleagues.

'She's one of their most valued employees, so this has been a very difficult decision for us to make. But after deliberating long and hard, we've decided to wipe the slate clean and start afresh together.'

There's silence all around. Bewildered faces. But Charles continues, his smile only growing brighter. His eyes find me and linger for a moment before continuing. 'Natalie has been keen for us to start a family, which everyone knows is just not possible working long hours in the City. And as her dutiful husband, it is my greatest honour to support her in her decision to leave her practice for the fresh start that she so deserves.' He holds up his flute. 'So without further ado, please raise your glasses to Natalie, my talented wife. I can't wait to see what lies in store for her next!'

The group is still speechless. Well, all except Luella, who smiles brightly, boasting about her first grandchild being on the way. We all obediently follow Charles's instructions, raising our glasses in Natalie's direction. But one slips to the ground, shattering into tiny pieces on the patio. It causes such a commotion that no one notices Natalie growing pale. And within seconds, she's unconscious on the floor.

It's only as I start to run towards her that I notice there's no flute in my hand.

Natalie

'Niaomi? Niaomi, is that you?' A young girl sits on the cold wooden floor, her knees to her chest and her face in her hands, quietly sobbing. 'It's me … Natalie.' I step a little closer, reaching out to touch her, twisting my fingers through her wild, tangled hair. 'What's wrong? Why are you crying?'

She raises her head, almost in slow motion. And when I see her face, I shrink back in fear, taking in her bloodshot eyes and ghostly white skin. But she says nothing. Just stares at me in silent despair, before raising her finger to her lips. 'Shh.'

I turn cautiously and feel a cold snake slither down my spine. My mother and Dr Baldwin sit on tiny rocking chairs, holding hands, swaying back and forth, with wide smiles on their faces. Dr Baldwin opens his mouth. 'This isn't real,' he says. 'None of this is real.' His voice is strange. Monstrous. Raspy. *What happened to the kind, gentle man I remember?* Luella tries to speak, but nothing comes out. Then, out of nowhere, I watch as she clutches her throat with her hands, looking desperately in my direction. Or behind me.

I turn around. Niaomi's eyes have transformed to a bright orange, a devilish glare at their centre. They remain fixated on my mother, as if in a trance. Her arms are horizontal by her sides, fists squeezing the air. And on the wall behind her, giant words are scrawled in what looks like fresh dripping blood. *HELP ME. HELP ME.*

My attention moves from the wall to the bed.

And a scream rises from me.

I wake to darkness crawling up the walls and lining the ceiling like black mould. My body feels wet to touch and a dull ache lingers. But the pain isn't just physical. It's a pain that has lain dormant in the depths of my mind, and now that it's finally free, it consumes me whole. I jerk my head back, scanning the walls. Looking for evidence of blood splattered on them. I narrow my eyes and stare in front of me, searching for any sign of Niaomi. But there's nothing here except my giant green wardrobe and the bed I'm lying in. Alone. Yet still I sense her presence clinging to me. Dragging me back to the place in my subconscious where I know we will be reunited.

I sit upright and force myself awake, knowing that I need my strength to stay alert. I've barely moved an inch since Charles brought me here, hours ago. Carrying me up the stairs like a damsel in distress, he my loyal servant. Through bleary eyes, I watched him lower me down. Lying still as if playing dead as he wiped the sweat off my forehead with his handkerchief and kissed me in the exact same place that he had rubbed clean. *Everything will be okay, Natalie*, he whispered. *If you just trust me.*

His words had lost their warmth and reassurance. They sounded razor-sharp, like a warning.

I hear voices below. The first is as deep and rich as roasted coffee. Undoubtedly Charles. The other is shrill, flapping about like an exotic bird. Mum? I'd assumed she'd gone home with the rest of our guests, and I'm anxious just thinking of the two of them alone together. But there are no raised voices. No whiff of tension in the air between them.

Tuning in, I catch dribs and drabs of conversation.

'I'm humiliated … didn't come to Seth's birthday … had to make excuses … pitiful glances … expected more …'

But I know I have to hear this properly, so I force myself out of bed and creep across the landing. And as I hover at the top of the stairs, every word becomes clear.

'This isn't like her, Charlie. The woman I raised would never have made a fool of herself in public like that. She would have come up with an excuse, taken herself inside to control her nerves. Something has changed since you moved here. Something is happening to her.'

'She's barely been sleeping, Luella, what with the hours she's putting in at work. I think she's been having nightmares. And that woman from across the road isn't helping – she was here last Sunday, remember? While I was in Miami. Poking her nose into our business. What was Natalie thinking, inviting her today? Amongst close friends and family.'

'Oh, *her*. Yes, I had a bad feeling about her too. Did you see what she was wearing? That cheap denim skirt. She stuck out like a sore thumb. Natalie has always chosen the people she lets into her life so carefully. That woman must have pushed her way in, taken advantage of Natalie's kind heart. Don't be disheartened, Charlie. Leave it to me. Let me talk some sense into her.'

I dash back across the landing and jump back into bed, smoothing down my hair and pinching my cheeks. It's not perfect, but it's the best I can do at such short notice.

She walks straight in without knocking. 'Natalie, darling. How are you feeling? Gosh, you look terrible, darling.' She shudders, placing her hand awkwardly on my forehead. I feel the subtle wrinkling of her skin, a part of her body not plumped by Botox.

Then, without waiting for me to answer, she launches into the silence. 'Well, as you might expect, Charlie isn't at all happy. Your reaction was completely uncalled for. You've embarrassed him. You've embarrassed yourself.'

I focus on my breath. Willing myself to remain calm. Still. For her words to bounce off me without piercing through my skin. It's the only way. But then I think of Niaomi. Her pale, ghostly face, dripping with tears. And how quickly her strength and determination took over, the bright orange flame flickering in her eyes. 'Stop, please just stop. Not now. Not after the nightmare I've just had,' I say, my features scrunching up with despair.

Her face drops. For once, her feelings are tattooed all over it. 'It's not …'

'Niaomi. She's back.'

The wheels are turning, heading down the highway at full speed. A crash is imminent. But somehow she manages to compose herself.

She comes closer. 'Natalie, you do remember, don't you, what Dr Baldwin said? How dangerous she is. What she did to you. We've worked so hard to put it all behind us. Think of everything you have now. Charles and your wonderful life together. Don't let her take it all away.'

She can't even say her name.

'Why was that, Mum? Why did we have to start again? You know that I've never been able to remember anything. And I'm tired. I'm tired of being in the dark.'

'Oh, Natalie. Why dredge up the past when you have so much to look forward to? We must never, ever go back to that place.' Taking a seat on the edge of the bed, she continues, her voice fading to a faint whisper. 'You've been so stable since

Charlie came along, but I think you're starting to relapse. Look, why don't we go back and see Dr Baldwin? Get you back on the medication. Charlie doesn't need to know a thing. It can be our little secret.' She smiles, before getting up and turning away.

But just as she's about to open the door, I hear her mutter under her breath, 'Everything I've done, Natalie, I've done for you. Only you. Don't ever forget that.'

Rani

Joel paces up and down our poky kitchen, waiting for the kettle to boil. He covers a lot of ground with his long strides. I wonder how many times he's trampled over the same path.

Stopping mid-pace, he turns to face me, perched on the end of the sofa. 'And you're sure about Charles?'

I nod, sighing anxiously.

'I dunno, Rani. I mean, he's a grade-A snob, let's be honest, but apart from that, you should have heard what he was saying to me at the barbecue. How he's never felt so happy and that it's all down to her.'

Joel has only met Charles and Natalie a couple of times. He barely knows them. But after the way Charles steamrollered over her at the barbecue, it's like I'm seeing him with fresh eyes and I can't stop replaying all our encounters in my head, filling Joel in at the same time. Charles holding Natalie like a child in the coffee shop after she fell. Her apologising to him over and over again. His dagger eyes in the car, almost running me over. And finally what he whispered in my ear at the barbecue. The threat within the words.

'Hmm,' Joel says, pouring boiling water into two identical mugs. 'The car thing, it was probably just an accident, and anyway, didn't he apologise? And maybe you misread the whole coffee shop situation.' I flinch as he comes toward me, setting the mugs on the coffee table. 'Please don't take this the wrong way,' he says, crouching down in front of me, 'but I'm worried about you. I think you're clinging onto something that just isn't there.'

Why does he have to make this about me?

'Okay, well how do you explain his speech at the barbecue, then? You have to admit that's a weird thing to do. Announce something publicly that you haven't even discussed with your wife.' I raise my voice. 'And Natalie fainting? Again. What if … what if he's drugging her?' As the words tumble of my mouth, something starts to click.

'That's insane, Rani! What's got into you? You can't go saying things like that about people you've only just met! Their garden is a suntrap; even I was feeling light-headed. And I don't think I saw Natalie have a single bite to eat!'

'Yeah …' I mumble, unconvinced.

'I'm sorry, but I don't see any red flags. And if I were you, I'd keep my distance from them. Let them sort it out on their own.'

'Don't you trust me, Joel?'

He sighs. 'I just think your judgement might be a little clouded, that's all.'

'I can see things just fine, thanks,' I snap, shuffling away from him.

'Oh, Rani. I'm sorry. I didn't mean it like that.' He scratches his head. 'I know I've hurt you, and that we're a long way away from fixing our problems. I just meant that maybe you shouldn't be wasting all this energy on *them*. Think about us … we have our first counselling session coming up; let's try and focus on that.

Ugh. I'm dreading it. But I have to try something. This isn't just about Joel and me. It's our girls' lives that will be affected too.

'Yeah, okay, fine.' I can tell that there's no point pushing it further, so I stand up slowly and take my half-empty mug to the kitchen. When I turn back, Joel is slouched on the sofa, feet up on the coffee table, watching TV, and I know he's already lost interest.

As an outsider looking in, Natalie's world seemed so transparent, so pristine. The successful career. The dream home. The adoring husband. But the more she lets me in, the more mysterious it seems. There are hints of something dark and disturbing that I can't quite reach, let alone understand. But I'm determined to find out what's going on.

Leela scurries into the room. She has a great big smile on her face, as if she's done something brilliant. 'Look, Mummy, look. Come see what I've drawn.' She takes my hand, leading me into their bedroom, and as I crouch down next to her colouring table, crayons scattered all over it, she hands me a sheet of paper. 'Look, I made this for you, Mummy.'

I take it and gasp, then quickly cover my mouth with my hand so as not to offend her. 'Thanks, chica. This is lovely.' Here we all are at the barbecue. She's captured every detail, even the champagne glasses in our hands. Well, all but one. My eyes drift to the fragments of glass by my feet. And just on the right of me is Natalie, lying on the lawn like a fallen angel.

There's a sound behind me. I turn around and my heart jolts into my chest. Lydia has changed into a dress in a similar shade to the one Natalie was wearing, and her lips are painted cherry red. But that isn't the most shocking thing. I watch as she dramatically feigns falling to the ground, mimicking the way Natalie fainted, and then rises to do it again. Leela cheers her on and she stops to take a bow.

I know it's just a game for them, but it's eerie to watch. Like a scene from a horror movie replaying over and over again.

Rani

I've tucked the girls into bed and am about to read them a bedtime story. Lydia insists on one with a blonde-haired, blue-eyed princess, and my heart breaks when I realise that this must be her idea of beauty. Someone who looks so different to me. So different to herself. As I open the first page, she stares up at me, pupils dilated.

'Mummy, is Natalie a real-life princess?'

I can't help but laugh, but the vibrations don't reach my insides. I want to do better by my children. I want them to have pride in their own unique selves, instead of longing to be someone else. But how I can ask that of them when I can't even do it myself?

After a couple of pages, the girls are already starting to drift off. I switch off their bedside lamp and walk down the landing towards our bedroom, staring out of the window at the house across the street, wondering how Natalie is doing. The curtains are drawn in her bedroom, but I can see a light on downstairs. Taking my phone out of my back pocket to send her a message, I notice two missed calls from Amber and a text. *I miss you.* I sigh through gritted teeth – how quickly she's moved on from 'I'm sorry'. Deleting it, I start to text Natalie, but I'm soon distracted by two figures appearing in the doorway of number 11.

A woman steps outside, a long trench coat belted tightly around her slim frame. Under the bright porch light, she could be mistaken for Natalie, but her plump lips and iron-smooth skin give her away. Luella. I watch as Charles kisses both of her cheeks. And as she turns away, our eyes meet, but only for a second, before she sets off briskly towards the station.

I follow her with my gaze, intending to stay put until she's out of sight. But my feet have another idea, and with no plan in mind, I find myself rushing out of the flat and galloping down the stairs to catch up with her.

Panting and spluttering, I stretch my hand out towards her shoulder, but she's already registered my presence and spins around before I have the chance to speak.

'Goodness me! What on earth are you doing sneaking up on me like that?'

I'm struggling to catch my breath. 'Sorry,' I wheeze. 'I wasn't thinking.'

'Look, I have a train to catch. So whatever you have to say, just spit it out.' She hisses at me like a snake. I'm surprised at how quickly she's lost her sugary-sweet demeanour.

'I … I just wanted to ask how Natalie is doing.'

'She's fine. Just a little tired, that's all.'

'Good,' I say, taking a deep breath to settle my nerves. This may be my only opportunity to speak to her alone. 'I know we've only just met, but Natalie and I have recently become friends and I'm worried about her. I don't know how well you know Charles, but there's something not quite right about their relationship. What he said at—'

'Now let me stop you right there.' She quickly lowers her voice as someone crosses the road towards us. 'How long have you known them? Days? Weeks? Well, that's not enough time to *really* know someone, is it? Don't you think I would want the best for my only daughter?'

'I'm just trying to—'

'Let me finish.' The lamp post above her suddenly switches on, and her face glows whiter than white, her features melting into it. I cover my eyes, blinded, but she continues, barely noticing. 'You may think you know Natalie, but trust me, you don't know *anything*. After what we've been through, Charlie is the best thing that has ever happened to her. He's everything she has ever wanted since she was a little girl, and nothing is going to get in the way of that. Least of all the neighbourhood busybody.'

Her words hit me hard, like a slap in the face. I swallow the bitter lump now lodged in my throat. 'Hang on a minute. That's unfair. I'm only trying to do the right thing by her.'

'Yes? Well, so am I. Why don't you let me worry about my child and you just focus on yours? Now, unless you're going to apologise for that outrageous accusation, I'm leaving.'

I'm so shocked by her outburst that I just stand there staring at her. Unable to move or speak. I hear her tut under her breath as she turns sharply away before disappearing down the steps into the station.

Rani

'This place. It's unreal,' I whisper, wide-eyed and open-mouthed, my voice echoing through the glossy Moroccan-themed interior of the Jedi Club spa. *God, Freya would love this*, I think, making a mental note to call her this weekend. It's been weeks since we last spoke, and with my head being all over the place, I've forgotten to respond to her messages. 'How much did you say this cost again?' I ask, turning back to Natalie.

'I didn't. It was a present from work. After what happened at the—'

'You're kidding?' I interrupt, sensing that she doesn't want to spell it out. 'Most people get flowers or chocolates. You get a day trip for two to the best spa in London.'

'No,' she says quickly, grimacing. 'The partners are all members here. We're probably just using their free guest passes.'

'Still … it's something else. I could get used to this,' I say, admiring the marble pillars and the gold statues. Staring at my reflection in the glistening infinity pool. 'Ooh, and it looks like we've got it to ourselves.'

'Yeah …' She seems nervous, cupping her phone in her hands. 'I think they're going to call me for my massage soon. You'll be okay here, won't you?'

'Are you mad? They'll have to throw me out!'

I can tell she's trying to smile, but it barely materialises on her face. 'Listen, you won't mention this to anyone, will you?

Charles … I haven't told him where we are. He thinks I'm at work,' she mumbles, her jaw quivering. 'I didn't want to worry him.'

'Of course not. It'll be our secret.' I touch her arm reassuringly, but feel her flinching at my words. I have no idea why this would even be an issue.

And then it hits me. It's not the spa trip at all; it's me.

We wander over to a duo of infrared heated loungers, a concept I had no idea existed until the lady at reception started gushing about them, her sparkling eyes looking only in my direction. 'Just thirty minutes of this and I swear you'll feel brand new.'

Slowly I unknot the belt of my dressing gown and hang it on the wall. Then, feeling suddenly conscious of my body and all its imperfections, I wrap a towel around my waist and lie back on the lounger. 'Aah, this is the life,' I say, relaxing my shoulders, letting all the tension drain out of me.

Natalie does the same, barely giving it a thought, and I can't help but stare at her. The cut of her minimalist white swimsuit and the gentle curves of her long, slender frame, not a bulge in sight. I sigh in relief. She can't be pregnant. But then I see something unexpected, a collection of bruises like ripe plums along the side of her leg. So stark on her flawless, white skin. It must be from when she fell. 'Ouch,' I say.

She glances down, embarrassed, before quickly turning her leg away. 'It looks much worse than it feels.'

'How are you doing? After the fall … and everything with Charles.'

Her jaw tightens and I immediately regret bringing it up.

'I'm fine. We're fine,' she says, staring at her phone. The light from the screen bounces up onto her face. I notice faint dark circles under her eyes that she's tried to cover with make-up. She catches me staring and looks uneasy. 'I haven't been sleeping that well. I keep having these nightmares.'

'Really? What about?'

She pauses, deep in thought. I can tell it's on the tip of her tongue, but then she brushes it off. 'Oh, nothing, just work stuff.'

I don't believe her for a second and want to press her further, but then she adds, 'I … I did get a strange email the other day, though.'

'Oh,' I say, my interest piqued.

'From my father.'

'What?'

'I know. He said he saw a photo of me in the paper, from this case I'm working on.'

'What did he say?'

She hesitates, before scrolling through her phone and holding it out for me to see. I skim-read the message, but hover longer over the email address. 'Oh … so he wants to meet you? That's it?'

'It looks like it.'

'But why now? After all this time?'

'I have no idea. Like I said, it's strange.' She lays the phone by her side. 'I'm not going to respond. After the way he treated Mum, and walked out on us, I don't want anything to do with him,' she says sternly.

I nod my head in agreement, but my mind is elsewhere, reflecting on how much Natalie has changed since the day we met. She seemed so perfect, so impenetrable at first. But how quickly after the fall and then her fight with Charles her spark began to fade. And I recall Luella's words. *After what we've been through*. She must have been referring to Natalie's dad walking out and the pain it caused them, still bubbling away beneath the surface.

And I worry about what his return will bring – whether it will be restoration or the tipping point.

Natalie

I hear a soft knock at the door, and a man enters.

'Good afternoon, ma'am,' he says, stepping towards me. 'My name is Suleman. I am delighted to be your therapist today.' He pauses, looking down at my hands. 'Ma'am, your rings. Shall I remove them for you?'

'Sorry. I completely forgot I had them on. Please go ahead.'

'Of course, ma'am. One moment, please.' Picking up a bottle of oil, he pours some onto his palm. Then, taking my hand, he massages the oil into it, teasing the rings from my fingers and dropping them into the pocket of my dressing gown. I hear them clash together and flinch at the sound as it echoes around the room. He cups his hand on my shoulder to relax me, and I try to calm my mind, breathing in the luxurious aromas of expensive lotions that waft through the air.

'So, ma'am, it's okay if I start now?'

I nod my head, but he's already kneading away at the balls of my feet with strong, smooth hands, deep in concentration. I hear it in his long, steady breath. I sense it in his firm grip. My stiff body soon begins to unwind, giving in to his touch, and I feel as light as a feather, as if I'm floating out of my shell, somewhere high above the ground.

Moving up my calves, he stops for a second, clearing his throat.

'I fell. While out running,' I mumble quickly.

I hear him tut under his breath, but he continues anyway, avoiding the spot neither of us wants to talk about.

As time passes, I reach that detached state between being awake and asleep, where your nightmares can't touch you and reality feels as though it's light years away. I have no thoughts. I have no fears. I exist only in the moment.

Clutching my left shoulder, he whispers into my ear, 'Ma'am, are you awake? Can you hear me? It is time to turn over, if you please.' I force my eyes open and turn my head, disorientated. The light above me shines down on my oiled body. My fair skin is several shades darker from the enhanced circulation, and for a moment I don't recognise it. 'Your back and shoulders, ma'am?'

Then I realise what he means me to do. 'Yes, of course,' I mumble, peeling myself off the massage table one body part at a time. It feels warm and sticky where pools of sweat have gathered. Suleman turns his head away, as if preserving my modesty, when we both know that he has seen it all already. It's not like clear plastic underwear leaves much to the imagination.

As I flop back onto the massage table, I bury my face in the deflated pillow and close my eyes, letting his magic fingers find the contours of my back.

'Ma'am, you carry a lot of stress here. Too many knots.'

I've heard this many times before, but I say nothing in response. This is a stress-free room. The last thing I want to do is invite stress inside.

His fingertips sink deeper into my flesh, as if teasing out every knot from my body, and I sense him edging closer, his body leaning over mine. I feel the force of his hands echoed in his breath, changing pace to short, sharp bursts, and the weight of him pressed against my thighs.

I tell myself that it's harmless, that he's only doing his job. But the more he homes in on the curves and crevices of my body, the more vulnerable I feel. My nose squashes up against the pillow and my breath becomes laboured as I gasp for air.

Before I have a chance to rationalise my thoughts away, I see him.

Charles. But not Charles. The coldness of his stare. The tightness of his lips. And I feel it in my bones, a paralysing fear that something terrible is about to happen.

In one mighty swoop, I turn and push him off me. There's a loud clatter somewhere in the shadows as his body collides with the collection of creams and lotions on the table behind us. I hear him shriek with pain, but don't stop to check if he is okay.

I'm in full survival mode.

All I'm thinking is that I need to get out. I need to save myself before he pins me down. Then, realising that the light is still shining on me, I leap off the massage table, grab my dressing gown from the chair and race out of the room.

Outside, a fresh-faced teen glides past me. She turns swiftly, taking me in. The gown wrapped loosely around my naked body and the sheer panic on my face. 'Madam, is everything okay?'

'He … he …' I point at the room.

'Do you mean Suleman? If you didn't like your massage, you're the first. He's the best we've got.' And then it hits her. 'No, no – there must have been a misunderstanding. Suleman would never touch a woman like that. He's not even interested in … Look, come with me and we'll sort all this out.' She weaves my arms into the dressing gown and ties the belt around my waist. She's several inches smaller than me, but I feel like a child next to her.

I stare at her in confusion. 'Suleman … who's Suleman?'

She takes a small step backwards, as if trying to distance herself from me. There is a look on her face that I haven't seen before.

Pity.

I reach into my dressing gown pocket for my phone and quickly switch it on. I wait for the screen to burst to life, desperate to call Rani so we can leave this place.

But a message flashes at me. *Natalie, where are you? Come home. Now.*

Rani

'Natalie, are you okay?' I manoeuvre myself into the seat next to her. She has a thick woollen blanket wrapped around her shoulders, and her hair falls in oily clumps over her heart-shaped face.

'I … I'm … so … cold,' she says, teeth chattering, her body shivering underneath the blanket.

I reach over and wrap my arms around her, rubbing her shoulders gently, transferring warmth. 'Excuse me,' I call out to the cab driver, 'would you mind turning the heating on?'

'Are you joking, love? It's almost June!'

'Please. Can't you see that she's freezing?'

I notice his eyes pop up in the mirror. 'She's not gonna be sick, is she? It's a nightmare to clean leather seats.'

I shake my head, and whisper into her ear, 'We're almost there, don't worry, please don't worry. You'll be home soon.' I press my cool hand onto her forehead. It feels red hot, causing me to flinch. *What the hell happened in that room?*

She stares up at me. Her pupils are dilated, larger than I've ever seen them before, and her irises are pools of blood. 'He … he … knows …'

'Who? Charles? What does he know?'

She nods her head. 'He … he … knows about me. I'm scared, Rani.'

'What? What does he know? Did you see him … in the treatment room?'

She nods again, ever so slightly.

Heat suddenly blasts through the fans either side of us. I look up at the driver and say, 'Thank you,' and he sighs noisily, muttering something inaudible under his breath. I can already feel myself sweating, and shrug my jacket off.

'But Natalie, there was no one else there. Just you and the masseur. And Charles is at work, isn't he?' Then I remember what I suspected after the barbecue, and I think, *This can't be a coincidence*. Her fainting in her kitchen and then on the lawn, the nightmares she was talking about earlier but then quickly dismissed as being work-related, and now hallucinations, too – it must be coming from somewhere. 'Natalie,' I say tenderly, taking her hands in mine. 'Are you on any medication at the moment, or ...' I hesitate, realising that I hardly know her at all. 'Do you do drugs ... like coke or something?' I remember going to Sasha's work drinks in Canary Wharf and watching her colleagues disappear off to the bathroom in tight huddles, returning minutes later with pupils dilated and their actions noticeably more erratic, restless.

She turns to stare at me, her mouth wide open. She looks stunned, I think, or is it something else? Panic? 'No ... no,' she whispers, shaking her head frantically. 'I don't ...'

'Okay. That's good. What about ... Did you have anything to eat or drink before we left for the spa?'

She eyes me curiously, unsure of what I'm getting at.

'Just in case,' I say, smiling to give her a bit of encouragement.

'Coffee. Just a black coffee. Charles is always making me cups of tea and coffee.'

I turn my gaze away, just for a second or two, so I can gather my thoughts. What if I'm right? What if he's been drugging her? This could have been going on for weeks, or even months. It sounds extreme, yes, even I admit that. But not unheard of. You only have to read the news to see that this sort of thing happens all the time. People who seem innocent, sometimes even charming, just like Charles, have been found guilty of the most harrowing crimes.

Seeing her expression grow more panicked, I quickly snap out of it – for now, anyway. 'Can't be food poisoning, then,' I say, forcing out a smile. The last thing I want to do is to alarm her, not after the shock she's had, and anyway, as it stands this is just a theory. I need hard evidence.

'You all right back there, girls? We're 'bout five minutes away now,' the cab driver calls, obviously eager to get rid of us.

Natalie jumps in her seat, shaking the blanket off her shoulders. 'I'm not ready,' she cries, before delving into her handbag and rummaging around. She seems different all of a sudden. In control, as if someone has knocked her back into place.

'Do you want to come to mine for a bit? Or is there someone else you can stay with, maybe?' I think of her mum; maybe she needs to see this for herself.

'No. It's okay, Rani, I'm fine,' she assures me, pulling out a brush and dragging it through the tangles in her thick blonde hair. Large tufts fall into her lap, and I see terror explode on her face before she quickly throws them into her bag. 'It's all my fault. I should have told him where I was going. I don't know what I was thinking,' she sighs, rubbing CC cream over her face and dabbing soft pink blusher onto her cheekbones.

'But you said …'

She stares at me, eyebrows raised in confusion. 'What? What did I say?'

'You said that you're scared of him.'

'Did I?' She laughs. It sounds way too genuine. 'How embarrassing. I don't remember that at all. It was so hot in that treatment room; I must be severely dehydrated or something.'

'Here we are, girls! Number 11, isn't it?'

As we pull up, I peer out of the window and see Charles pacing up and down, his floppy brown hair bouncing on his forehead. I watch as he marches up to the car, his features sharpened like kitchen knives, and I start to feel faint.

'Natalie. Where have you been?' he asks, pulling at the door handle, reaching out for her. 'I called your office and they said you'd taken the day off … something about a spa trip? Gosh, look at you. You're so pale. What happened to you?' Then he notices me sitting next to her. 'You. What are *you* doing here?'

'I …' My face burns up. I feel like I'm suffocating.

He turns back to Natalie. 'Come here, darling. Come here, I've got you now,' he says, his voice now tender. She flops into his arms, and he holds her tight, patting down stray wisps of her hair. 'Don't you see, darling, how worried you make me? But it's okay. It's all forgotten.'

Hands trembling, I reach for the handle on my side and force the door open, panting for breath.

'You all right there, love?' The cab driver turns to face me.

'Yes. Yes, I'm fine,' I say, staggering out. 'I just need some air.' And when it hits my face, I gulp it down, trying to steady myself.

'Mate, how much? I'll get this,' I hear Charles say, as I walk around the boot towards Natalie. I'm scared for her. I'm scared about what he might be doing to her.

'Natalie, are you okay?' I whisper as Charles pays the driver. But she doesn't respond. She just stares blankly at the cab as it reverses and makes a sharp exit.

When it's out of sight, Charles turns towards me. I notice his forehead creasing. 'Can't you see, Rani, she isn't well. And … you're making it worse.'

'Me?' I falter. *I don't understand. All I want is to be there for her, for her to be okay.*

'Please, Rani, just leave her alone. Leave us both alone.' His manner is firm, but there's an edge to his voice that I haven't heard before. A faint vibration in his vocal cords that sounds almost like despair, as if he's clinging on to something that, deep down, he knows is long gone.

Natalie

'Niaomi. It's me. It's Natalie. Where are you going?' I'm panting hard as I race towards her, trying to catch up with her. The
cold, wet wind splatters against my face. 'Niaomi, please. Wait!
Wait for me!' I scream and shout at her, my cheeks inflamed as
I jerk my head from side to side, taking in my surroundings.
I thought we were in my garden. I thought I saw the giant oak
tree at the end of the lawn, but the ground beneath my feet
feels rough and wild. The terrain is never-ending.

I don't recognise this place at all.

She turns back to look at me. Just for a second. The same
bloodshot eyes, the same pale skin. In that moment, I feel
every ounce of pain that she carries inside her gushing into
my stomach like scorching-hot lava. It almost cripples me, but
somehow I keep going.

Because she needs me.

I'm all she has.

She runs faster, darting amongst the trees. But I do too, with
all the strength left in my body. I feel the air being squeezed out
of my lungs, but still I run, until the space between us starts to
close and I can reach out to touch her. I want her to know that
she's not alone. That she'll never be alone.

Then suddenly, out of nowhere, I feel a violent force pulling me back. I try and shake it off. Lashing out. Kicking and
screaming. But it's no use. It's just too strong, too determined.

And I watch in terror as Niaomi fades away into the distance, my face drenched in tears, my heart sinking heavily in my chest.

Falling to the ground, I cry out to her. Hoping she can hear me. 'I'm sorry, Niaomi. I'm so, so sorry.'

I wake up feverish. My body shivering, skin tingling. But still I feel her presence in the room. My hands reach out in front of me, eager to touch her, to hold her. 'Niaomi,' I whisper, 'is that you?'

A dark, shadowy figure moves around me. I follow it with my eyes, watching it drift away through the gap in the bedroom door and out onto the landing.

I hear footsteps down the stairs. Heavy. Solid.

Charles? It has to be Charles. And I shudder.

How long was he standing there, watching me?

How much did he hear?

Rani

'And what about you, Rani? How have you been since that night?'

How does she think I've been? My ex-best friend won't stop calling, and I'm terrified about what's happening to the woman across the street, not to mention that I feel guilty about spending money on these stupid sessions that we can barely afford. But I don't know how else we can move on from what happened. I don't know how else to fix us. I glance up at Sandrine, in her ditzy print dress with the ruffled collar and her tortoise-shell-rimmed glasses, leaning back on a sand-coloured bouclé armchair in the loft room of her three-storey townhouse in Muswell Hill, and I shrug. 'I'm fine.'

Joel clears his throat.

'What?' I glare at him. 'I *am* fine. What's wrong with that?'

'We talked about this earlier, Rani. *Fine* isn't good enough here. But if you really are fine, then tell us why.' Sandrine gives me a patronising, primary-school-teacher smile that makes me want to wipe it right off her face.

I breathe in and out through flared nostrils. 'Okay. Okay. I feel like … not much has changed, really. Between us. We've gone back to the same old routine, as if nothing happened. Except something did happen.'

'What happened, Rani? Tell me how it was for you.' She shifts towards the edge of her seat, now fully engaged.

'I don't know,' I say, staring at my hands, twiddling my thumbs. 'It was shocking, of course it was. She ... Amber was my best friend. I never thought she and Joel could ever ... but you know, what happened sort of confirmed what I've always thought about myself, and us.'

'Go on,' Sandrine says, scribbling away in her notebook. Barely looking up.

'That we're ... we're unequal.' I take another deep breath, fighting back the tears.

'What?' Joel gasps, reaching for my hand.

'Wait,' orders Sandrine, waving her pen in the air. 'Let her finish.'

'I felt it before, back when we first met, but it was different then; I was going places. I was going to be someone. But now ... I get it, Joel. I get why you'd be interested in someone like her. I mean, look at me. I'm ... I'm ...'

'No.' He shakes his head. 'How can you say that?'

'It's how she feels, Joel. She's telling you how she feels.'

He lowers his gaze, wiping away a tear with the back of his hand. 'I'm sorry. I don't think that about you, I've never thought that. You're amazing, Rani. You've raised our two girls practically by yourself. Just look at them.'

I say nothing. For once, I'm glad Sandrine is here to break the silence.

'But Joel, what *you* think about Rani won't change how she feels about herself.'

'Then what will? What will, Rani?' he pleads, tears filling his eyes. I turn away. I can't bear to see his face. 'Please. Tell me what I can do.'

'Okay,' Sandrine says firmly, uncrossing her legs and leaning towards us. 'Let's go back to what you said before, Rani, "the same old routine". Joel, you said something similar earlier. How you felt that you never really talk to each other any more, and that Rani has grown distant over the years. Have I got that right?'

'Yes. It's been that way for a while, but I dunno, it seems to have got worse over the past few months. Before what happened with Amber. And then there's her weird sort of … I dunno … obsession with our neighbours.'

'Right …'

'Obsession, Joel? Really?' I glare at him. 'I've tried to tell you, but it's like you're not even listening. When that stuff happened with Amber, I didn't have anyone else to talk to about it. You did that, Joel. I lost my friends because of what you did. But Natalie was there for me. And now something awful is happening to her, and you think I'm making it up. Do you know how that makes me feel?' Before I know it, I'm standing over him, spitting out words through clenched teeth, my cheeks flaming hot.

'Rani, it's okay,' Sandrine says. 'Sit down, please. I think we're going off-piste a little.' She waits till I sink back into my seat. 'Having children changes you, your identity, especially for mothers. And Rani, you were so young when you became a mother. It seems like what you're saying is that you missed out on a whole phase of your life. But you know, it's not too late.'

I nod, but I'm barely registering what she's saying. It's nothing I haven't heard before – and at least that advice didn't almost bankrupt us.

'So what if you're parents? You're still young, so *be* young. Go on dates, have wild sex, get to know each other again, and then see what happens after that.' She smiles, as if she's done her good deed for the day. 'And Rani, what you feel about yourself, no one else can change that. It has to come from you. But – and we can talk about this more next week – there are things you can do to help yourself. For some people, even small but meaningful changes to their routine can make the world of difference. Does that make sense?'

'Yes,' I mumble under my breath, edging out of my seat so we can wrap this thing up. Has she even been listening? It was a date that blew everything up in the first place! I'm not buying any of her 'happiness comes from within' bullshit – it sounds like it came from a psychology-for-dummies cheat sheet. Try spending years of your life stuck in a tiny flat with only tiny humans for company and then tell me you're still happy, Sandrine. And now even they have more of a life than I do. A little self-care isn't going to change that.

Fists clenched by my sides, I jump to my feet and hurry towards the door, knowing that I have to leave before I say something I'll regret.

Natalie

I'm leaning over a mountain of paperwork, massaging my temples, when out of nowhere I hear footsteps marching towards me. My hands start to shake, and I quickly hide them under the desk.

'Hello, Natalie! Nice to see you've decided to grace us with your presence.'

It's Derek, our head of litigation. He was supposed to be working from the New York office this week. I sit up tall and blink my eyes wide open. I've barely slept all night. I don't know if I can face him without bursting into tears.

He pauses to look at me with slightly raised eyebrows. 'You seem ... hmm, different,' he says quizzically, clearing his throat.

'Sorry. I haven't been too well lately,' I mumble, cupping my palms together to steady myself.

'Now, that's not like you,' he says, stealing a look at my stomach. I can feel my jaw tightening. 'Do you have a moment?'

'Now?' I ask, wondering what this could be about. I doubt he cares enough to check on my well-being, so it must be another chat about partnership, and I feel nauseous just thinking of what Charles will say if he finds out. When I woke up after the spa visit, the house was deadly quiet. He must have moved his things into one of the guest bedrooms when I was asleep, and has barely said a word to me since. Leaving for work earlier than usual. Shutting himself in his study in the evenings.

The silence is deafening.

I follow Derek towards Threadneedle – all the meeting rooms on this floor are named after the streets surrounding our office in the Gherkin. They're identical in decor. So clean and clinical that I'm always aware of my minute imperfections. A subtle crease on the sleeve of my blouse, unruly wisps of hair coming loose from my clasp.

When I step inside, I see someone from HR, whose name escapes me, sitting at the table. *This can't be good.*

'Thanks for joining us at such short notice, Natalie,' Derek says, pulling out a chair and pointing to one opposite. 'I hear there's been a small bump in the road on the Fidel matter, so I don't want to keep you too long.'

I sit down, hands pressed together to hide my nerves.

He clears his throat. 'So ... no point beating around the bush, I suppose. I'm guessing you already know why I arranged this meeting?'

'Actually, no. Sorry. I have no idea.'

'Right.' He clears his throat again. Either he's got something stuck there or he's irritated. I've irritated him. 'Look, there's no easy way to say this, Natalie. When were you going to tell us that you're leaving the firm?'

I quickly open my mouth to explain, but I can't seem to find the words.

'I must admit, we're really disappointed to hear this. Not least because you're on partner track, as you know, but also because, well, we thought you respected us enough to come to us first.'

My eyes sting from the pressure of holding back tears. *Pull yourself together, Natalie.* 'Sorry. I ... I don't suppose you could tell me who told you that?' My colleagues Hannah and Priya were both at the barbecue. Witnesses to Charles's big reveal.

'That's not the point really, is it? I assume you've been head-hunted.' He sighs deeply, shaking his head. 'Don't tell me it's Arlington & Price. If it's more money you're after, I'm sure there's room for negotiation.'

'No!' I cry. 'I'm not going anywhere. I think there's been a misunderstanding.' I take a deep breath and continue. 'Charles and I have been privately discussing the possibility of me taking a back seat career-wise, that's all. I can assure you that I won't be joining another practice.' I stare down at my hands. 'But nothing's been decided yet. And whatever happens, you'll be the first to know.'

The woman from HR chimes in. I'm interested to hear what she has to say. 'Are you sure that's a good idea? You're so close now, Natalie.' She glances at one of the corner offices. For partners only. The rest of us minions sit open-plan. 'Are you really willing to give all this up, when you've worked so hard to get here?' She pauses, and when I don't reply, she carries on. 'A female partner in a City law firm. Under thirty. It's unheard of.'

'Like I said, nothing's been confirmed.' I stare back at her. This almost-stranger who is judging me. 'And I know exactly what I'd be giving up.'

They glance at each other, conversing silently with their eyes. *We need to drop this before we overstep.* 'Right, okay. That's all ironed out, then.' Derek smiles, tight-lipped, fiddling with his tie. 'And Natalie, if you do decide to leave, *please* let's have a chat about it first.'

'I will, I promise. And I'm sorry for the misunderstanding.'

I jump out of my seat and head straight to the bathroom down the corridor, bowing my head to avoid the lingering stares of colleagues as they walk past. I hurl myself into a cubicle and slam the door shut. Now that I'm alone, it doesn't take long for the tears to flow. I have an urge to yell and scream, but I can't. Not here. Not now. So I settle instead for a childhood failsafe.

Closing my eyes, I anticipate the harsh but satisfying sound of the palm of my hand meeting the flesh of my cheek. *Slap*. I'm greeted by a familiar rush of pain, followed swiftly by a tingling sensation that takes over my whole face for a few triumphant seconds.

I do it again, and again. Harder. Faster.

Slap. Slap. Slap.

Taking pleasure in my ability to control every movement, every sensation. Remembering how enjoyable this used to feel. These little acts of rebellion that would send Mum into quiet chaos.

When my head starts spinning, I quickly unlock the door and step outside the cubicle, scanning the bathroom for colleagues. Thankfully, it's still empty.

The person staring back at me in the mirror is unrecognisable. She looks so vulnerable, her cheeks puffy, her skin puckered and red. *You're nothing*. I run the tap until it's ice cold and splash water on my face to bring myself back to life. This will have to do. But now that the initial burst of satisfaction has subsided, I'm left feeling as conflicted as before.

I know I need to speak to someone, and Charles should be that someone. But he's become the cause of the problem rather than the solution.

When I get back to my desk, I mumble to a colleague about craving an iced latte from the coffee shop downstairs. Then, grabbing my bag, I head out of the office into the glass lift. The cool breeze that greets me outside is a refreshing surprise. Until now, I hadn't realised how overheated my body had become, conflicting emotions driving around within me like racing cars.

I wander amongst the other suits and trench coats, passing rows of brightly coloured coffee shops and eateries. Tight huddles of tourists amble out of them with steaming cups of coffee and bags of pastries in their hands. I stop and stare at them, feeling my shoulders loosen, my breath slow to a relaxed pace, and it occurs to me that I've never felt like this before. So free and unfettered. I realise that up till now, the decisions I've made, the actions I've taken, have never felt like my own.

As I continue walking aimlessly down the street, I realise that I'm no longer alone. I don't mean the crowds of people, who rarely infringe on my personal space, but someone else who has entered uninvited. I feel their eyes on me, noticing my every move. And I throw my head back, hoping to catch them off guard, but no one reveals themselves.

Suddenly the outside world doesn't feel so safe any more, and I find myself longing for the security of the office filled with familiar faces. I turn briskly around and head back as fast as I can, retracing my steps. Dashing in between the groups of people, who stare at me in annoyance. When I reach the entrance, I walk past the security screening and bag search. The guards know me by name, so they always let me through. One of them nods at me as if to ask if I'm okay, and I just about manage a smile.

In the lift, my heart is racing. I take several deep breaths to compose myself, filling my lungs with all the oxygen I can muster. It takes me the whole journey up to the thirty-fifth floor to compose myself. As I exit, I pull my phone out of my pocket, preparing myself for a flurry of emails. Straight away, I see a message from Charles, and for the first time since we met, I'm scared to open it. Terrified of what he has to say.

When I finally find the courage, I take in its contents. His words are harmless, but they still send shivers through my body.

Let me take care of you.

Rani

I scroll through my last few messages.

How are you feeling?

Is everything okay after the spa?

Natalie, it's Rani. Call me.

Each text remains unanswered, unread. I'm running out of options. Charles told me to back off, but I can't just leave her there with him. Alone. Not after what she said in the cab on the way back from the spa. *I'm scared.* It was a cry for help, even if she denied it afterwards. I can sense that she feels conflicted because she loves him and wants to believe that he loves her. And maybe he does, in his own way. But his love is laced with something toxic.

My phone vibrates in my hand. I quickly open the message, then sigh, my throat rumbling with frustration. It's not Natalie's name on the screen, but Amber's. Again. *Why can't she give me the space I asked for?* I drum my fingers over the screen to steady my nerves, inhaling loud and deep, focusing on my breath. Between her daily messages and the lingering tension at home, my head is still drowning in the aftermath of their betrayal. On the surface, Joel and I are holding it together. Half-smiles around the kitchen table, seamlessly coordinating drop-offs and pick-ups. We're co-parents, at best, doing what is necessary for our children.

But outside of the counselling sessions, we've barely said a word to each other. Neither of us feels ready to make a decision about our relationship, our future. And we're trapped in this farcical charade until we do.

The laptop whirs into action, blowing warm air onto my fingertips, and as I wait for the screen to load, I stare at the house across the street. It looks so different now. Almost threatening, with its blackened windows and bright orange bricks. Feeling nausea creep over me, I quickly look away, flicking through the pages of my notebook. I bought it on a whim a while back, thinking I could use it to prepare for interviews. But as the rejections kept piling up, it just sat there at the bottom of my bag, the pages creased yet unused.

I've been using it a lot this week, though. Ever since our spa trip – witnessing Natalie racing terrified out of the massage room, clumps of her luscious hair falling out into her lap – I've been recording every conversation, every expression, every sighting of them since our first meeting.

A chronology of their relationship.

And how it went up in flames before my eyes.

But I know that I have to be smart – not like the other night with Luella. I can't make a habit of firing off wild accusations with nothing to back them up, especially if I think he's drugging her. I need to speak to someone who can attest to his true character, someone who knows him well enough for it to be credible. *Charles must be edging close to forty by now*, I think. A man like him could have had several relationships before Natalie. And then it dawns on me. Of course, he was married before. How could I have forgotten that Darcy mentioned his first wife when I spoke to her at the barbecue? Until now, I've been so distracted by what happened afterwards. But snippets of our conversation are slowly coming back to me, like I'm vacuuming them up from the corners of my mind. I'm sure she even mentioned her name as well. Jessica. Joanne. Something classically English like that.

I bring up the Facebook homepage. It's been so long since I've logged in that my memory immediately lets me down. My fingers fail to move over the keypad in the way they used to, pressing the right combination of buttons like it's second nature. And after a string of unsuccessful attempts, I'm locked out of my account. 'Damn,' I mutter, slapping my palm against my forehead.

I jerk back my chair and open the drawer in my desk, looking for inspiration, my fingers rustling through old receipts and other useless junk. Something glitters in the corner and I pull it out, intrigued. My fake diamond ring. *No.* Serena's sparkly wedding band. And it occurs to me then that maybe I don't need my account after all. Maybe this is a job for Serena Rhodes.

I'd already set up an email address for her before calling the estate agent, so it doesn't take me long to create a Facebook account. In fact, I relish it. Inventing her persona from scratch – searching for a profile picture in online magazines and sharing and liking posts that I know she'd enjoy. I even find a nice man called Rahul in Bangladesh who gives me two hundred fake friends for £7.99.

Once I'm satisfied that she looks and feels like a real person, I begin. Hovering the cursor over the search bar. Typing in *Charles Riley*. It's a common name, and the list of profiles the search brings up is daunting. I don't know how on earth I will narrow it down, but then I see it. The colours. The pixelation.

The warm Tuscan sun, shamelessly calling out to me. That same photograph I saw in Natalie's downstairs bathroom, encapsulating everything he wants the world to see. It makes sense that Charles would have a Facebook account. Only it's nothing like mine, left to fester through years of disuse and neglect. If you looked hard enough, I'm sure you'd find several dozen photos of me that I wish had never seen the light of day, trapped in cyberspace for eternity. But Charles's account is different. It's a clone of the live, physical version of him. Every part of it has been curated with purpose.

Though that's not what intrigues me most. Unlike most of us, who whacked on our privacy settings as soon as we'd left university to join the real world, his page is public. As if to say, *This is the real me. I have nothing to hide.*

I click on his profile photo, and it abruptly enlarges, expanding over my whole laptop screen. His piercing green eyes stare back at me, and my hands start to tremble. I force myself to take a deep breath, before cautiously peering across to their bedroom window.

The house is empty, of course. I know he's at work – I saw him leave this morning – but my mind plays tricks on me. Seeing his face pressed up against the window. Watching my every move. *Focus, Rani, focus. You're almost there. You can't give up now.*

I push through the fear, clicking on his list of friends, and use the search engine to type in the name Jessica. There's only one entry, who looks old enough to be his aunt. I delete the letters one by one, all except the J, which I use to spell out Joanne.

Then I close my eyes as if in silent prayer, and as I blink them open, I see three entries with that name. The first looks like another older relative, but the other two are carbon copies of Natalie, with porcelain skin and golden hair. I copy and paste the first name, Joanne Buckle, into the search engine. Google tells me she's in her mid-twenties and works in finance. A work contact, perhaps, but definitely too young to be a first wife.

So, Joanne O'Brien, am I looking for you?

I notice that her feed is busy and disorganised. She has a simple profile picture, taken out of focus without much thought or care. Her face is blurry, but she looks like she could be the right age. That's promising at least. I briefly read her bio, which tells me that she lives in Surrey and works as a receptionist at a local GP surgery. But there's nothing else of substance.

I click on Facebook Messenger and, holding my breath, send her a quick message. Casual. Nonchalant. The last thing I want is to scare her off. *Hi, Joanne. You don't know me, but I'm a friend of Natalie Riley. Her husband, Charles, I believe is your ex. I was wondering if you had time for a quick chat.*

The dots move as if she's typing.

I wait a few minutes, nerves firing through my body.

But then they stop. No response.

Jumping up from the desk, I pace up and down my bedroom, my breath quickening as I raise my hands to my head in horror. What if she's speaking to Charles right now? Reading out my message to him? What if he puts two and two together, and knows it's me? Have I put myself in danger? Natalie too?

I think quickly, knowing that I need a plan B. And fast. Is there someone else who might listen to me? Who might care enough about Natalie to help? My mind flits to Luella, but I don't know how I'd get hold of her, and after our last conversation, I doubt she'd believe me anyway. And then an image pops into my mind. An email. The message is fuzzy, but the address above it is crystal clear.

Eyes glued to the screen, I sink back down into the chair and open a new browser, heading straight to Serena's email. The words come flying out of me as if I'm in a trance. I tell him what a wonderful person his daughter is, how poised and successful, and how much she cares for others. Then I tell him that something is happening to her, and that she needs his help. Finally, I give him my number, asking him to get in touch.

Just seconds later, I hear a beep. My heart jumps. Has he replied already? But it's a new friend request, from a woman called Erin Preacher. I feel deflated. The name doesn't ring a bell. Her profile picture is a cartoon character, and she's restricted her settings so I can't access her page. It's probably spam, or another fake friend created by Rahul. But I accept it anyway. Because what harm can it do? Serena isn't real.

Within seconds, there's another beep. This time, a Facebook message from the Erin Preacher account. *Hi Serena, it's Joanne. Perhaps we can meet in person? Are you London-based? Bring Natalie if you can. She needs to hear what I have to say. J.*

I bury my face in my hands, my pulse still racing. I know I have to act quickly, but the doubt still weighs heavy inside me. Natalie is already at breaking point. She hasn't answered any of my messages. What if she's not ready for this?

What if I've gone too far?

Natalie

Mum turned up on our doorstep last night, clutching an overnight bag to her chest, her eyes sunk into their sockets like they'd been submerged in quicksand. 'He started raising his voice, Natalie. I thought he was going to … hit me.' She's always been melodramatic. But Gerald? He wouldn't hurt a fly, let alone a grown woman who towers over him in four-inch heels. But before we had a chance to question her story, she flung her bag in my direction and dived straight into Charles's arms, burrowing into his chest.

I flinched as he scowled at me over her nest of hair, growling under his breath. 'Now, now, Luella. I know it's a Friday, but it's rather late, don't you think? A phone call would have been nice.'

'But … but I have nowhere else to go,' she pleaded, eyelashes fluttering, before lowering her tone. 'And didn't one of the guest beds arrive the other week?'

She's been like this all my adult life. Showing up unannounced at various flat shares around London, giving my housemates something to snigger about. I never would have invited her, with everything being so fraught between Charles and me. I don't think I could face her disappointment as well. But now that she's here, I can't help but feel a sliver of relief that I'm not alone with him any more. We may sleep in separate bedrooms and eat at different times – this house is big enough for us to lead wholly separate lives – but still,

I feel his presence everywhere. His dark shadow following me up the stairs. Looming over me while I sleep. The text he sent earlier this week felt like an attack, the threat within the words screaming at me.

With work being so busy, I've barely had the head space to digest it all. I can't even face talking to Rani about it – she's been texting all week and I've ignored every single message. But each night as my head hits the pillow, I wonder who this man is. The person I've chosen to spend the rest of my life with.

I open my eyes, blinking in the late-morning sun. My head feels heavy, like it's filled with cement. I can almost taste vodka on my tongue, what I so desperately need to numb the pain. Charles lies next to me, breathing deeply. He may have relinquished the guest bedroom to Mum, but it still feels like we are miles apart, and it dawns on me, watching his lips pressed tightly together even in sleep, that at least behind closed doors, the tension between us stays hidden from the outside world like a guilty secret. But now that Mum is staying with us, there's nowhere to hide. I'm at his mercy. Trapped somewhere between reality and expectation, with two people who are family, yet feel more like strangers.

Rolling out of bed, I pull out a pair of linen shorts and a merino wool jumper, and tiptoe into our en suite to get changed. That's all I seem to be doing these days, tiptoeing around the house, treading on eggshells. I catch sight of myself in the bathroom mirror and lower my gaze in horror. I'm unrecognisable. I can hardly bear to look at myself. Thinning hair, lifeless, hollowed-out cheeks, a greying complexion. My mother cannot see me like this.

As I dive into my make-up bag, pulling out item after item, I see my phone light up on the sink. It's Rani calling me. I let it ring out, but she calls again. Maybe she's upset – something to do with Joel – so I swipe the screen to answer it and whisper, 'Hi.'

'Natalie! Are you okay? I haven't heard from you all week. Wait – why are you whispering? Is everything all right?'

'Charles is asleep.'

She pauses, lowering her voice. 'I'll be quick, then. I know it's last-minute, but do you fancy grabbing a coffee this afternoon? I'll be on the South Bank.'

'Oh.' I really need to get out of this house – it feels like the walls are closing in on me – but I'm worried about what Charles will say when I tell him, especially now that Mum is here.

'Just for an hour or so,' she says, as if she can read my mind.

I picture her warm face, her comforting smile, and sigh. I have to see her. I'll deal with the consequences later. 'Okay. Text me the details.'

Once I'm dressed, I creep downstairs and into the kitchen to pour myself a tall glass of water, a poor substitute for the drink I'm craving. And as the cold liquid slaps against my dry throat, I realise that I'm not alone.

'Don't you look lovely, darling.' Mum emerges from the shadows, wafting up to me and stroking my hair like I'm ten years old again. She's lying, I can see it in her face, and my body tenses up with every touch. But I smile brightly at her.

'Thanks. I hope you don't mind, but I'm popping into town for a bit. I said I'd meet Priya for a coffee – you remember her, from work? She's having some issues with a client and wanted my advice. I won't be long, though.' I hear Charles reach the bottom step and my heart starts to race as he follows the direction of our voices.

'What's that, Natalie? It's not even midday and you're already thinking of leaving us?' The tone of his voice is interlaced with humour, but his lingering fury seeps into the atmosphere.

He strolls into the kitchen to start the coffee machine. I hear the low whir of the coffee beans, and the kitchen is filled with that delicious lazy morning smell. It soothes me, and I start to relax a little. But when I look up, I notice that Charles and Mum have positioned themselves directly opposite me, both staring at me with the same restless expression.

I've been cornered.

'If you really don't want me to go, I'll cancel. But she sounded upset. I won't be long, I promise. A couple of hours at the most. How about I make it up to you both by cooking dinner?'

Charles breathes out loudly through his nostrils. 'It's selfish of her to take up your weekend like this, but you only have yourself to blame. You spread yourself too thin with people you shouldn't be wasting your time on.'

'I know. I'm sorry. I wouldn't go if she wasn't desperate. Why don't you show Luella around …' I stop mid-sentence, realising what I've just done. Charles's weekends are so precious to him. I'm sure playing happy families with Luella is the last thing he had in mind for today.

He smirks at me. 'Yes, Natalie. What a great idea.' His voice is laced with sarcasm. 'Luella, it'll be my absolute pleasure to be your guide. Shall we kick off in an hour or so?'

The shorts I'm wearing are light and airy, but I can feel the sweat coating my inner thighs, sticking to the fabric. As I walk out of the kitchen, Charles takes a loud gulp of his coffee. 'Hold on, Natalie. Are you really thinking of wearing those into town? A bit short, don't you think?'

Drops of sweat trickle down the insides of my legs, and I swallow the hurt, the sense of shame.

'I think she looks lovely. Keep them on, Nat—'

'Oh for God's sake, Luella, just butt out! This is none of your business. She already attracts enough attention without her flashing her legs as well.'

Am I doing the right thing leaving them together? It's only been a few minutes and they're already bickering. Maybe I should cancel. But Rani has been there for me, and I want to do the same for her.

'Actually, it's so hot, they're damp already. I'm just going to head up and change before I leave. Have a lovely afternoon. Behave yourselves!'

I cobble together a cheeky grin before sprinting upstairs, wishing I could leave this house for good and never look back.

Rani

'So … tell me about yourself?' Joel says, breaking into a boyish grin. He looks almost twenty-two again.

'What are you talking about?' Feeling restless, I turn my head away from him, staring out of the café window at Crouch End Broadway, watching the locals pottering about with Waitrose shopping bags and takeaway cups of coffee.

'Come on, Rani. Look at me. You heard Sandrine.' He leans closer; I can smell his hot coffee breath on my face. 'Please, Rani.' His hazel eyes shine brighter.

'Okay … fine.' I shrug, trying to blot out the last time we were sitting across the table from each other like this as I scan the menu in my hands. Banana pancakes dripping in maple syrup. Avocado and poached eggs on sourdough. It all sounds so OTT. 'What do you feel like getting? I think I'm just gonna go for the peanut butter on toast.'

'No.' He clicks his tongue. 'You can have that any time. Come on, push the boat out. It's my treat.'

I roll my eyes at him.

'Sorry … I just meant, forget about money for a change. What about the pancakes?' He breaks into a smile. 'Do you remember when you were pregnant with Lydia and you couldn't get enough of those buttermilk ones – I used to do weekly trips to the Sainsbury's Local and empty the whole shelf into my basket!' He laughs. 'The manager hated me!'

'I can't believe you remember that.' He's trying. He's really trying.

'Of course I do,' he says earnestly, reaching his hand towards mine, brushing my fingers lightly. My cheeks burn up, my skin tingles, and for the first time in weeks, I don't pull away. 'I remember everything, Rani. When you thought you were finally done with morning sickness, but then we went on the bus journey from hell and you threw up all over that grumpy old man who looked like Stephen Fry! And that time after Leela was born and we were both so tired that we fell asleep mid ...' His smile fades and he stares longingly at me, reaching out to tuck a strand of my hair behind my ear.

I start to feel nauseated, wondering if he did this with Amber too, and pull my chair back abruptly. 'No. I'm not that hungry. Toast is fine for me.'

He looks disheartened, but then quickly recovers, clearing his throat. 'Okay then, toast it is.' He signals to the waitress, who comes over to take our orders.

Smothering the sourdough toast with the café's home-made peanut butter, I listen to the chatter around us. It's mostly young families here. Children about the same age as Lydia and Leela, and it feels strange without them, like I'm missing a part of myself.

Joel catches my gaze. 'It's weird, isn't it? Just the two of us. I like it, I like being alone with you, but it feels like we're incomplete.'

I nod my head. He's right. We're not the same people any more. We won't ever be again. But maybe that's okay.

'Oh, I forgot to tell you,' Joel says, his eyes widening as he slices through his avocado toast. 'Aman … he's leaving. He got a job out in Melbourne.'

'No way!' I cry, chewing slowly. 'I'm sorry.'

'I know. End of an era, right? But I'm super-chuffed for him. He needed a change, I think, after Marissa. I kind of envy him, actually. A change of scenery would be nice.'

'Yeah. It would be. But Marissa, she was really, umm, how do I put this kindly … bat-shit crazy!' We laugh together, and I feel a warmth settle inside me. Maybe that's what we need too, a fresh start somewhere new. 'Didn't they break up over a year ago, though?'

'Yup.' He nods, swallowing. 'But it turns out she's been stalking him for months, and she even sent him death threats. He had to get the police involved and everything.'

'What?' I gasp, shaking my head. 'That's horrendous. Poor Aman.' My thoughts suddenly race away from sandy beaches towards this afternoon. I feel sick to my stomach thinking about what Joanne has to say about Charles.

'Is everything okay, Rani?' Joel asks, eyebrows raised.

'It's just … Doesn't matter.' I take a long sip of my orange juice, hoping it will dissolve the lump forming in my throat. 'How's your avo toast?'

'It's decent, actually. Although it feels a bit ridiculous paying fifteen quid for something I could have made at home. Hey, I've got an idea, why don't we pick up the girls from Jemima's and head into town? We could go to Hyde Park and feed the ducks. Leela will love that.'

I stare down at my half-eaten toast, my appetite gone in a flash.

'Only if you want to … otherwise we could just stay at …'

'No. Sorry. That sounds nice, but I already have plans.'

'Oh?'

'With … umm, Natalie.' I bite my lip.

'Rani, how many times?' He rubs his forehead, fine lines resurfacing. 'Didn't we just discuss this with Sandrine the other day? I don't understand why you're still thinking about her after everything *we're* going through.'

I jerk my head back against the chair, sighing through my frustration. Not again. 'Because she's my friend, Joel. She's the only person I can talk to.'

He exhales sharply out of his nostrils. 'That's just it though, Rani. You should be talking to me.'

'Can we just drop this, please?'

'But Rani—'

'Leave it, Joel,' I say curtly, pushing my plate away and standing up. 'I'm done, can you just get the bill? I'll meet you outside.'

Natalie

I sprint down the escalator, leaping into the nearest carriage, and as the doors slide towards each other, I feel my shoulders start to sink and my jaw relax, the lingering tension draining out of my body. I may be on my own, surrounded only by nameless strangers, but I'm not lonely any more. That feeling left me the moment I cupped my hand over the chunky brass knocker and pulled the royal-blue front door firmly shut behind me. And now, standing on a moving train, hiding amongst the hustle and bustle of people going about their busy weekends, I'm filled with possibility. I feel free.

It's only a short journey from Highgate to Waterloo, so I take a seat and scroll through my phone, reviewing any new emails that have come in overnight for the case I'm working on. With all the sleepless nights and my volatile home life, my concentration at work has been waning. I know Derek has noticed. I can see it in his face – narrowed eyes attempting to mask his disappointment. I'm surprised no one else has said anything. It's only a matter of time before I make a serious mistake or break down in front of my colleagues. I need to pull myself together before I lose control of everything.

As I escape into the world of fraud and embezzlement, the fine hairs on my arms and legs prick up, as if on high alert, sensing a change in the atmosphere. I peel my eyes off the screen, scanning the seats around me. A couple of love-struck teens are sitting opposite, way too preoccupied with each other to notice anyone else, and the passengers either side of me are all minding their own business – heads in books or glued to their phones. I shake off the paranoia, reminding myself that Charles is at home. *He's not here. He's not following you.*

But as I lower my gaze back to my inbox, there it is again, that same eerie sensation I experienced near my office of someone watching my every move. Eyes dotted all over me, a marked target. I jerk my head from left to right, straining to see to each end of the carriage, but I can only make out blurred shapes and colours. I feel exposed. My breath becomes faint and laboured, oxygen squeezing out of my lungs, and my chest constricts like it's in a vice, clamping and tightening. I grip the armrest to steady myself. But it does nothing to reassure me.

'Are you okay?' the woman sitting next to me asks, touching my arm.

I nod my head, then stand up and stumble along the carriage, trying to ignore the rows of eyes that brush over me as I walk past. My cheeks are burning and sweat glazes my brow. I wipe it away with the back of my hand just as the automated train voice announces, 'Next stop Charing Cross. Alight here for …' It's not Waterloo, but it's close enough. I've held on for too long. I have to get out.

Throwing myself out through the doors, I weave in and around the crowds of people as fast as I can, walking briskly up the escalator and instinctively jerking my head back as if I'm looking for someone. Occasionally I see a man with chestnut hair, which feeds the panic, but I don't stop. I keep moving until I reach the barriers.

The air outside is fresh and warm. I bask in it, letting it flow freely through my body before ducking behind a row of cabs and pressing my back up against one of the cars in wild relief. It's just gone half past one. I'm meeting Rani at two – plenty of time to cross the river towards the café. And the walk there will do me the world of good, I tell myself. Settle my nerves before I see her. I want to be able to hold my head high. I want to offer her advice, be her shoulder to cry on instead of cowering by her side.

Taking a long, deep breath, I rejoin the crowds heading down towards Embankment station and across Hungerford Bridge, losing myself in anonymity. Feeding off the energy, the laughter, the merriment. I lock eyes with beautiful strangers and shiver with intrigue, aware of them turning their heads to take another look. With every glance, my crumbling marriage fades further from my mind. Even if Charles doesn't want me any more, I feel confident that I'll survive this. I'll be just fine on my own again.

As I pass the National Theatre, I pause to sit on a bench, watching well-dressed couples strolling inside arm in arm to catch a matinee performance. A year or so ago, Charles and I would have been among them, taking baby steps towards our first proper date. The name of the play we went to see escapes me. I spent most of the three hours staring at his hand locked in mine, fighting the urge not to squeal with joy. He was my one chance at happiness. Someone even Mum would approve of, knowing what it could offer us. There was a time when I thought my life couldn't get any sweeter.

But that was before we moved into the house. Before I met Rani. Before Niaomi started visiting my dreams again.

I can sense there's something the world is trying to tell me, something I'm not seeing. I may not have all the pieces yet, but I know I'm getting closer.

A ray of sunshine falls over my face, blinding me, and I rest my palm on my forehead before peeking out from underneath it. Blurred shapes and colours settle before me, and suddenly I'm filled with dread again, because I recognise them from the carriage. The very same colours. The very same shapes. I hold my breath as they become sharper, warmer, and then a figure emerges out of the bright light, staring directly at me. Haggard, bruised skin, messy hair with streaks of grey. He wears a battered old trench coat wrapped around his bony frame and carries a newspaper rolled up in his hands. I don't recognise him at all.

I jump to my feet and start edging away, but he raises his arm while quickening his step, shuffling towards me. 'Who are you?' I call out. 'What do you want?'

'Natalie … Natalie, wait.' His voice is deep and croaky.

'You know my name?' I cry. 'Is it Charles? Has Charles sent you?' I swallow down the lump forming like a pebble in my throat. Then I turn away, scanning the area for somewhere to escape to, somewhere to hide.

'Charles? Who's Charles?'

I pick up the pace, dashing past bewildered faces, listening out for his footsteps. I think I've just about lost him when I hear a voice, slicing through the background noise. 'Natalie!' he shouts. 'It's Robert. I'm your father.'

His words spasm through me and my body jerks to a standstill. Then, as I replay them in my mind, I find myself turning slowly towards him, whispering as he approaches me, 'It was you, wasn't it? It was you, at work and then on the train. You've been following me.'

'I'm sorry.' He lowers his gaze. 'I just wanted to see you, that's all.'

I shake my head, clenching my fists by my sides. 'I thought … I thought it was someone else. I was terrified.' I swallow hard. 'I don't understand,' I say. 'Why are you here? Why now?'

The crowds continue to throng the pavement. Groups of teenagers, smoking and laughing. Couples walking side by side, brushing past us, drowning us out. Robert waves the newspaper in his hand before smoothing down the creases and holding it out to me. And I recall his email – how he came across an article about the case I'm working on and saw my name underneath the photo of the legal team. But it doesn't answer my question. I don't know this man, and he knows absolutely nothing about me.

'Do you even know what I've had to tell myself over the years?' I say, cold and expressionless. 'That my father must be dead, that something terrible must have happened to him, because it's the only reasonable explanation I have for what you did, what you put us through.' I turn and walk away, forcing my head upright. But I feel him behind me, I sense him closing in on me, and abruptly I swing round to face him, unable to control my emotions any more. 'Why can't you leave me alone?' I cry. 'I have nothing more to say to you. I don't want to see you ever again.'

'But … but your friend. She said you're in trouble, that you need my help.'

'What? Who?' I ask, my mouth wide open.

'She said her name was Serena. That you'd be here today.'

'I don't have a friend called …' And then it hits me. Rani. She's the only person who knows I'm here, the only person I've talked to about this. My cheeks burn red hot. I can't believe she would do something like this. What if Charles and Luella are right about her? I catch Robert looking at me, pity written on his tired face. 'Look, I'm fine,' I say quickly. 'I don't need anything from you. Just leave me alone.'

He edges closer. 'You don't look fine. Natalie, please hear me out. Five minutes and then I'll go. I'll be out of your life for good, I promise.' He gestures to a bench nearby.

I glance nervously at my phone. 'Okay,' I say, because I don't have the energy to fight any more.

I perch at the very edge of the bench, legs crossed and leaning away so that our bodies can't touch even for a second. *This man is a stranger. He's nothing to you.* But then as he turns his gaze towards mine and our faces align, I can't help but look into his eyes and see tenderness and warmth. It doesn't make sense. He doesn't seem anything like Luella described. 'I'm sorry,' he begins. 'I'm sorry for everything.' He reaches his hand out towards mine, but then quickly pulls it away. 'I didn't want to leave you, Natalie. I swear to you, it was never my intention.'

I say nothing, because I still don't know if I can trust him. And what does it even matter, anyway? It's all in the past, one great big void.

'I left, yes.' His thin lips press together. He looks solemn, mournful. 'I had to. It was too much. You were only young, too young to remember. But I was coming back. I was always coming back.'

'Then why didn't you?' I ask.

'What?' His mouth drops open in disbelief. 'You don't remember? Your mother, she didn't tell you?'

'No,' I spit. 'I don't remember anything. She won't tell me anything.'

'I visited you both for months, Natalie. We played in the garden together, I read to you on the sofa.' His expression is wistful but calm.

He's lying. Of course he's lying.

'You must remember – a part of you must remember me. You're living in that house. Our house.'

I turn away, my insides trembling. I don't know what to think. I don't know who to believe any more.

Then it hits me. If he returned, then why hasn't he been part of my life? Why is he still a stranger? I jerk my head back. 'So what happened, then? If you came back as you say, where have you been all this time?' I ask, cuttingly.

'Oh, Natalie. I tried, I really did.' He shuts his eyes for a second. 'We'd arranged for me to pop by again. I was so hopeful, I thought maybe your mother and I might be able to work things out … that we could at least be civil. But when I knocked on the door, a strange woman answered.' He looks straight at me. 'You'd left, and another family had moved in. I asked around, but no one knew where you'd gone.'

'What?' A coldness passes through me.

'I didn't give up there, though. I looked for you both, for years.' He sighs deeply, like he's ashamed to keep going. 'But I guess as time went on, I had no choice but to accept it as my punishment for abandoning my family. What kind of a man does that? And then I told myself that it was better for you both if I just stopped looking … that is, until that day I saw you in the newspaper.'

His words wash over me. My mind is like murky water, and I don't have the energy to process, to make sense of it all. 'I don't understand,' I say, rubbing my temple. 'So what are you saying? That you've been here, in London, all this time?'

He nods his head.

My mind is a blur. I can't think straight. 'So, why now? What do you want from me?'

'Nothing.' He looks shocked. 'I don't want anything from you, Natalie. I just want to know that you're all right.' He edges towards me.

'I'm fine,' I cry, standing up. 'I told you, I'm fine.' Torrents of mixed emotion expand and collide inside me, and I feel as if I'm going to explode. I have to get out of here. Glancing at my phone, I realise that I'm running late to meet Rani. A part of me doesn't want to go any more, after what she did. But I can't go home. 'Look, I'm sorry. I have to be somewhere.'

'Yes, okay. I understand. But Natalie … you'll be okay, won't you?'

I don't answer him, I just turn and run, because the truth is, I don't know. I don't know if I'll ever be okay.

Rani

She bursts through the door of the coffee shop, panting for breath. I watch as her eyes scan the room, searching for me, distress lingering within them. When she sees me, she marches over, her hands screwed into tight fists. But I was expecting this.

'What the hell?' she asks through gritted teeth. 'A heads-up would have been nice, Rani. Or should I say *Serena*?'

I feel my cheeks start to redden. 'Oh God, I'm sorry. I can explain …'

'How could you do that to me?' Her hands shoot up towards her head, gripping her temples.

I look up at her, pleading. I knew this was a risk.

'He cornered me,' she says. 'You both did. I just don't get it, though. Why contact him when I told you how I felt about it? And a fake name, Rani … really?'

'I know. I'm sorry. It's stupid. It's all so stupid. I honestly thought I was doing the right thing, that deep down you wanted to see him. And then when he said he was so excited about meeting you, I had to do something. He cares, Natalie.'

She sighs and shakes her head, suddenly looking drained.

My palms are clammy. I'm burning up, knowing what is coming. Will this be too much for her? Will it tip her over the edge?

As she goes to take the seat opposite me, she notices a coat and handbag resting on it. I can see her mentally backing away. 'Is someone else here?'

I'm just about to answer her when Joanne emerges from the toilet and makes her way over. I can feel myself growing more and more anxious as Natalie turns her head, almost in slow motion, then jolts it back.

'Natalie, I can explain,' I say hurriedly. 'I don't think you've met before. This is Joanne …'

She looks at me, confused, and then back to Joanne. 'You're Charles's ex-wife,' she says slowly. 'I've seen your photograph at Seth and Darcy's house.' She glares at me. 'What is this? First my father and now this … What's going on?'

'She's come up from Surrey to speak to you. Please, just hear her out.' I manage to coax Natalie into the seat next to me, being gentle but firm like I am with my girls. Then, sliding the oat milk latte that I ordered earlier towards her, I give Joanne a nudge.

'Charles and I met in sixth form,' Joanne begins. 'He was charming even back then.' She smiles as if reliving it. But how quickly her smile disappears. 'It was a difficult period in my life. My parents were going through a messy divorce and none of my friends seemed to get it. One weekend, they dragged me to some house party. I remember sitting all alone in the garden, and then Charles appearing out of nowhere next to me. He knew exactly what to say to me to comfort me, to make me laugh.'

As she speaks, I flick my gaze between the two of them – with their golden hair and translucent skin, they could be sisters. But where Natalie's eyes are dark and mysterious, Joanne's are the colour of crystal-clear seawater. Where Natalie is expertly put together, Joanne looks like she's thrown on the first clothes she could find.

'I followed him to Durham for uni. We were inseparable. I didn't really make any friends. He made me feel like I didn't need anyone else.' She lowers her gaze, fiddling with the hairband around her wrist. 'After uni, I started working in HR, and he proposed pretty soon after that. It took me completely by surprise. We'd talked about marriage and having children now and again, but I always assumed it would happen much later, after we'd lived out our lives a little.'

Natalie looks shell-shocked, as if she can't believe what she's hearing. The similarities in their experiences. I can see the cogs slowly turning, but she's speechless. Even if she had something to say, I don't think the words would come out.

Joanne takes a long breath. Her bottom lip starts to quiver, and I watch her bite down on it. Even after all this time, I can tell how difficult this must be. 'We were happy for a while, but then slowly he started to change. At first it was little things – telling me what to wear, what to eat and who to hang out with. He said it in such a clever way that I barely noticed, or just saw it as him looking out for me. But when he persuaded me to leave my job, I realised what was going on. He was trying to turn me into his mother – the perfect housewife. Someone he could have on his arm at parties, but who would also have dinner ready on the table when he came home from work.' She drops her gaze and sighs. 'But I still couldn't leave him. Even after all that. I guess I was in denial. He seemed so devoted to me, and my parents adored him – how could I let such a good thing go? It wasn't until about a year later, when I started getting closer to someone I met at the gym, that I finally found the courage to leave.'

'The personal trainer? Charles said you ran off with him. You broke his heart. It took him years to get over you,' Natalie pipes up accusingly.

'You mean Simon?' Joanne looks confused. 'No, Simon's gay. Charles knew that. But I owe him everything. He was outside in the car the night I told Charles I was leaving him. If I'd been alone, I don't know what would have happened.'

I feel my neck tense up. 'What do you mean? What did he do to you? Joanne, did he ever … drug you?'

She shakes her head at me. I notice the panic in her eyes. 'No. I … I don't think so.' Then she reaches across the table towards Natalie, who withdraws her hands, adjusting her position in her seat. 'I'm sorry. I know it's a lot to take in. But I'm almost done.' Her voice is shaking now, but she continues staring at Natalie. 'I realise that I don't know anything about you, or your relationship with Charles. But I was worried when Serena told me how quickly you got married, and how things between you started to change after that. I've tried and failed to help friends in similar situations in the past, but I thought maybe this time I *can* help … because I understand, I really do. So if anything I've said sounds familiar, then please, it's not too late. Find a way to leave, and do it quickly. You see, Charles has a type. He preys on vulnerable women. Women who need sav—'

There's an ear-piercing screech as Natalie pushes her chair back abruptly and then hurries away in the direction of the bathroom. I jump up and follow her. And as I push open the toilet door, I see her unravelling tissues from the dispenser, scrunching them up into a makeshift ball and dabbing it lightly over her eyes. 'I feel so stupid,' she whispers. 'I really thought this was it … my one chance. But I should have known it was too good to be true.'

She looks at me, and all I see is torment on her face.

'I don't deserve to be happy, Rani. I'm nothing.'

Rani

We sit side by side as the train chugs and squeaks its way back up the Northern Line. Natalie spends most of the journey in silence. A million miles away. I can tell that she's still processing everything, her mind replaying the movie of their relationship, from the night they first met to the present day. And I want to honour her silence. But there's so much we need to talk about. So much I want to say.

Taking my notebook out of my bag, I run my gaze down the research I've been doing over the last few days. Common signs of abusive relationships. Charities to contact. A list of local support groups. I'm eager to broach this with her, but I don't know if she's ready after the day she's had. *Baby steps*, I remind myself, recalling the final bullet point in the article I read this morning.

I close the notebook and rest it on my lap. Then I tilt my face towards her and softly brush her arm. 'Natalie, are you okay? Do you want to talk?'

She turns towards me, still lost somewhere outside reality. 'You know, it's funny.'

'What is?'

'How similar I am to the father I barely remember. The same dark eyes. The same perpetual disappointment.'

I take her delicate hands in mine and look up at her. 'Natalie. What Charles is doing to you, you're not to blame. It's all him. Please tell me you get that.'

'No. *You* don't understand.' Her lips press together in frustration. 'She's right. This is my fault. It's all my fault.'

'What? What are you talking about? Who's right?'

But she doesn't respond.

When we reach Highgate, we take the escalator out of the station. Natalie suddenly picks up the pace, darting ahead of me, lost in the crowds. I can just about make out a flash of blonde hair bounding up the steps, taking them two at a time.

So that's that then.

By the time I reach the top, I've reassured myself that this is common in domestic abuse. Denial. To Natalie, it's about survival, whatever she can do to get herself through each day. But as I tap my bank card to let me out of the barriers, I'm surprised to see her standing there smiling at me, as if this afternoon never happened.

'Sorry, Rani, I didn't mean to run off like that. It's just that Mum is staying at ours, and I promised her and Charles that I'd be back in time to cook dinner.' She hesitates. 'Also, I know it's a bit delicate, but it's probably best we don't mention we saw each other today. Please don't take it personally. You know how overprotective family can be.'

Space. Give her space. But not so much that she can't come to you for help.

'Sure. Why don't I walk the long way back, so there's no risk of them seeing us together?'

She nods her head gratefully.

'But Natalie … if you want to talk, about anything, you know I'm here, don't you? And I'm sorry again about today.'

'Thank you. That's really kind. But honestly, I'm fine. Everything will be fine. I'm sure of it,' she says, before turning and walking away.

I follow the opposite exit, which takes me out onto the hustle and bustle of Archway Road. Buses and cars pelt past at full speed, groups of people monopolise the pavements. I start to feel even more anxious, wondering what Natalie could be walking into, and find myself craving a quiet space to digest my thoughts.

It's still early, so I decide to take a detour through the Parkland Walk – a railway-line-turned-nature-trail that has become one of my favourite local spaces. I love that it hasn't been pruned and refined like most London parks. It has its own unique beauty. Brambles left to creep over the pathways. Disused platforms untouched. Graffiti crawling up crumbling walls. I don't come here often, but when I do, I'm always on my own. I haven't even told Joel or the girls about it, and I like that feeling. Something that is only mine.

As I walk along the path, Natalie's words reverberating in my head, my phone chimes in my bag. It's another message from Freya. It must be early in the morning over there. She's probably coming back from a party on the beach. What a life.

I miss you sooo much xxxxx

Is someone having a good night? I reply. *How's Will? ;)*

He told me he loved me yesterday (!!!) How are you???? I haven't heard from you for ages. I was worried you'd gone MIA.

It occurs to me that this is the longest I've ever gone without speaking to her. I've been so preoccupied with Joel and Natalie that I've neglected my own sister. Again.

I miss you too. I'm fine. I've just been busy, that's all. Shall we speak next weekend? I know the girls would love to see your face. PS OMG. Did you say it back?

As I walk down the steps to Stanhope Road, still engrossed in my phone, someone calls my name. I look up to see Jemima chuckling at me, her beautiful printed scarf blowing in the breeze.

'Jemima, hi. Sorry about that, I was just texting my sister. No Scruff today?'

'No, sadly not. He's not doing too well. The vet says it's kennel cough.'

'Not serious, I hope?'

She shrugs, then changes the subject. 'You're looking well, my dear. How funny, I just saw Natalie sprint past. You know, I met her mother the other day. They look almost identical, don't they? Like sisters.'

'I guess so … What did you think of her?'

'Oh, er, she seemed nice enough,' she says casually, but then glances away, her smile melting. 'It's strange, I could have sworn she used to live next door. Years ago … although she flat-out denied it when I asked her. I can't imagine why.'

'How strange,' I say, feeling a little light-headed. I wonder why Luella would lie about something like that. Of course, it's entirely possible that Jemima could be mistaken. But in all the time I've known her, her memory has never let her down.

Natalie

The rain hits me. Hard and heavy, like gravel falling from the sky. I rub my hands down my wafer-thin nightdress, trying to retain the heat. But it does little to comfort me, as the water continues to seep through to my bare skin, now coated in layers of ice-cold dampness.

The lights are on inside.

I can hear them. Intermittent giggles. The scraping of pots and pans with wooden spoons. I catch the scent of apple and cinnamon wafting through the closed patio doors, and my mouth waters just thinking about the sugary-sweet taste on my tongue. But my belly remains empty, stinging with raw hunger. I call out to them. 'Hello? Mum? Can you hear me? Can you open the door … please?' I stand on tiptoes, banging on the glass with my fist. 'I'M COLD. LET ME IN. PLEASE LET ME IN.' Maybe they've forgotten that I'm here. That I'm locked out. Again. But their backs remain turned. It's like they can't hear me.

Like I don't exist.

My throat starts to close. My teeth feel too large in my mouth, chattering through my words. And as hope dwindles, I find myself inching away from the house. Staring out into the garden, trying to make sense of the blackened shapes behind me. Then, with barely another thought, I sprint for shelter under the giant oak tree at the end of the garden. Gasping for breath,

I sink to the ground. The branches vibrate in the wind, contorted shapes glaring down at me. Terrified, I curl up into a ball on the carpet of dead leaves, shrinking further into the rough, thick trunk. Then, taking a deep breath, I picture the vastness of the skies beyond, praying to whoever lives up there to reach down and swallow me whole.

Tremors shoot through my body, jolting me awake. But the nightmare lingers. So vivid. So real. Niaomi darting through the trees. Her wild blonde tangles flying in the wind. It's like she lives inside me, her heart beating simultaneously with mine. I know how hard I worked with Dr Baldwin. All those long, exhausting afternoons. The weekends he gave up for me, sometimes even through the night. How he patiently guided me to see things clearly, reassuring me that Niaomi was someone I invented as a means of survival, an alter ego onto whom I transferred all my pain and anguish. And that it was okay to let go. With my marriage at breaking point, it makes sense that she would return. But if that's the case, why do the dreams feel so real? Why does *she* feel so real?

I force myself out of bed, creeping softly across the landing. The study door is closed, and Charles is inside. I assure myself that he's on a deadline, hoping to convince Mum of the same. The last thing I need is for her to suspect what is happening between us. I know it will only add to her worries.

Last night's dinner was an absolute disaster. I'd decided to make a tomato sauce from scratch to serve over layers of diced aubergine, mozzarella, and glugs of olive oil. Parmigiana di melanzane. It was the same recipe Charles and I had discovered on our first weekend away together, and I'd selected it especially. An ode to better times. A labour of love. The olive oil was sizzling away in the pan. The onion had been blitzed into tiny bite-sized chunks. I was all ready to go, but as I opened my notebook to cast my eyes over the recipe, I saw it. The elegant loops and squiggles of his handwriting, in solid black marker. *Not enough salt. Too much garlic. Needs sugar.* None of what I had written was mine any more.

This time, I felt rage as well as hearing the voices. I pulled a beef tomato out of the paper bag and squeezed it hard in the palm of my hand. *You'll never be good enough. You're nothing.* The juice spurted out in every direction. Over the marble counter and onto the tiled floor. I watched the seeds drip down my pristine white dress, but I didn't care. It felt so good to let out my anger without even making a sound. I grabbed another one and squeezed harder, feeling power and energy shooting through my veins. And just like that, Charles didn't seem so terrifying any more.

Finally, I stepped back to admire the scene before me. At first glance, it looked like the aftermath of a murder. Once forensics had been and gone, and the bodily ruins had been bagged up and taken away. I examined my hands, tracing the sticky juice all the way down to my fingernails.

If this was a murder, they'd be pointing the finger at me. And I'd have happily gone with them, flying high on adrenaline. Because nothing else mattered except this wonderful feeling.

But then a key rattled in the door, and I plummeted back to reality with a thud. There were seconds between us. I had to act fast. Tying a spotless apron around my waist and neck, I threw some deli olives into a bowl and grabbed a bottle of wine.

Then I shut the kitchen door behind me and ushered them into the lounge with an award-winning smile, my jaw aching from all the lies.

Just under an hour later, Mum and Charles were sitting side by side at the dining table. I walked towards them carrying a steaming baking dish bursting with promise and expectation. And as I set it down in front of them, I imagined Charles diving into the story of how we'd discovered the little taverna off the beaten track, and the funny old man with the wafer-thin moustache who serenaded us with Italian folk tunes as we ate. It had been way out of his comfort zone, but it didn't seem to bother him. That was the old Charles. Wooing me with rustic candlelit dinners, barely blinking an eye when I polished off my meal.

But last night he wasn't in a talkative mood. As I watched him sinking the spoon into the gooey interior, my heart was beating so loud I was surprised they couldn't hear it.

'It smells delicious, darling, well done,' Mum squealed, bursting with pride. 'I can't wait to—'

'Hmm. But how does it taste?' Charles loaded up his fork and took a large mouthful.

I waited with bated breath, watching him make the most of the chewing process. Eventually swallowing, with an air of discomfort. Then, turning the plate around emphatically, he helped himself to the accompanying salad. 'I don't want to lie to you, Natalie,' he said sternly, shaking his head. 'This isn't great at all. It doesn't even come close. Didn't you read my notes?'

I apologised under my breath. But beneath the table, my hand pulsated over an invisible beef tomato.

Natalie

'Watch out!' I shout at her, pointing to a thick root jutting out of the ground.

'Thanks, darling,' she beams, stepping over it before weaving in between the tall trees. Just watching her makes me feel more anxious, as the lies close in on me, and I turn sharply around, pelting up the steep hill, my thoughts firing me away from her. *Robert didn't walk out on us. He came back. He came back for me.*

'Wait for me, darling,' she pants. 'I'm struggling to keep up with you!'

When I reach the top, I stop and hover at the edge. It's not a vertical drop, but it's terrifying all the same. A slippery slope of rough, crumbly terrain. Giant trees and sharp, prickly bushes. I close my eyes. One leap is all it would take.

Mum presses her hand onto my back, causing me to flinch. 'Natalie. Please don't tell me this is where you fell. You must be more careful. You'll injure yourself again. This time it might be your face,' she adds, horrified, as if that would cause her extra pain.

I back away from the edge, thoughts still swirling around in my head. And before I can stop myself, they spill out of me. 'Do you ever think about my father?'

'What?' Her smile is gone in an instant. 'Why are you asking me this? I've told you what happened. What he did to me.'

'So he never came back? You never heard from him again?'

'Stop. Just stop! He left, Natalie. He *left*.' Rage pours out of her, and the veins on her neck start to quiver. 'But I'm still here. I've always been here. Am I not enough for you?'

'No, no. That's not what I meant,' I assure her, guilt lodging in my throat. *What was I thinking, trusting a stranger over the one person who's been here for me my whole life?* 'I'm sorry. You've always been enough, more than enough.' I swallow, but the guilt is still there, unrelenting. 'Please just forget I said anything, it was stupid of me.' I reach for her, taking her hand, hoping she'll forgive me. 'Come on, let's head back,' I say. *She's right. She's always right. It's Niaomi messing with my head, making me doubt myself. I can't let her win.*

As we turn back, following the well-trodden path through Queen's Wood, my stomach twists and turns. Charles must have emerged from the study by now. But what mood will we find him in? I feel a strong sense of déjà vu. This fear of my own home, like it's been deeply entrenched inside me for a long time but is only now starting to resurface. He hasn't laid a finger on me. But I've seen his rage. Heard his insults. Throwaway comments that individually mean very little yet collectively fester within me, growing like a balloon being pumped full of air. There's only so much air a balloon can hold before it bursts.

I reassure myself that I've given him space. Recalling what happened the last time we fought and how he was fully restored upon his return from Miami. *Deep breaths, Natalie*, I tell myself, squeezing Mum's hand for support. Remember Charles as you used to know him. The coffee in bed. The fresh flowers.

The impromptu picnic on the living room floor. That man must still be in there.

'Darling, are you okay? You've been awfully quiet.'

'Sorry, I'm just tired. It's the case I'm working on. There's so much to do, it's always on my mind.'

'Okay, well don't let it ruin our weekend. Soon we'll be two ladies of leisure. What fun we'll have together!'

'I can't wait,' I say, forcing out a smile as my phone buzzes in my pocket. 'One second, that could be Charles calling to see where we are.' I let go of her hand and rummage around in my jacket pocket, pulling out my phone. Rani's name flashes on the screen. My jaw clenches as I think about what happened yesterday.

Luella peers over my shoulder. 'Oh, it's not that nosy little neighbour, is it? Go on, answer it. Let's see what she has to say for herself,' she says, nostrils flared.

'Hi, Rani. I'm just out in the woods with Luella,' I say quickly, so she knows I'm not alone.

'Oh, sorry, should I call back another time?'

'No, it's fine. Is everything okay?'

'Yeah. I was just ringing to see how you are … after yesterday.'

'Oh.' I start to feel a little dizzy.

'Listen, Nat, I know you're busy, so I'll be quick,' she says, lowering her voice. A part of me is desperate to talk to her about everything. Joanne. My father. Niaomi. I feel like I'm two people, and Rani is the only person who might understand them both. 'Your dad messaged me. He really wants to see you again. I think he's worried about you.' She pauses. 'You know you can call me, don't you? Any time. And … you don't have to stay there. In that house. With him. We can find you somewhere safe.'

Blood rushes from my head.

'Emotional abuse … it's still abuse …'

I flinch as her words slash away at me. I can't deal with this now, with Luella here next to me. *We've just had a fight, that's all*, I tell myself, brushing the fear away. Couples fight. It's normal. 'Thanks, Rani, that's very kind, but we have plans this afternoon. Let's catch up soon.' And then I hang up quickly, before turning to Mum, the brightest smile on my face. 'I'm so happy you're here,' I sing, taking her hand again and squeezing it tight.

Rani

Deflated, I hurry out of Angel station. There must be more I can do to help her, someone else I can speak to. As I walk towards Camden Passage, I try to ignore the crowds brushing past me. Friends in matching Lululemon leggings meeting for post-Pilates smoothies, bleary-eyed couples joining the never-ending queues for brunch. All deliriously happy. It makes me want to vomit.

I pause outside the café, scrolling through Charles's Facebook page. I'm a few minutes late, but Sasha will understand. He's been tagged in a photo on a beach in Cannes, captioned 'The good old days'. I quickly click on it to see a youthful Charles and someone else I vaguely recognise in the foreground, laughing together with bottles of beer in their hands.

There's a row of people behind them. I zoom in and see a young Joanne in the middle, with long blonde hair just like Natalie's. They really could be sisters. She seems withdrawn, clinging to the woman next to her, who's just about recognisable as Darcy. But it's Darcy's expression that catches me by surprise. Her eyes are like daggers, focused in one direction, and I remember her words at the barbecue. *He never changes ... We don't see her any more.* I didn't realise at the time how close she and Joanne were. Is Darcy aware of what happened to Joanne? Could she know what Charles is capable of?

I click on her profile and decide to add her as a friend on Serena's account. They'd probably get on in real life, both well-dressed, powerful women. I drop her a message. Completely casual. *Hi. We met at that party the other weekend. I'm a friend of Natalie Riley's.* Then, remembering that she works as a stylist, I add, *I'm thinking of a wardrobe cleanse. Would love to pick your brain sometime.* As I hit send and look up from my phone, I catch sight of a flash of bleach-blonde hair in front of me. Amber. What is she doing here? We've had this date fixed for a while, but I didn't think she'd have the nerve to show up.

I hover outside the door, contemplating whether to stay or go. I could easily just switch off my phone and make the most of a child-free afternoon. But what do *I* have to be ashamed about? I'm innocent. I should be able to stride in there with my head held high and take a seat at the table next to my best friend. The one who didn't betray me.

Peering through the window, I try to spot them first, get a sense of how they are with each other. But I'm not subtle enough. Sasha's warm eyes stare straight into mine, and she stands up, gesturing me over, the sleeves of her cream silk blouse billowing. She's more expressive than usual, knowing I'll need a lot of encouragement to make it through the door. As I walk in, I recall the words of an old teacher, who drummed into us the importance of maintaining good posture. *Ladies: neck long, chin away from your chest.* It was a state school but housed in a former convent, so they were old-school like that. Mum hoped it would assimilate me fully into British culture. Shake off that strong Indian accent I'd inherited.

Sasha lunges at me, squeezing me tight. I inhale her rich perfume. She always smells so good.

Hugging me still closer, she whispers into my ear, 'So sorry, Rani, I didn't think she'd actually come.'

I sit down in the empty chair next to her, my eyes flitting in every direction to avoid Amber's face. But she doesn't read my signals. And it soon becomes impossible to look away.

'Rani, please just hear me out,' she pleads. 'Just for a minute. Look, I know you weren't expecting to see me …'

I nod my head. *Too right*.

'Okay. Just say the word and I'll go.'

I laugh out loud. I can't help myself. Of course she would say that. Try to seem like the bigger person. But if she really cared about my feelings, she wouldn't be here in the first place. 'I'm hardly going to ask you to leave, am I?'

She smiles softly in acknowledgement, but her eyes tell a different story. It's her privileged silver-spoon upbringing that makes her so accustomed to getting what she wants. I never saw it before, because what we wanted had never been in conflict. But now I can't even stand to look at her.

'Okay, ladies, before we order, you gotta hear about the dates I went on last week,' Sasha blurts, attempting to break the tension. Her voice is forced, upbeat, while her gaze swings anxiously between the two of us. 'Seriously, you can't make this stuff up!'

I nod. Willing to give in simply for the distraction.

'So, Tuesday there was Claudia, this raunchy redhead from Argentina who had a fetish for … wait for it … sex in cemeteries.' She pauses, expecting the hysterical, falling-out-of-our-chairs laughter we used to be known for. But I can barely manage a smile. 'And Wednesday …' she continues, determined, 'boy oh boy, Deja. She was fine. That body. Wow. Until I realised, she could only climax listening to David Attenborough.'

She's met with awkward silence and stares at the floor, out of her depth. The elephant in the room is just too enormous. Trampling heavy-footed over our past. Driving its trunk into our present.

The food arrives, and we dive straight in, barely coming up for air. I can't face the pressure of another second at this table, so after we're done, I look gratefully at the waitress as she clears our plates and I ask for the bill.

Amber stands up to leave, claiming she has to be somewhere, and I begin to relax. But as she heads towards the door and turns around to say goodbye, she meets my gaze, and it hits home for us both. This isn't just goodbye for now.

It's goodbye to over ten years of friendship.

Goodbye to a person I thought would be in my life for ever.

I know Sasha must feel it too. It was always the three of us, after all. But when the door chimes shut and the flash of blonde fades into the distance, she looks at me. 'So ... got time for cake?'

'God, I love you. Yes. One hundred times yes.'

We're in the middle of slicing our forks through a triple-layer vegan Sachertorte when Sasha looks up at me. 'How are you really doing, Rani?' she says, taking a bite.

'I'm okay, actually. Joel and I have been having counselling. We went on another date yesterday – okay, it was just breakfast, but still, it was nice.'

'That's great, Rani ... so great.'

'Oh, and I've been hanging out with my new neighbour, Natalie. I told you about her, the one who moved into the house across the road? She took me to the Jedi Club spa,' I add, enjoying having something else to talk about.

'Ooh. Check you out!' She nods her head, intrigued.

'It's strange, though, because her life seemed so perfect, but it turns out she's dealing with some really difficult stuff, and I'm helping her through it. It's nice to be that kind of friend for a change.'

'Aw, Rani, it's lovely of you to be there for her when you have so much going on,' She pauses. 'I just … I hope you aren't using it as an excuse not to deal with your own stuff.'

I force a laugh. 'Have you been speaking to Joel? You sound just like him.'

'No, of course not. But you know, I hate to admit it, but he's right. This is the time for you to get back on your feet, not worry about someone you barely know.'

I'm annoyed that she's taking his side, and feel it burning the backs of my ears. 'I really thought you'd get it, Sash. How hard it can be to fit in. To find people who get you.'

'Why, because I'm a Black lesbian who works in the City?' she says, roaring with laughter so contagious that I can't help but join in. 'Look, you know I only want the best for you. But I really think you have to find contentment … purpose in your own life, instead of living through other people. You have so much going for you. Two beautiful children. A partner who, yeah, fucked up a bit, but who clearly loves *you*, wants to be with *you* – and anyway, nothing actually happened with Amber, did it? Okay, so you're not travelling around the world as an investigative journalist, but that's the price you pay for stability.'

She stops and stares into the distance. I notice the soft lines around her eyes and at the corners of her mouth. 'And let me tell you, you're not the only one who's had to make sacrifices, Rani. Why do you think I'm always the first one in the office and the last to leave? Because I don't have a life outside my job? No. I have to work twice as hard to get recognised, for clients to see me as a senior associate and not a partner's fucking secretary.' Then she snaps out of it, flicking her long braids out of her face like she means business. 'Now, before I spend the rest of this gorgeous weekend in the office, I'm fricking gonna have another slice of this cake!'

She's right. Deep down I know she is. Meeting Natalie has changed my perspective, has shown me that no one's life is perfect, no matter how it may seem. But now that she's let me in, I owe it to her to stay. Because I'm all she has.

'What are you going to do about Amber?' Sasha says, as she presses a finger into the cake crumbs.

I shake my head, sighing deeply. 'I don't know, Sash. I really don't know.'

She doesn't push it; instead, she reaches across the table and squeezes my hand. I can't help but smile back, feeling so grateful to have her in that moment.

By 6 p.m., we've parted ways. Her to the office, despite it being a Sunday. Me back to the flat. My mind skips past Joel and settles on the girls. They feel like home to me, and this sense of clarity makes me want to kneel on the ground and cry. I know I need to be with them. But I also need my independence. My own identity away from being just a mum, just a housewife. Is it possible to have both, or will I *always* feel this conflicted?

I take the long route to the station to decompress my thoughts. My surroundings look like a scene change during a play. Those who have spent the day lying in the sunshine or having lunch with friends make way for the night owls, who parade down Islington High Street, heading for the rows of bars and pubs. I gaze at them enviously. Short skirts. Legs out. Eye make-up game strong. Brimming with confidence, without a care in the world. The tip of my tongue feels heavy with the words I want to scream at them.

On the Tube back home, I turn the pages of my notebook, reflecting on Natalie's beautiful but cold home. As I head up the escalator, I hear my phone beep in my jacket pocket. It's a Facebook notification. From Darcy. I notice that she hasn't accepted my friend request, but there's a message from her in my inbox.

My heart races and I quickly click to open it.

It's Rani, isn't it? I spoke to Joanne. Thank you for being discreet, but look, I'm sorry, I can't get involved. You don't know Seth. What he's capable of. He could take away my children, or worse. You must understand, I can't risk it. Just get her out of there. And please don't contact me again.

Natalie

There's no sign of Charles greeting us at the door. At first, I'm deeply concerned about what we're walking into, but as we move through to the living room to cool off from the heat, the comforting smell of roast potatoes wafts in from the kitchen. I hear him whistling away as he chops vegetables, and close my eyes, breathing a long sigh of relief. This all sounds promising. Whistling. Cooking. The old Charles returning. Maybe Joanne was wrong. Maybe Charles loves me enough to put it all behind us.

'Hello, ladies, how was your walk?' He grins at us from the door, twin dimples popping. 'It looks lovely out there; perhaps we should have lunch outside.'

I'm still taken aback by his sweetness, but manage to squeeze out a response. 'Really nice, thanks.'

'Gosh, doesn't it smell delicious in here? Luella pipes up. 'You're spoiling us, Charles.' She stares up at him in admiration.

I keep quiet, moving through into the kitchen and reaching for a pile of plates. Charles presses the palm of his hand into my shoulder. I have to consciously stop my body from tensing up.

'Let me do that, darling. Why don't you and Luella head into the garden? I'll bring everything out.'

We sit down to eat, and I can't stop staring at him. Half in adoration. Half in bewilderment. He's so attentive, laying the table with our best crockery. Carving the roast chicken and serving up his handiwork onto our plates. There is only love and adoration in his eyes as he caresses my face, reminiscing about this time last year, when we were on our way to Florence. Sipping Aperol while overlooking the Fountain of Neptune. Roaming through cobbled alleyways to lose the crowds. How can this be the same man as yesterday, who refused to eat the meal I'd cooked because I hadn't followed his adjustments to my recipe? Who belittled me in front of my mother over an outfit that hung just above my knees? I must be living with two versions of the same person. My very own Jekyll and Hyde.

After lunch, Charles and I make our way to the living room, while Mum heads upstairs to rest. I close the shutters, blocking out the late afternoon light, and switch on the Vitra Akari reading lamp, which emits a cosy glow.

Charles settles down on the sofa, flicking through the weekend papers. I hover at the other end, unsure of what to do with myself. But then he looks up at me, smiling in a way that used to make me feel safe.

'Come over here, darling,' he says, throwing the papers to the side before patting the spot next to him. I'm still a little anxious but feel a touch of warmth inside me as I reflect on the afternoon just gone. Perhaps this is Charles's way of apologising, waving the white flag on our period of conflict.

I sink my body down, nuzzling my head in his lap, enjoying the sensation of his fingers running through my hair, lightly massaging my scalp before moving down towards the curves of my bare neck and shoulders. His pressure is light and gentle, and I feel my pulse slow to a soft purr, the tension in my body drifting away.

Suddenly I can sense where this is heading, and jerk my head up, remembering that I forgot to take the pill this morning. Curling my legs off the sofa, I stand upright, gesturing to Charles that I'm heading upstairs. But he grabs my hand.

'Where are you going, darling? Come back to me.' He winks and pulls me towards him. 'We don't want to miss this ovulation window.'

'What?' I say, frowning. Surely he hasn't memorised my menstrual cycle when I barely keep track of it myself?

'Well, you're going to be leaving work soon anyway.' He nuzzles my belly. 'Aren't you?' His voice suddenly becomes firm.

I shake my hand out of his. 'Charles, we've talked about this. I'm still trying to get my head around quitting, but a baby is one step too far. I'm not ready for that now.' *Or ever,* I add in my head.

'For God's sake, Natalie, I don't know how many times I have to tell you. I'm going to be forty next month. I want to be around to see our kid grow up!'

I take a step away from him, but he reaches out again, with both hands this time, and as he pulls me towards him, I feel his sharp fingernails digging into my skin. My mind flashes back to the spa, and I feel that same sense of claustrophobia, of fear. 'Have you forgotten that I'm going to be funding your life, Natalie? This is the least you can do. You owe me.'

Within seconds, he has ripped through my dress, wrenching down my underwear. I attempt to wriggle out of his grasp, but he pushes me backwards onto the sofa. From the look on his face, he's applied more force than he intended, but his eyes glimmer as he feels pleasure in my pain. And as my body sinks into the velvet fabric, I think back to the days when he only strove to please me, seduce me, when his fingertips used to caress my body with love and affection. 'Charles, please. Don't do this. Please.' I hear desperation in my voice, and my eyes sting with tears, though I refuse to let him see them.

Within seconds, I've escaped my body, until I'm floating in the air, watching it happening to some other body, some other woman.

But I feel nothing. This is not me.

Rani

I head up the stairs to the flat, distracted by the sounds com-ing from inside. Muffled words. Adult voices. One of them sorrowful, as if it's drowning in tears. As I insert the key in the lock, the door unexpectedly opens from inside, and Joel is standing there, pale-faced, with frown lines criss-crossing his forehead. I'm about to ask him if he's okay when I notice Natalie hovering behind him. Her face is drained of colour. Her skin lifeless like a mannequin's. She's wearing a turquoise dress that once would have dazzled but now looks like it has met one hell of a sorry end. Carelessly ripped at the edges and suffocated by one of Joel's crumpled old jumpers. For a moment I ask myself what's going on between them. Is there a *them*? I hate myself for thinking it, but I can't help it after what happened with Amber.

Joel senses my suspicions and gently takes my arm. 'Rani, I think you're going to need to sit down.'

'What's going on? Where are the girls?'

'They're fine. Don't worry, they're with Mum. She picked them up just before you got here.'

'Okay ...' I say, but I feel even more nervous now – Joel would never have asked her at such short notice unless it was an emergency. I turn my head towards Natalie, searching for an explanation, but she just stands there frozen, except for her hands, which tremble uncontrollably by her sides, as if crying out for help. I grab hold of one of them and squeeze it tight. 'Natalie, what's happened? What has he done to you?'

Silence.

Wrapping my arms around her, I gently guide her towards the girls' bedroom and tuck her into Lydia's bed. I bend down and kiss her forehead. 'Just rest now,' I whisper. 'I'm here when you're ready.' Then I switch off the lights, leaving the bedroom door ajar.

Joel is waiting for me in the hall, pacing back and forth. I follow him into the kitchen and slouch down at the table, holding my head in my hands. I'm too late. It's too late. He closes the door behind us before sitting down next to me.

'What happened?' I whisper.

'I have no idea.' He shakes his head. 'We were on our way home from the park when Lydia spotted her running towards us. You know how she thinks Natalie's a princess?' His mouth breaks into a soft smile, but it passes in seconds. 'She looked like a madwoman, Rani. With her dress torn, and her hair all tangled up. Some kids were pointing and laughing. I had to get her away from there.'

'Oh God,' I say, clenching my teeth. 'Did she say anything?'

'No. Not really. She kept asking for a pharmacy. We took her to one opposite the station, but she wouldn't let us come inside.' His gaze shoots to the floor. 'Rani,' he sighs, scratching the back of his head, 'I think you were right to be worried about her. Something is going on. I'm sorry. I should have listened to you.'

'It's okay, Joel.' I shrug it off. This isn't about us. He nods gratefully at me. 'Do you think it could have been Charles?' I ask.

'Maybe he did something to her. She has bruises on her arms and thighs. They look brand new.'

'I don't know.' He stares at me, anxious. 'I couldn't get much sense out of her. She just kept apologising and repeating, *"What have I done?"* It must be the shock. We need to let her sleep it off.'

Suddenly the doorbell starts to ring continuously, like a car alarm. We look at each other with matching expressions of confusion and fear. Neither of us is expecting visitors. Joel walks over to the intercom. 'Wait,' I say. 'Don't pick it up in case it's him. He can't know we're at home.'

I tiptoe towards the window and pull back the curtain ever so slightly. The doorbell stops, but then my phone begins to ring. And that's when I see him. Standing on the pavement outside, phone to his ear, staring up at our window, eyebrows scrunched up in fury. 'It's him, Joel. Charles. Should we call the police?'

'And tell them what? We don't know what happened.' He pauses, looking worried. 'Look, as much as we want to help her, we're out of our depth, Rani. And we've got Lydia and Leela to think of. We need to get her out of here.'

We're interrupted by noises coming from the girls' bedroom. The walls are wafer thin, so the minutest of sounds can be heard all over the flat. And for a moment, I drift back to the newborn days, when there was no need for a baby monitor because I could hear everything, from the softest gurgle to the loudest of screams. As if they were inside my head. I tiptoe into the bedroom and see Natalie sitting upright on the edge of Lydia's bed, clutching her phone to her ear as she weeps softly into it.

'I'm sorry. I'm so, so sorry.' When she sees me, she drops the phone on the bed. But I notice the name on the screen. It's not Charles she's speaking to.

Lowering myself down next to her, I fold her head into my chest. I don't want her to see my face, the guilt eating it alive. Maybe if I had pushed her harder to leave him instead of enjoying having a friend whose life was as fucked up as mine, this wouldn't have happened. 'Natalie,' I whisper. 'What did he do to you?'

'No. No.' She shakes her head vehemently, quick to defend him. 'This is all my fault. I lied to him. I did this. And now … it's over.'

'What do you mean? What did he do to you?'

She says nothing, but her silence is all the confirmation I need. 'You can't go back there. I'll find you somewhere to stay until we figure out what to do. But what about your mum? She's staying with you, right? Do you want me to call her back?'

'No, please, no! She doesn't want to talk to me right now. I've let her down.'

'Natalie, I'm sure she doesn't think that.'

She nods her head in shame. 'You don't understand. If only I had listened to her. She's right. She's always right. And now it's over … it's all over.'

Joel hovers outside the door. 'Rani,' he says softly, 'I've just seen Charles pull out of their drive.' He pauses, as if contemplating something. 'Listen … what if we dropped her at Amber's? She's been through something like this in the past, hasn't she, with that hedge fund guy … She might be able to help Natalie see sense.'

My mind instantly rejects the idea. I can't believe he would even suggest it. 'What? No way.' But then I look at Natalie, so shaken up and helpless, and I know that Joel is right. I have to look beyond my own pain. I have to think about what's best for her, and right now, Amber is the one person who might be able to understand what she's going through.

As I'm figuring out what to say to Amber, Joanne's words echo in my mind. *He preys on vulnerable women.* On the surface, Natalie didn't strike me as vulnerable, but I wonder if Charles saw through her right from the beginning, and that's why he wanted her. Joanne and Natalie aren't that different. Both beautiful, intelligent women with deep-rooted insecurities. Both fell for his charms, saw him as their saviour, their second chance at happiness. With Joanne, the abuse happened slowly, over a number of years. Whereas with Natalie, he seemed to reveal his true nature in a matter of months. It could be his desperation, his fear of growing older, losing his power. But something tells me there's more to this. Another layer hidden somewhere below that is slowly starting to trickle to the surface.

Natalie

'Natalie, it's Amber. Are you awake?' Her voice is the sound of songbirds at dawn, a gentle lilt flying through the air to greet me. I could listen to it all day. Escape my reality in its harmonious rising and falling.

She follows up with three soft knocks at the door.

I am awake. But to say that would be misleading. Implying that I had slept, when I've spent all night staring up at the bare ceiling, wondering how on earth I've ended up here. Hiding from my husband in the spare room of a woman I've only just met. The bruises on my body have turned a deep shade of purple. The colour would be mesmerising if it didn't bring it all back to me. That sense of sheer helplessness. Knowing there was nothing I could do but wait for it to be over.

If I wanted evidence of what happened, this is it. I could have shown it to the pharmacist, who failed to hide his disgust, shaking his head disapprovingly at my wedding ring before reluctantly handing me the morning-after pill. What he must have thought of me. A woman who showed no remorse after cheating on her poor husband. If only. Perhaps if I'd told him the truth, he would have urged me to speak to the police. They would have asked me to make a formal statement, carried out an examination. Would this be enough for them to arrest him? Most likely. But then what next?

I know Charles. He won't let himself be publicly shamed. His reputation tarnished with my slanderous accusations. He'd throw all the money he has at this case. Proclaiming his innocence, sweet-talking the jury. Hiring lawyers and private investigators to drag up all the dirt they can find on me. Even the dirt I'm not prepared for, that Mum has tried so hard to wipe clean.

My name would be leaked to the press. Somehow. It always is in cases like these. My face splashed across the papers, accompanied by headlines like 'Blonde Slut Had It Coming' and 'She's No Angel'. Perhaps worst of all is what my lawyers would make me out to be. An innocent woman trapped in an abusive marriage.

But I am not a victim. I will never be a victim.

I shake myself out of my dark thoughts. 'Hi, Amber. Come in.'

She pushes open the door with the back of her heel. It seems like a strange thing to do until I notice the tray in her hands, and the soothing smell of freshly made coffee wafting past me. I close my eyes for a second, inhaling deeply.

'I thought you might fancy something for breakfast. Rani said you haven't eaten for a while, so …' She lowers the tray onto the table beside me. 'Don't get your hopes up. It's nothing special. Just coffee, a banana and a slice of toast. I've never been much of a cook.' She smiles, but then her cheerfulness drops. 'How are you feeling? Wait, you don't have to answer that.'

I observe her through tired eyes. She's tall, tall enough to pull off the boho-style maxi dress that she's thrown over her slender frame. Her hair is blonde like mine, but several shades lighter. And short, framing uber-high cheekbones. She's so effortlessly beautiful that I can't stop staring at her. This is how I've always wanted the world to see me, except on her it feels entirely genuine. 'Thanks, but you really didn't have to.' I look around the bed, patting the covers, feeling for my phone. 'I don't suppose you know what time it is?'

'It's just gone eight. I've got to head to the office soon, but I'm working from home this afternoon. Rani said she'll swing by too.'

Eight o'clock? I leap out of bed, frantically searching the room for the clothes I was wearing last night. *Shit. I'm going to be late. I'm never late.*

'Wait. Where are you going? You can't possibly think that … not after …'

'I have to. They're expecting me.'

'Natalie, stop. Charles knows where you work. Plus, you've been through absolute hell. Just stay in bed and rest. You're safe here. I can call them if you want me to.'

I pause, reflecting on her words. She's right. The last thing I want is for him to turn up at my office, causing a scene. I don't need to draw any more attention to my crumbling relationship.

When I eventually find my phone, I quickly tap the screen, but it stays black. 'Thanks … it's all right, I'll message my secretary. But could I …'

'Charger? Yes, of course. There's one in the kitchen. It's one of those savvy multi-phone models. Ric left it behind when he moved out. Come with me, I'll show you.' She's perceptive, deceptively so. 'And before I forget, the guest bathroom is just through there. I've left you a fresh towel behind the door, and there's a toothbrush in the holder. It's brand new, I promise!'

I follow her downstairs into the kitchen, taking in my surroundings as if for the first time – I could barely see straight when I arrived last night. It's an elegant maisonette filled with natural light. I think I could be happy with something like this. One day.

She takes my phone out of my hand and inserts the charger cable. After a couple of minutes, it comes back to life. 'He's going to message you, Natalie, if he hasn't already. Look, I know we've only just met, so forgive me if I'm overstepping here, but I want you to know that I understand. I think that's why Rani asked me to help.' She turns to look at me with warmth and sincerity. 'It does get better, I promise. But you need to take the first step and leave.'

I nod to let her know that I'm listening, but I can't manage anything else. There's so much more to this than she can imagine.

She glances at the phone. 'Argh crap, I'm going to be late. Sorry to leave you here alone, but there's a meeting I just can't get out of. Feel free to snoop around. *Mi casa, su casa*, and all that. And help yourself to anything that takes your fancy from the fridge. I've just done an Ocado shop, so you're in luck!' She flashes me an apologetic smile. 'I mean … oh God, I'm sorry. I have this hideous habit of saying and doing the wrong thing. You'll soon get used to it.' She touches my arm for a brief second before swiftly turning away, her dress billowing around her like a parachute.

As soon as I hear the door close behind her, I pick my phone up from the counter, ravenous for any messages I may have missed from Charles or my mother. I hate myself for crawling back to them, but it feels so natural, like we're connected by an invisible thread. There's radio silence from Charles, so I reread the message he sent yesterday evening. *Natalie, where are you? I'm worried. If I don't hear from you soon, I'll have to call the police.* This must be a threat. A threat in disguise.

Terrified of what he might do if he doesn't hear from me, I drop him a quick one-liner, letting him know that I'm staying with a friend for a few nights to clear my head. Then I notice a flashing icon: my voicemail box is full. I check my missed calls. Every single one of them is from Mum. I start to feel light-headed, my pulse racing, but I can't help it. I have to hear what she's thinking. Holding my breath, I click play.

Sunday, 6.32 p.m.: 'Darling, it's me. I just heard the door slam. Is everything okay? Charles has locked himself in your bathroom. He's not answering. Call me back.'

Sunday, 7.15 p.m.: 'Darling, please pick up. Let me know you're okay. Whatever has happened, I'm sure we can fix it. Just come home.'

The first handful of messages have the same tone. Tame. An anxious check-in. But I know Mum; there's more to come.

Sunday, 8.33 p.m.: 'Natalie. What happened? Charlie is fuming. He's throwing things against the wall. What have you done?'

Sunday, 10.47 p.m.: 'Is that your neighbour I just heard? Don't listen to her lies. You've been so tired, Natalie. You must have fallen asleep, had another nightmare. Charles would never hurt you. He loves you.'

Monday, 12.05 a.m.: 'I can't bear it. Why are you doing this to me? After everything I've done for you.'

Monday, 2.45 a.m.: 'Natalie, you're killing me. Do you want my blood on your hands? Go back to him. It's not too late. Tell him how sorry you are for what you've done. Do it, Natalie. Please.'

I hurl the phone against the wall. It breaks in two as it drops to the floor, but two pieces that can easily be put together again. Indestructible. Feeling disappointed, I grab chunks of my hair and pull at them ferociously until strands come loose. They feel dry and brittle in the palm of my hand. I slap my cheeks hard until they're flushing with pain. But I don't care any more.

Wandering helplessly around the kitchen, I search for something to knock me out cold. I know Amber is right. I can't go back to Charles, not after what he did. But Mum's words are like magic, making me doubt myself.

I open the fridge door. *Come on, Amber. A woman like you must have what I'm looking for.* Then I find it, expertly concealed behind a bag of salad leaves. An unopened bottle of vodka. Chilled. Just the way I used to drink it.

I pull it out and head into the living room, rummaging through drawers, pawing over trinkets, anything to distract myself. When Mum's voice creeps back into my head, I pause my foraging to take a long swig from the bottle, waiting impatiently for the clear liquid to seep down my throat and into my empty stomach. It isn't long before my vision blurs and I start to lose my balance a little. This is all starting to feel frighteningly familiar. Life before Charles. Alone in my flat. Drinking my misery away, straight from the bottle. But this time it's Monday morning instead of Friday night – I haven't just done a one-eighty, I've reached a whole new low.

Just as I'm about to head back to bed, I spot an area of the wall decorated with a collage of framed photographs, and stumble over to take a closer look. There are several photos of

Rani and Amber together, alongside a black woman who must be Sasha. So many happy moments. Treasured memories. It feels like being repeatedly punched in the stomach.

This is what normality looks like, something I've never experienced and now never will.

One of the photographs stands out among the rest. It's not the people in it, but the scenery that makes me stop. I want to continue staring, but the room starts to spin around me and I'm struggling to grasp my train of thought. I unhook the photo from the wall and clamber upstairs, clutching the bottle in the other hand. Then falling into bed, I hover it above my face, my hands shaking from the weight of the frame.

It's a fairly recent photograph. Amber looks the same as she did this morning, but with longer hair. She's lying on a picnic blanket with her head in the lap of a man, presumably an old boyfriend. But it's the way they are positioned, with the expanse of still water directly behind them, that captures my attention. Identical to the photo of Mum and me in my downstairs toilet. The place that she claims was a weekend getaway yet has no recollection of.

Natalie

'Natalie, hello? Where are you?' I hear voices calling my name. Somewhere far in the distance, footsteps stampeding towards me. Then, 'Shit!'

The voices become louder until they surround me. I feel hands on me, little shots of electricity bringing me back to consciousness. My mouth is metallic, causing me to smack my lips together in disgust.

Someone flips me over. Someone else strokes my face with a dampened towel. My senses are slowly returning.

Warm hands cup my wrist. 'I think she's okay.'

'Fucking hell, she's polished off over half that bottle. I was saving it for a party on Saturday. Her hangover is going to be insane.'

'What? No way. I've *never* seen her drink.'

When my eyes eventually open, I can just about make out their blurry faces staring at me, flushed pink with worry.

'You're awake. Thank God you're all right.' She speaks too soon, though, as the slice of toast leaps from my stomach into my throat.

'Wait. I think I'm going to be …'

Too late.

As I sit up, I see the yellowy-green bile dripping down Amber's dress. She stares down at it in disgust, and for a moment I think she's going to scream at me. But then she turns to look at Rani, and surprises us both by breaking into fits of giggles.

Then Rani joins her. And they don't stop.

Once they've caught their breath, I reach out to touch Amber's arm. Waving the photograph of her and the man in my hand.

'This photo. Where was it taken?'

'Huh?' Amber looks confused, her forehead wrinkling. 'Oh God, umm … somewhere in the New Forest, I think. The lake, it had a funny name … what was it? Oh yeah.' She clicks her tongue. 'Hatchet Pond?' But it means nothing to me. Not even a fragment of a memory. 'Anyway …' she continues, eyeing the front of her dress, my vomit crusting over it. 'I'd better go take a shower.'

I shrug in response, a frown settling on my face. I'm too ashamed to apologise.

As Amber leaves the bedroom, I sense Rani glancing over my shoulder. 'That lake … it's so familiar.' She bites down on her bottom lip. 'Hang on … it's in that photo, isn't it? The one hanging on the wall of your toilet?'

I nod, smacking my dry tongue against the roof of my mouth, grimacing at the sourness of it.

'But it's you and Luella in the photo, isn't it?'

My chest is heavy with her insinuation. *Why don't I know where it was taken? Why don't I remember?* The past is a black hole, growing in force, pulling me towards it, destroying any chance I have of a future. I'm terrified of what lurks there, hidden in the shadows, behind the flicker of memories that have already revealed themselves. But with everything that has happened with Charles since we moved into that house, I don't think I have a choice. I can't keep this up, living this double life. If I have any chance of moving on, finding peace, I can't keep scratching at the surface any more. I have to confront the past head on.

Heaving myself upright, I curl my knees into my chest before gesturing at the empty space next to me on the bed.

Rani shuffles on, leaning back against the wall, her lips pursed with worry. 'Nat … are you okay? What's going on?' She brushes her hand lightly over my shoulder.

I feel like sinking into her. But instead, I stare up at the blank cream wall of Amber's spare bedroom, playing with words in my head, trying to figure out where to begin. 'When I first saw the house, it felt like fate,' I say slowly, tuning in to the faint whir of the shower going next door and Amber humming to herself. 'I was in such a good place with Charles. He made me feel loved and secure. I could see my future, and the door to my past, together. I thought I was ready for it all; I thought I could finally let someone in, that I would feel happy … complete.'

'Nat, what are you saying? Your house …'

'It was my childhood home.'

'But I thought … didn't you say you grew up in Kent?'

'Huh? Oh yes, I did. I mean before, before Kent. And Mum refuses to talk about it. It's too painful for her.' I turn to her, reaching for her hand as the fear bubbles inside me. 'I'd planned to tell Charles everything. I hated lying to him about it, about who I really am. But the house, Rani, it's nothing like I thought it would be. Ever since we moved there, it feels like my life has been unravelling.' The words burst out of me. I can't stop myself. 'Charles. The nightmares, so vivid, like memories. I don't know why she's back, and I don't know how to make her leave.' I shrink away, cupping my palm over my mouth.

'Who's back, Nat? Who are you talking about?'

'Mum knows. She's so worried.' I ignore her question – it's too much to deal with. 'Charles was our one chance at happiness, to put it all behind us, and now it's over. I've blown it, Rani. I lied to him. I pushed him over the edge. It's all my fault.'

'No, no.' She gently touches my arm. 'You have to trust me, Nat. You've done nothing wrong. Only Charles is to blame. Do you think he could have been drugging you? It might explain the confus—'

The sorrow spills down my face. 'No, Rani. Of course not. He wouldn't. This is all *my* fault. If you only knew what else I've kept from him …' I freeze mid-sentence. I've already said too much.

But she doesn't seem to notice. 'What can I do, Nat? Tell me what I can do to help you.' She grips hold of my hand, staring up at me, her dark brown eyes sparkling with kindness.

It ignites me, somehow, having someone to confide in, to share this with. I spring off the bed and turn to straighten the covers. 'That photo. What did Amber say about where it was taken?' I ask her, the desperation clawing away at me. 'That place is all I have now, Rani. It's all I have of the past. I need to go back there.'

Rani

I reach up high on my tiptoes and grab the holdall resting on top of the wardrobe. As I yank it down towards my chest, a mountain of dust follows closely behind. My nose immediately itches. My lungs start to constrict. I quickly drop the bag on the bed and rummage in my bedside drawer for an inhaler. After two generous puffs of steroids, clean air powers through my body again.

So much has happened in the last twelve hours, I can hardly believe it. I stayed the night at Amber's. It felt strange, the two of us united again with so much left unsaid, but I couldn't leave Natalie in the state she was in. She seemed so distressed and alone in the world; blaming herself for what Charles had done to her; mumbling about running through fields and lying under trees. I couldn't make sense of it.

When she woke this morning, the colour had returned to her cheeks, but the tension still tainted her half-baked smile. We took the train back to Highgate together. Number 11 was completely still. Nothing stirred. In silence, we walked through her front door, passing the scene of the crime, and up the stairs to their bedroom. Charles wasn't due back from work until the evening, but I could feel his presence everywhere. His musky scent marking every room like he had only just left it.

I wonder what will become of this beautiful house now that it has taken on the persona of their broken marriage. I wonder if I will ever look at it in the same way again.

Pulling open a drawer, I think about what I'll need to take. Where we're heading is only a couple of hours' drive from London, and the forecast looks warm and dry. I fold in a pair of beige cargo shorts and an assortment of plain T-shirts to accompany the leggings and jumper I'll wear on the drive there. The colour scheme is bland and neutral. My uniform of choice for blending into the background. Feeling frustrated by the limitations of my wardrobe, I wonder if I might be able to squeeze into something Natalie brings with her.

But then the image of her lying in a pool of her own booze-infused sweat comes back to me, and I'm forced to accept the real Natalie. No longer shiny and perfect, but seeped in mystery and torment.

My phone vibrates on the bed. It's a text from Joel, responding to my message about our road trip. *I don't know, Rani. It's so last-minute. What about the girls? And you have no idea where you're going, what you're walking into.*

I type out my frustration. *You didn't believe me before and look what happened. She's going with or without me. I can't let her do this on her own.*

That's fair. I'm sorry. But don't you think you should get the police involved first? What if Charles follows you there? They need to know what he did.

I've tried. She doesn't want to hear it.

Well, try again.

Okay.

It's a few minutes before he finally responds.

Be careful, Rani. I love you.

I start to text back, but then decide against it, my eyes tearing up. It feels strange to be heading somewhere without Joel and the girls. This will be the first time I've been away from them for longer than a night since Lydia was born. I feel guilty. Of course I do. But I know they'll be fine without me.

I'm just about to put my phone away when I notice a missed call from Jemima that I didn't see before. She rarely calls unless it's urgent. Maybe something has happened to Scruff – she mentioned he was ill, and he is getting on a bit. I glance at my watch. Twenty minutes until I'm due to meet Natalie outside number 11. That's plenty of time to check in on Jemima.

I sling my travel bag over my shoulder and grab my keys from the desk before leaving the flat, instinctively searching Natalie's bedroom window for movement. But it stares back blankly. Crossing the road, I push open the gate to Jemima's before heading down the path to ring the bell. It's only then that I notice her front garden. It's a long way from its usual standard. The rose bushes look like they've gone too long without watering. Sizzled to a crisp. Weeds are starting to sprout over the lawn. Concerned, I press the door bell with my index finger, lingering over it in case she doesn't hear it the first time.

There are a few half-hearted yelps from Scruff inside, but no sign of Jemima. How strange. I peer in through the windows, but all I can see is darkness. Maybe she's not at home. I decide to give it one last try, bending down and calling through the letter box.

'Jemima. Are you there? It's me, Rani.' Suddenly, she emerges from the shadows. Pale, like she's seen a ghost. 'Is everything okay, Jemima?'

She ignores my question. 'Are you alone?' I'm surprised by the sound of her voice. So faint, like a whisper.

'Yes, it's just me.'

She opens the door just enough for me to slide inside. Scruff hobbles up to me, eager for attention. I reach down and nuzzle the sweet spot under his chin, and he whimpers contentedly.

'Jemima, what's wrong? You look terrified.'

She leads me into the kitchen at the back of the house, the only room where the curtains haven't been drawn. It's unusually cold in here. 'The last few days, I've had this awful feeling that I was being followed. I was going to call the police, but whoever it was, well, they seemed to stop. I assumed I was just being paranoid. You know? Silly old Jemima and her overactive imagination. But then earlier this morning ...'

She turns. My eyes follow. And that's when I see it. Cardboard taped where the glass would normally be.

'Someone threw a brick through the back door.'

'Oh Jemima, that's awful. I'm so sorry.' My mind wanders. Could this be connected to Natalie and Charles? Does he suspect that she overheard them arguing that day, and the night before last? But I say nothing. I don't want to worry her any more than necessary. 'I can't imagine anyone would have a reason to target *you*, Jemima. It's probably just some kids playing a harmless prank. You know how cruel they can be these days. And with the school holidays starting soon, I'm sure they're thinking of ways to amuse themselves.'

Her face starts to relax a little, her cheeks regaining colour.

'It's probably nothing to worry about.' I pause, deliberating what to say next. How to press her further. 'But I'm just thinking out loud here … maybe you know something that might cause some … I don't know, tension?'

She lifts her gaze. Palm over her rosy cheek. 'No, I don't think so.' Then she turns her face towards mine, still reflecting. 'Unless … Natalie's mother … I'm sure I recognised her, that she used to live next door. But she wouldn't have done this, would she?'

'I doubt it. It doesn't seem her style.' Except now that I know Luella, a part of me does wonder. But I continue brushing it off, not wanting to worry her. 'And wasn't Natalie there when you asked her, anyway? So it's all out in the open.' Then, hoping to join up the dots, I ask hesitantly, 'Jemima … if it was Luella who used to live there, I don't suppose you remember why she left?'

Part Three
The Secret

Natalie

She walks towards me, an overnight bag swinging defiantly from her shoulder, bouncing off her hip. Her nose pointed up into the air like a hound following the scent of raw meat. It's not an expression I've seen on her before. Powered by determination. Hungry for the truth at all costs. As she squints into the car, I can almost hear her wondering which Natalie she will find here. The one who caught her eye from the moment she moved in across the street? Or the one slumped on her friend's bed, a pungent odour of sweat and vodka steaming off her?

I watch as she breaks into a smile, absorbing my freshly washed hair, my immaculately painted face. I know she's pleased that I'm the one sitting here. All glossy-haired and squeaky clean. The other Natalie shocked her. She was unpredictable. Unstable.

Who knows what she was capable of?

Rani knocks on the window, gesturing at me to wind it down. 'Nat. I've just come from Jemima's. You're not gonna believe it!' Her pupils are dilated. She's barely breathing as the words fly out of her. 'Listen, Amber's photograph was taken at Hatchet Pond in the New Forest, right? Well, I just googled it, and it's close to where Jemima said you moved to. A village called … Beaulieu, or however the hell you pronounce it. Your mum mentioned it to a neighbour. Apparently she couldn't afford the rent here when your father left.'

'Oh?' I know I should be relieved that we're getting closer. That the pieces are finally coming together. But all I want to do is bury my head in the sand. I didn't want to be right. I didn't want to believe that Mum was capable of all these lies. All these secrets. And it makes me wonder what else she is hiding.

'Yes! It's so strange, don't you think? Why she would want to keep this from you. And why she lied to Jemima.'

I shrug my shoulders. 'Maybe she wanted to protect me.' But even as I say the words, I'm not sure I believe them any more.

'Well, whatever the reason, we're not going to find it hanging around here. You ready?'

I set the satnav to our end destination. The village where I supposedly spent years of my childhood. It's strange to feel connected to a place yet hold no real memories of it.

Rani slumps next to me, fidgeting away. She takes off her trainers and stretches her feet. Rummages in her bag for a packet of popcorn, crunching her way through the silence. I can tell that she's itching to reach our destination, for us to be one step closer to finding out the truth. But all I want to do is grab her by the shoulders and shake her. *This isn't a game, Rani. This is my life. We have no idea what we are driving into.*

As we turn onto an A-road just past Wembley, I see a short traffic jam ahead and get ready to pull on the handbrake. The car slows down, grinding to a halt.

Rani turns to face me, lightly brushing her fingers over my arm. 'Nat. Sorry for bringing this up now, but we haven't had a chance to talk about what happened … with Charles. How are you feeling? Ugh, sorry, I know what a stupid question.' She hesitates, as if contemplating what to say next.

I remain fixated on the road ahead of me, trying hard to quieten my mind. I can't go back there. I won't go back there.

'You know, there's still time to go to the police – if that's what you want, that is. You're not alone, Nat, I promise you. I'm here,' she says, squeezing my hand.

Memories force their way through the darkness, and my body tenses up. There's a tightness around my chest, a piercing ringing in my ears, and I feel that same sense of sheer helplessness. I shake my head adamantly.

'Are you sure? It's just, I'm worried he might be looking for you.'

'Rani. Just drop it, please,' I say, one eye on the rear-view mirror. 'I've got too much going on inside my head. I can't think straight.'

She lets it go, but I can tell that it's still preying on her mind. It's preying on mine, too, weighing heavy on my shoulders. Not to mention the guilt I feel about staying quiet. I know I should report him. If not for me, then for someone else further down the line. People need to know what he is capable of, even if I pushed him to do it. Even if it was my fault. But right now, it's impossible. I can't move forward. There *is* no forward. I can only go back. Back to the beginning.

As we make our way out of London, the lump in my throat starts to dissolve as my body drains itself of the city. I remember this sensation of leaving everything behind. I'd tasted it on weekends away with Charles, but it always felt artificial. Knowing that I was still attached to reality like a dog on a lead. And that at any moment, it could pull me right back.

I think of our house in Highgate, standing tall and proud. It's what every hard-working Londoner dreams of owning. And I used to be just like them. Shuffling back and forth from my shoebox studio on Bethnal Green High Road. A miserable existence – and I was one of the lucky ones, earning over double the average national wage. But it was all I could afford after multiple student loans, and of course, Mum's monthly allowance.

On weekends when the weather was good, I'd take the Underground away from east London and spend all day walking aimlessly along tree-lined streets and cobbled pavements, gazing at beautiful, lofty townhouses draped in wisteria. Every so often, I'd catch a glimpse of an elegantly dressed woman at a window. Her hair piled loosely into a bun. A lustrous pearl in each ear. And I'd imagine what it would be like to be her. To gaze up at those high ceilings. To glide around rooms laden with designer furniture. Occasionally, I'd meet their eyes. But rarely would they acknowledge me.

At the time, I put it down to an air of superiority. The fact that they could see right through my cheap clothes and fake designer handbags. But now that I'm one of them, I know it wasn't that at all. They couldn't smile back at me because they'd forgotten what happiness felt like.

Rani

'So where are we heading to first?' I ask.

'I have no idea. Apart from that lake in the photograph, I'm going in blind like you.'

We're on a long, winding country lane, a never-ending expanse of grey surrounded by identical green fields and a canopy of trees above our heads. I catch sight of wild ponies and cows grazing on the edges, dangerously close to our blind spot. Natalie leans back in the driver's seat, one hand clenched tightly over the steering wheel while the other glides through her hair, smoothing out the tangles. She looks immaculate again, like a Bond girl. Flawless-faced and dressed in a cream linen shift dress. Not a crease in sight. I grimace at my faded black leggings and oversized denim shirt, in dire need of an iron. *How does she do it?* But that thought goes nowhere as her gaze lingers too long off the road in front of us and the car swerves from side to side at high speed.

'Whoa! Slow down, Nat!'

She grins playfully at me, lowering her free hand back onto the steering wheel. Her body language seems way too relaxed, like this is all just fun and games to her. But her eyes tell a different story. Shrunk deep into their sockets, repelling the light. Every day I spend with her, I lose sight of who she is. Beneath that glamorous, serene exterior there's a whirlwind of conflicting personalities. Shifting from the submissive and vulnerable to the wild and carefree, almost as if she too is in the process of self-discovery. And I want to ask her, *Who are you really, Natalie? And what are you hiding?*

'Shall we find a hotel, get that sorted first?' I suggest.

She doesn't respond, lost in thought. Thinking that Google Maps might be our best bet, I pick up my phone from my lap. The screen flashes with a message from Joel asking how we're getting on. Typical. We're only a few hours into our trip, and already he wants me home again. Back to the laundry, the dirty dishes, the packed lunches. He ends the text with the same two words he sent earlier. *Be careful*. I don't know why he's so worried. It's the New Forest, not a war zone. What could possibly go wrong here amongst the quaint English cottages and the pretty tea rooms? We're miles away from London, in a place that Natalie has no recollection of. How will Charles be able to find us here?

I ignore him, opening the app and typing in the search box. 'Ooh, I've found somewhere we could try. Beaulieu Palace Hotel.' I zoom out. 'Looks like the only option. Great reviews, though.'

'Great,' she says, firmly back in the present. 'And before you say anything, this is on me. It's the least I can do for dragging you down here.'

'Trust me, Nat, you're the one doing me a favour. You have no idea how much I've missed just being able to pack a suitcase and walk out the door.' I zoom in again to see what sights are nearby. 'Interesting. So the hotel looks like it's bang in the centre of the village. How about we grab some lunch nearby, then in the afternoon we could swing past the local school? It's called … Village Oaks Primary. I'm guessing that doesn't ring any bells?'

She shakes her head.

'Well, it looks like the only school in the area, so you must have gone there. Unless there's a posh private school nearby.'

'Not a chance. Mum could never have afforded that.' She laughs. 'I went to the local grammar school in Kent.'

'God,' I say, sighing, 'I can't believe how wrong I was about you.'

'What do you mean?'

'Don't be so modest, Nat! You must know. When you and Charles moved across the street from us, I couldn't believe it. That someone like me could live opposite people like you.' I lower my voice. 'But to think what you were having to deal with. I thought he worshipped you. That he could never ...' The words fly out of my mouth before I can stop them. I can't help it after the last few days and everything she's trusted me with. It makes me feel special.

Her expression immediately darkens. 'I was wrong about him too, Rani. I really believed he loved me, that we could be happy together. What a mess. My life is such a mess.' She blots her eyes with the back of her hand.

I quickly turn to face her, lightly squeezing her shoulder. 'Oh, I'm such an idiot. I never should have said anything. But honestly, Nat, he's not worth it. Look, let's just concentrate on what we came here to do. We can deal with him later.'

'No, Rani, you were right about Charles, and about me. I've been thinking about it a lot over the last few days. I know I'm not perfect, far from it. But for so long it's how I've wanted people to see me ... or rather, it's the only way I knew how to be seen.' She glances at me with a solemn smile. 'So when I saw you that day,

I couldn't believe it. How real you were, how at ease with your pain. I was in awe of you. I still am.'

'What, me? You're joking. I can't imagine anyone seeing me that way, let alone you.'

'Of course. That's why I couldn't understand it when you pretended to be Serena. It doesn't seem like you at all.'

'Yeah. Not my finest moment. I kept telling myself it was to hide my identity in case something went wrong, when deep down, I enjoyed it. I enjoyed being someone else for a change. Someone people could look up to. You know ...' I gulp, regretting the words as soon as I say them, 'I went to view your house. Before you bought it. That's the first time I became Serena.'

'Oh, Rani.' She looks at me again. I expect to see pity or fear written on her face, but all I see is empathy. 'I wish you could see yourself the way I do. You're an amazing mother. Teaching your children the truth about life, instead of, well, sugar-coating it. Inspiring them to be whoever they want to be, and not who you want them to be. To me, that's everything.'

'No one has ever put it like that before.' I nudge her affectionately, laughing through teary eyes.

A few minutes later, we turn into the hotel car park. My heart races as I open the car door and step outside, admiring the ivy-clad red-brick exterior, steeped in character and history, the epitome of the English countryside hotel. Rustic meets romantic. Boutique yet luxurious. A world away from the B&B we head to every summer on Brighton seafront, with its sterile white backdrop chipping away into moody greys.

Natalie struts straight through to reception, barely giving the outside a second glance, her Chanel bag hanging from her shoulder, wheeling a matching designer suitcase behind her. I follow her inside, hearing her chat away to the plump, rosy-cheeked woman on the reception desk, spouting words like *afternoon tea* and *girlie weekend* as if she's forgotten why we've come here. No one would guess what she has just been through. Her pain camouflaged by bright eyes and radiant smiles. It's scary how seamlessly she puts on her mask, as if it's her favourite party trick.

The receptionist notices me enter, and her gaze hooks onto me suspiciously. I try to visualise how she must see me. A battered khaki travel bag branded with the girls' peeling Disney stickers, hanging from my shoulder. Scruffy black Converses on my feet, and my greasy hair falling out of a loose pineapple bun. I smile at her reassuringly, but she returns it with caution, as if to say, *You're not our usual clientele, but I'll be with you in a moment.* I want to mouth to her, *It's okay. I'm with the beautiful blonde*, but I know she won't believe me. Brushing my hand over the ornate furniture, gazing through the windows into the gardens bursting with new life, I close my eyes, imagining that I am someone else entirely. That this is the airbrushed world I live in, with nothing and no one holding me back.

Natalie calls me over, bursting my bubble. 'My friend Rani's staying too. Both rooms on my card, though, please.' She winks at me, fiddling with the clasp on her bag. 'A birthday treat without the men. Let's hope they manage without us. Ha ha.' Her laughter rises high, echoing off the wooden beams above us.

'Oh ... I see. You're together? I didn't realise, sorry.' The receptionist's cheeks flush pink. 'Let me see what we have available.'

She scrolls through the computer, pretending to look for vacant rooms. It's the start of the week, for God's sake. 'Ooh, you're in luck. We have two rooms available next to each other on the second floor, our four-poster suites at £325 a night. Would that work?'

She directs her question at Natalie, ignoring me completely. I give Natalie a nudge, thinking that's an insane amount for rooms we'll barely be using. 'Perfect, thank you,' she says, completely calm, and the receptionist smiles smugly as she finalises the booking.

'Breakfast is served between eight and ten. It's the usual full English, but you can order pancakes and waffles at the bar if you fancy it. I hope you have a lovely stay.' She manages her whole spiel in one breath, barely blinking. I stare hard at her throughout, but her eyes do not leave Natalie's face. Then she hands her both sets of keys and rings the bell for someone to take up our luggage.

Once we reach the lift, I turn back. She's already on the phone to someone, balancing her mobile between her ear and her neck as she files her nails. She notices me staring and laughs out loud before turning away, her voice drifting further out of my reach.

As the lift door shuts firmly behind us, Natalie breathes a huge sigh of relief. Her body slumps against the wall and her face resumes its raw state.

'How do you do it?' I ask her. Dead serious.

'Do what?'

'Be so damn delightful even when you feel like utter shit. Doesn't it get exhausting having to pretend all the time?'

She stares at me, expressionless. 'For a while, it used to, yes. But I've been doing it for so long, it's second nature to me now.'

Natalie

I stand in the doorway, on high alert. Listening to her fiddle with the chunky key to open the door to her room, gasping with excitement. I picture her wriggling her toes over the soft cream carpet and flopping with relief onto the four-poster bed.

It must have been a year ago now, the first time I stepped into a room just like this one. Charles had been messaging all week. I'd ignored every single one, because what had I left to offer him beyond that one night of passion? I was nothing. A fraud. Beneath my skin-tight dresses and expertly made-up face, I was just a lonely woman wasting away.

By Friday morning, the messages had stopped. I thought I'd finally managed to shake him off for good. But as I stumbled bleary-eyed out of the office, there he was. Leaning against the pillar outside the revolving glass doors. An overnight bag slung over his shoulder and a sparkling Rolls-Royce parked behind him.

We drove through the evening to a quaint boutique hotel in the heart of the Cotswolds. Stunning beige stone walls dressed in purple wisteria and ripe green ivy glistening in the evening sunlight. As we walked hand in hand towards the entrance, we were greeted by a smiling gentleman in a bright red coat who guided us around the hotel, holding open every door. The moment I entered the deluxe suite was a turning point in my life.

I almost squealed in wonder at the grand four-poster bed dressed in satin and silk and laden with an array of pillows, the tea bar with a selection of china tea pots and a range of flavours that would rival Fortnum & Mason's, and the deep free-standing bath overlooking the floor-to-ceiling windows with stunning views of the countryside. I saw the doorway to a world that was suddenly open to me. And I knew right then that I never wanted to leave it.

But now, as I observe my surroundings, my vision is tainted by the blunt truth that no amount of beauty can rewrite how you feel inside.

The phone on the bedside table bursts to life, emitting a sharp ringtone. My heart jumps. Could it be Charles? Has he tracked me down already? I tread with caution, picking up the receiver as quietly as possible. Waiting for the person on the other end to announce themselves.

'Natalie! This room! Just. Wow. Have you tried the bed?'

I breathe a sigh of relief. Of course, it's Rani. Who else would it be?

'Do it. Do it now. Honestly, it's like lying on a blanket of clouds. I'm never going home. Joel will have to drag me out of here kicking and screaming.'

'What I would do to see that! Rani, what on earth? Don't tell me you're bouncing on it?'

'Of course. It's all part of the initiation process. Don't mock it until you've tried it. Anyway, what time shall we head out? Ten more minutes of this and I'm all yours.'

I've never heard this emotion in her voice before. Pure, wholesome elation. And it's all down to me. Is this all she needs to feel herself again? A break from the mundane? A taste of luxury?

I feed off her giddy excitement, hoping it will set the tone for the next few days. I convince myself that the dark clouds are only inside my head. Maybe all that will come of this trip is an embarrassing childhood story and the foundations of a life-long friendship.

I want to believe it. I throw myself wholeheartedly into this belief. Because right now, it's the only thing stopping me from curling up under the duvet of this grand four-poster bed and never coming out.

Natalie

'Is everything okay?' As we settle in our booth at the pub across the road, I notice Rani's mood suddenly change. She's buried deep in her menu. Biting her nails as if she's cramming for an exam. Every so often she emerges, jerking her head from side to side. 'Would you rather we leave?'

She pops her head up again. 'No, no, it's fine. Really. I'm just ... acclimatising.' Her voice drops to a low hush. 'It feels like we've stepped back in time. You know, the only brown person in the village sort of thing. Highgate is bad enough, but at least in London people understand diversity. They appreciate it.'

She gestures towards our fellow diners, a homogenous crowd of locals. I hadn't even noticed them until now.

'I grew up in a village just like this one. But that was in the nineties. I can't believe how little has changed. I mean, did you see the way the receptionist looked at me earlier?'

'No, I didn't. But you're right, Rani. Now that you've mentioned it, she was quite standoffish. Sorry. I had no idea it would be like this.'

'No, don't be silly. It's not your fault. You shouldn't have to apologise for being white! It's just been a while since I've been to a place like this. The demons are usually inside my head. *My skin is too dark. My accent's a bit foreign.*' I stay quiet. Nodding my head while she gets it off her chest. 'I remember when I fell pregnant, we'd stay at Joel's mum's place in

264

Hertfordshire for a break and I'd catch her staring at me ... like I disappointed her. I think she'd secretly hoped that Joel would end up with someone more like her; someone who knows her Merlot from her Rioja, who grew up watching reruns of *Birds of a Feather* instead of old Bollywood movies – I mean, of course we watched *Birds of a Feather* too, who didn't? It used to drive him crazy, having to reassure me that I was part of the family.' She laughs, shaking her head. 'Ugh. I don't know where that came from ... Sorry, just forget I said anything, okay? I know these OAPS are harmless!'

It's strange. I've never really thought of Rani as Indian before. If someone asked me to describe her, I don't think it would have come up. Dark eyes. Jet-black hair. Smooth olive skin. These are the adjectives that spring to mind. But different, foreign? No. It occurs to me now, though, that when people look at me, it's usually with envy or lust. They want to be me. They want to be close to me. Yes, they make assumptions about who I am, where I came from, but they never look at me like I'm an outsider.

I think about what it must feel like to be her, to be a brown woman in a white man's world, and it feels like I'm seeing her for the very first time. Caught between two cultures but never truly belonging in either. Always on the outside looking in. I want to reach across the table and take her hand, tell her that I understand her pain. That I'm an outsider too. But this isn't just about me. Not any more. I wanted to get close to her. I chose to entice her from her normal life into my messy, unravelling one. But I never once considered the sacrifices she's made to be here, to intertwine herself in my fate. And I have a strong sense of impending danger.

Not to my life. But to hers.

Rani

'Listen, this is on me,' I mumble, picking at crumbs with my fingertips.

'No, Rani. I can't let you do that.'

The waitress puts down the bill. We both go to grab it, but I get there first. 'Are you kidding me?' I cry. 'These must be magic burgers. Are they going to give me legs like a supermodel?' I grin at the waitress. She stares back at me, rolling her eyes before walking away.

'Why don't we go halves?' Natalie says, not even looking at the bill.

'No, seriously, Nat. I never get to treat my friends. Not that it's even my money,' I scoff, 'but I can pretend, right?'

'What do mean? You have a joint account, don't you? So, what's Joel's is yours, Rani. And you more than pull your weight looking after the girls.'

I fiddle with the receipt, my eyes focused on the table in front of me. 'Yeah, I know. He's never said anything to me about it, but I can't help how I feel. This endless guilt. Knowing that it's always him that fills the account with his hard-earned salary and me that empties it.' I feel my cheeks grow warm. 'What happened with Amber, it's made me realise how powerless I am. How dependent I am on him. For everything. And he could take it all away, just like that.'

She frowns. 'Oh, Rani … I had no idea. I do get it, though, I do. Maybe not in the same way. But feeling powerless. That's what Charles wanted. To control me. Strip me of everything. I know that now.'

I nod, reaching over to touch her hand. 'He can't do that any more, Nat. No one can.'

She looks at me for a lingering second. I can tell she wants to say something. But then the waitress arrives with the card machine and the moment is gone.

As I pay for the lunch, Natalie scrabbles around in her handbag. She takes out her phone and stares at it curiously. 'Withheld number. It must be someone from work. I'm going to have to take this, sorry.'

I watch her answer the call, and her face immediately drops. 'I'm sorry. I just needed some time to think.'

I listen closely. It doesn't sound like Charles on the other end.

'No. He won't. He'll be fine without me for a few days.' Her expression becomes more and more anxious, her skin paler. And I remember where I've seen her like this before. In her kitchen, on the phone to Luella. Moments before she fainted.

'I'm fine. I just need some time to myself. There's something I have to do.' She stares at me with pleading eyes, a cry for help. But then suddenly they change, becoming wider, deeper. A flicker of a flame burning within. 'Actually, there is something else. My house. We lived there together, didn't we? You, me and Dad. I don't understand why you would lie about it.' I notice that her tone of voice has changed too, like something dangerous is stirring beneath the surface. 'Why are you lying to me? I'm sick of it. I wasn't going to say anything, but I don't care any more. I saw Robert … Yes, that's right. My father. And he confirmed it. All of it.'

She's yelling now. I've never heard her like this before. 'What? No. Stop. Please stop. I'm not going back. You can't make me go back. I don't need them any more. I feel more myself now than I've ever been. I remember that house and I know you do too.'

The waitress glares at us suspiciously. I think she wants us to leave before we cause a scene. I brush Natalie's hand, and she looks up at me. Her face is stark white, like she's been possessed by a ghost. 'The truth, Mum. I just need the truth.'

Standing up, I reach for my jacket, hoping Natalie will follow. But as I turn towards the door, I notice a man standing outside: tall, broad frame, thick chestnut hair. His back is turned, so I can't his face, but the stance is chillingly familiar, and I feel my jaw clenching.

Natalie notices me staring. She stops speaking, lowering the phone, Luella's voice echoing out of it. But before I can warn her, she's looking in the same direction, her face distorted with panic, her voice trembling with fear.

'Charles,' she chokes. 'He's here. He's found me.'

Natalie

'It might not have been him, Nat,' she says, pouring me a cup of tea. 'Maybe it was just someone who looks like him?'

My mind is all jumbled up. I can't think straight. But I shake my head anyway, just in case. I need her to feel it too. This sense of impending danger. 'I saw his trench coat. And his hair. I'd recognise that anywhere.'

'Yeah,' she says, a little more hesitant, resting her cup on the bedside table. I watch the steam evaporate into the air. 'It's just, I don't know how he could have found out where we are. You didn't tell your mum, did you?'

I shake my head, covering my face with the palms of my hands. 'What's happening to me, Rani? Maybe Mum was right and I'm spiralling out of control. Maybe I need to go back on the medication. I can't bear it. I really thought that was all behind me.'

She sits down next to me on the bed. Drapes an arm around my shoulders, squeezing me gently. 'What you're going through is completely normal, Nat. It's shock. I don't care that he's your husband and that he claims to love you. But he abused you. That shit doesn't leave you. Listen, I do think you need to see someone when we get home, but not to dose yourself up so you feel nothing. You need to talk about what happened. Process it.'

'So you don't think I need to see Dr Baldwin again? Mum was so sure that it was happening again.'

'What's happening again? What were you taking, Nat?'

'I can't remember what they were called. I was on them for years and they always seemed to work.' I hesitate for a moment, looking down at the floor. Thinking about what to say next, how to frame something I've never told anyone before. 'Do you remember at the spa, when I told you I was having nightmares?'

'Yeah. I remember. You said they were about work.'

'No.' I turn to face her, looking deep into her eyes. 'When I was young, I think around 11 or 12, I started having dreams about this girl, Niaomi – I think I mentioned her to you, my make-believe friend? But honestly, Rani, they felt so real.' I shuffle a little closer. 'At first, I kept them to myself. I was lonely back then, I didn't have many friends, so I loved her company. I didn't want her to leave. But then the dreams started taking over my life. I was exhausted all the time. I could barely function at school. It was like she was haunting me.'

'Oh Nat, that sounds awful. I can't imagine.'

I nod my head. 'Dr Baldwin, my psychotherapist, said it was quite common amongst children who have experienced some kind of loss or trauma early on in their lives. They create a person or a separate identity as a way of processing difficult emotions while remaining detached from them, a sort of self-preservation thing. And the nightmares I experience are my deepest fears bleeding into my subconscious.' I sigh, releasing a little tension from my shoulders. It feels strangely comforting being able to speak openly about such a huge yet hidden part of my life, like I'm peeling off the layers one by one. 'Anyway, I've been off the medication for a while now, and I'd been doing so well over the past year. I think it was the reality of a fresh start with Charles that seemed to settle me. But these last few weeks, I've been dreaming about her almost every night. It's like moving into my childhood home and then everything that happened since has triggered something within me. Opened a door into my past.'

'Look, Nat, who am I to argue with a professional? But it sounds to me that what you're experiencing is PTSD. I went through something similar after Mum died. I kept dreaming about what I saw. The cancer sucking the life out of her. It was pure hell. I'm just thinking out loud here, but what if the nightmares you experienced weren't part of your imagination? What if they were memories tied to your childhood in some way? You said you can't remember much.'

I stare at her. Shocked. 'No. No. They can't be memories. Niaomi isn't real. She can't be. Dr Baldwin is the best there is. He works on Harley Street, for God's sake! Honestly, Rani, if you met him, you'd understand. He's only ever wanted me to get better.' I pause for a second, thinking about our time together. His kindness, sensitivity. All the hours he put in, day and night, and the money Luella spent. Most of Gerald's army compensation money. It couldn't have been for nothing. 'No, he was right. I'm sure of it. Because if he wasn't … I can't go there, Rani, I just can't.'

She looks unconvinced, but her eyes flood with kindness. 'Okay, okay. Sorry. You're probably right. Forget I said anything.' She squeezes my hand. 'Maybe once you're home, you can get a second opinion. Don't worry. We'll get to the bottom of this.'

'Thanks. But I'm the one who should be saying sorry, for wasting your time. If it wasn't for me, we could have gone to the school this afternoon.'

'Don't be silly. One day won't make any difference. We can head there first thing tomorrow.' She picks up my cup and hands it to me. 'Now, how about I leave you to rest?'

I stare at the tea. Its milky brown surface. This just won't cut it. 'Actually …' I say, wiping the tears off my cheeks, 'fancy sharing a bottle of Rioja instead?'

She smiles. 'Just what the doctor ordered!'

As I watch Rani call for room service, I feel a burst of hot, delirious energy rising within me. Could it be the result of finally being myself, no longer having to hide, or something else that I can't quite reach? Whatever the reason, it seems to grow in force with every second, and I know that I have to let it out before I go insane. Getting to my knees, I pick up the remote from the edge of the bed, then rise to my feet.

Rani turns to look at me, mouthing, *What are you doing?*

'What do you think I'm doing?' I shout back at her. 'You practically begged me to give this jumping thing a go!' Pointing the remote at the TV, I flick through the channels. Eventually I settle on a nineties hits show on MTV. Natalie Imbruglia's 'Torn' blasts through the surround-sound speakers, and I join in with gusto, throwing my hands up in the air, swishing my hair from side to side.

'You may need to turn it down a notch,' Rani shouts over the music. 'You're going to get us kicked out.'

I laugh. 'I'm going to have my fun, whether they like it or not,' I say, gesturing at her to join me.

She sighs, reluctantly putting down the phone. But then her mouth breaks into a smile, her eyes twinkle, and she takes my hand and steps up onto the bed. And together we prance around deliriously, like two convicts on the run enjoying our last night of freedom.

Rani

'How are you feeling? Did you manage to get some rest?' I ask as we hurry down the stairs towards the hotel reception. I'm subtly prodding at Natalie's shiny exterior, hoping she'll let down her guard with me again.

Her eyes flit about, scanning our surroundings. 'Barely. I was too scared to sleep,' she says. 'What if it *was* Charles I saw yesterday? What if he's here?'

'Oh Nat, it's unlikely. I doubt he could have tracked us down here so quickly.' I touch her arm, feeling her body tense up. But her appearance doesn't give her away. Somehow she still manages to look fresh-faced and doe-eyed. She's dressed head to toe in cream silk, and her hair smells like it has just been washed, tucked away into a low bun, with a bright orange Hermès scarf tied around her head. It's not an outfit I would choose for a visit to the local primary school, but she wears it with purpose. 'Even if it was him, he can't touch you here, not in public. I swear to you, I won't leave your side.'

We pass the room where they serve breakfast. Holiday-makers tucking into rounds of toast, pancakes and scrambled eggs. I glance wistfully at them, envious of the simplicity of their lives, ticking along at a leisurely pace. But Natalie walks straight past, nourishment far from her mind.

As I follow her through the front door leading out into the car park, I turn my head to look at the receptionist. It's the same woman as yesterday, the one who eyed me up suspiciously before deciding I was irrelevant. She's still filing her nails. I manage to hold her gaze for a few seconds, eager for her to acknowledge me, to hear an apology in her tone.

'Morning!' she calls out, smiling awkwardly, as if wondering what I'm after. 'Off to discover the wonders of the New Forest, are you? You've picked a great day for it.'

'Yeah, something like that,' I say without stopping, attempting to cultivate the air of importance that I know she must be used to with the other guests. Maybe she'll finally take me seriously.

Within a few breaths, we've reached the school gates. Through thin metal bars, I take in the brick building set against a backdrop of flower beds and shrubbery. From the vast red doors and the majestic steeple, I can tell that it's a place seeped in history, filled with secrets. If only buildings could talk. I nudge Natalie, who stares at it intently, as if scraping through the reserves of her mind. 'Anything?'

'I have a feeling, that's all. It's not quite a memory, but it's close.' She looks at me, her face growing even more anxious, terrified about what this might mean. Inching back, she stands behind me. *As if I could be a shield for anyone.*

'Are you sure you're ready for this, Nat? We could always head back to the hotel for a few hours … grab some breakfast – it might help settle your nerves.'

But before she can answer, a tall woman strides towards us. She looks like someone who once might have been described as pretty, but over time her surfaces have become worn away like a shrivelled-up old peach. I notice the stern expression on her face. If I was a young child, I'd be shaking right now. 'Can

I help you?' she demands. 'We don't tolerate loitering here, I'm afraid. It upsets the children.'

I turn to look at Natalie, waiting for her to explain our presence. But she just stands there, mute. I can tell by the flickering of her long eyelashes that she wants to say something, but she's struggling to find the words to make it all sound believable.

I know I have to speak up before we lose our chance. 'Sorry … do you have somewhere private we can talk? It's difficult to explain, but I assure you, we're not wasting your time.' I nod towards Natalie. 'You see, my friend here is trying to trace her childhood, and she thinks she might have been a student here.'

'Right. Well, couldn't you have called or emailed first?'

'Yeah, I guess we could have, sorry. It just that we've … she's had a tough few days, and this trip, it was very last-minute.'

She shakes her head, tutting under her breath. 'It's quite an inconvenience, really. We've got Sports Day this afternoon.' She pauses, studying Natalie. 'But okay, I suppose I can spare some time. I'm the headteacher, Mrs Springer. You can call me Kate. It's … nice to meet you.' But she's not convincing anyone.

She opens the gate to let us in, shaking our hands in turn. Her handshake is firm but forced. I can tell she isn't entirely sure about us, but I've caught her attention, and human instinct thrives off intrigue. We follow her through the red doors and down a long corridor. I peer into the classrooms to my left and right, scanning the walls around us. I don't know what I'm expecting to find: a piece of Natalie's artwork, or a sports cup with her name engraved on the front displayed in a glass cabinet? Silly to even think this. It's been years since she would have wandered these corridors. If there's any record at all, the only person who might be able to confirm it is this woman. I turn to look at Natalie, who treads cautiously behind me. Her mouth is wide open, taking it all in. But she says nothing.

When we reach the end of the corridor, Kate opens a small wooden door and hurries us through before closing it firmly behind us. I take one of the seats opposite her. Probably reserved for naughty children or their apologetic parents. Natalie mimics my movements exactly, slipping into the seat next to me as if she's forgotten how to think for herself.

I take a few minutes to observe my surroundings. A wooden desk fills most of the small space, with a large filing cabinet behind it. It seems they haven't quite mastered digitalisation here in the sticks. I notice that the desk is flooded with paperwork. There's barely any surface area left. It reminds me of my desk at home, covered in Lydia and Leela's homework, and I smile, wondering how Joel is getting on with solo parenting.

'Can I offer you anything to drink? A glass of water, or a hot drink perhaps?'

Natalie shakes her head.

'That's kind of you, Kate,' I say, 'but I had a cup of tea in my room this morning. We're staying at Beaulieu Palace Hotel; you know, the hotel just down the road?'

Her eyes light up. 'An expensive choice. I hope you're taking some time out from your quest to enjoy the facilities. Sorry, but does your friend speak? I mean, *can* she speak?' She smiles sheepishly in Natalie's direction, realising how blunt she must have sounded.

'Yes, sorry,' Natalie says, sitting straighter. 'It's just a lot to take in. Being here again after all this time. I don't remember much, but I feel connected to this place.'

'Right …' I can tell Kate doesn't want to hear some long-winded sob story. Just facts. Straightforward, easily digestible facts. 'Do you have something more concrete? Like the year you might have joined the school? Then I can search through some old class registers to find your name. I should explain, I only arrived here last year. I took over from the old headteacher, Clarissa Paxton.' She pauses, as if the name should mean something to us. 'Come to think of it, she might have been around when you were here. Maybe you could speak to her as well. I'll write down her number for you. She still sits on the board of governors. You know what it's like when you've worked somewhere for so long, you never seem to retire.'

'Sorry …' Natalie mutters under her breath. I nod at her, offering encouragement, and she continues. 'I'm not sure when exactly, but definitely before 2006. Maybe we could try between 2002 and 2005?'

'Great. That's helpful.' Kate pulls a key out of her desk drawer, swivelling her chair to root around in the filing cabinet.

Silence swallows the room. Natalie and I wait in quiet anticipation, listening intently to the sound of the cabinet creaking and Kate shuffling through files of paper. 'Right, I've found them. A little dusty, as you might expect. Let's start with 2002. I'll look at Year 1. What name am I looking for?'

'Natalie. Natalie Sabian.'

She adjusts her glasses and runs her forefinger down the list of names. 'Right. We have Georgina, Abi, Katie, Christine, Niaomi, Danielle, Caro—'

'Wait. Did you say Niaomi?'

'I did. But you said your name was Natalie, didn't you?' Kate observes her suspiciously.

'Yes … sorry.' Natalie looks at me from the corner of her eye. I can tell she's confused, but she doesn't bring it up again.

'Here, why don't you look through these? I shouldn't really give them to you, but perhaps it'll save us some time.'

I pick up one of the registers, labelled Year 2. Natalie takes another, and we skim through the lists of names.

I'm about halfway down the page when I see it.

Natalie Sabian, staring back at me in bold marker pen. My stomach jitters with nervous excitement. We're another step closer.

Natalie

With trembling hands, I dial the number on the yellow Post-it note the headteacher gave me. My vision is so blurry that the digits seem to be merging into one, as if conspiring against me. I squint hard to try and separate them.

Rani holds out her hand, offering to help. But I shake my head. She's done more for me than she'll ever know. Without her, I would never have found the courage to make it this far. I'd still be in the dark, on my hands and knees, clutching at fragments of my broken marriage. Choosing between two doomed fates. A life of imprisonment with Charles as my gatekeeper, or back to my lonely existence as Luella's perfect daughter.

The number starts to ring, and I hold the phone up to my ear. But it goes on and on. Minutes feeling like hours. I'm about to hang up when I hear a click on the line and the faint croak of a woman's voice, huffing and puffing like she's come back from a run. 'Hello, Paxton residence. Clarissa speaking.'

'Hi,' I say quickly. 'Sorry to disturb you, but I think I was a student of yours, years ago. You probably don't remember me, but I'm Natalie Sabian.'

Silence.

I wonder if the line has gone dead, but then I hear the gentle huffing of her breath, and clicking sounds as she fiddles about with something on the phone line, muttering to herself in frustration. After a short pause, she returns, loud and clear. It's a voice I've heard before, I'm sure of it, but I don't know if I can trust my memory. 'Natalie! Goodness me, is that really you? Rosy-cheeked, golden-haired Natalie. Of course I remember you. How could I forget? I can't believe it. I thought I'd never see you again. You left so suddenly all those years ago. I just … My goodness, this is wonderful!'

I don't know what to say. I'm taken aback by her tone, so open and warm. Feelings that I'm unable to reciprocate. 'Yes, it's me, Mrs Paxton.'

'Now, now, I'm not your teacher any more; you must call me Clarissa. So tell me, what brings you back into my life?'

'Well, you see, the thing is …' I stop myself. I don't know this woman. I don't know how she'll react if I launch into the truth. 'I'm on holiday in the area, with a friend. It's the first time I've been back here actually, since … and we have some free time this afternoon. I don't suppose you might be free to catch up? We could meet somewhere in town.'

'Gosh, yes. I'll never forget what happened. Not a day goes by that I don't think of it. Of her.' I wait for Clarissa to continue, but her voice sinks into silence, and I'm left on the outside. Again. I want to ask her who and what she is referring to. But something tells me I'm not ready to find out. Not now. Not like this.

'Thank you,' I say eventually.

'Oh, I would absolutely love to see you, Natalie. What are your lunch plans? I was going to make a salad with the vegetables from our garden … nothing fancy. I don't suppose you'd be interested in joining me? Karan is out playing golf. He hasn't stopped since he retired last year.'

Rani is listening intently. I mouth the word *lunch*, and she nods emphatically. She's enjoying this more than I am. But then why wouldn't she? It's the secrets of my past that will soon be unravelled; it's my future that may soon be blown apart. She's just a spectator with a front-row seat.

An hour later, we're parked up in front of a row of identical chocolate-box cottages over in the next village, a short drive away from the school. It's the kind of street that tourists would go crazy for. Snapping away on their iPads like they're capturing a pride of lions while out on safari. It screams quintessential English country living, with storm-grey thatched roofs and walls dressed in ivy. The only feature that distinguishes the cottages is their painted front doors.

Clarissa's cottage is right in the middle. Its bright turquoise door stands out next to the grey and navy of her neighbours'. I can just imagine the scandal when she decided to upset their uniform colour scheme. They probably gathered on the street watching the transformation take place, posted nauseatingly polite notes through her letter box. *It must be as interesting as life gets in the countryside*, I think, smiling to myself. Until I remember what I'm here for, that something happened here all those years ago. Something that Clarissa has never been able to forget.

Thankfully we're a couple of minutes early. I have time to collect my thoughts, prepare myself for whatever this visit will bring. Pulling my work phone out of my bag, I notice that the notifications have multiplied. Emails. Missed calls. Voice-mails. My life in London taunting me. But there's nothing from Charles. Could that be because he's already at the hotel? Sitting in reception, sipping a cup of coffee and skimming the papers as he waits for me?

Rani seems eager to get going, smoothing down her T-shirt and reaching for the door handle.

'Wait a second,' I say. 'I just need to check my messages.'

'Okay, but be quick. We don't want to be late. Oh, and listen, about that register. Niaomi. I saw your face earlier. It's probably nothing, okay? A coincidence. I'm sure your old teacher will fill in the blanks, anyway.'

I shrug before looking away. Her tone of voice is starting to grate on me. Every time we pick up a new thread, I notice a change in her, a glint in her eye and a spring in her step. I'm grateful to have her by my side, and deep down, I want her to be happy. But at what cost? I can't help but wonder if our fates were intertwined long before she came into my life. Maybe what ties us together isn't our mutual hunger for the truth at all, but rather that her success is in direct correlation with my demise.

As I scroll through, I notice the same number come up a few times. And there's a voicemail to go with it, from a few hours ago. I decide against pushing the speakerphone button, thinking about what recent history has taught me. People can let you down. They don't always want the best for you. Love can be toxic. Instead, I hover the phone up to my ear, pressing the volume button all the way down to a low whisper.

'It's Robert … your dad. I've tried calling you a few times. You must be busy at work. I've been thinking a lot about our last meeting and there's something I need to talk to you about urgently. It's been preying on my mind and I can't seem to make sense of it. Can I come by your office later today, or the house? Just let me know.'

I lower the phone. Slowly, so as not to cause alarm.

'Anything?' Worry flashes over her face. 'It's not Charles, is it?'

I shake my head. 'Nothing important. I'll deal with it when we get back to the hotel.' My voice is calm, but fear presses into my temples as I fight the urge not to cry out with panic.

Natalie

The bright turquoise door swings open. I step back in disbelief, bumping into Rani behind me. From the soft, raspy voice I heard on the phone, I expected a frail old woman with hunched shoulders and spindly legs, frumpy clothes drowning her tiny frame. But the woman who greets us is nothing like this, and I'm worried that we might have knocked on the wrong door. 'Clarissa …?'

She has smooth, supple skin and perfectly crafted cheekbones. It's partly due to her heritage, I think. Somewhere exotic I can't quite place has gifted her the glow of graceful ageing that no amount of money can buy. But it's the way she carries herself, too, wearing her idiosyncrasies like crown jewels. I marvel at her bright Indian-style tunic and her thick hair wrapped in a crimson headscarf. Several wisps breaking free along her hairline. They may be greying, but I can tell that doesn't bother her at all.

'Come in, come in. Gosh, let me look at you,' she says, gesticulating wildly before pulling me into a hug, pressing me so close to her chest that I start to feel dizzy. This extravagant welcome feels strange, foreign. Mum has never been tactile. She prefers to admire me from afar, like I'm a mannequin in a shop window instead of a real person brimming with insecurities and fears. 'I can't believe you're standing here on my porch after all this time.'

Everything in me wants to like Clarissa. She's warm and loving. Being around her is like being kissed by the sun. But as I breathe in her scent, a mixture of sugar and spice, I find myself pulling away. 'Clarissa, I need to be honest with you. We're not here on holiday like I told you on the phone. The truth is, I … I don't remember living here at all, or why we left. I've asked Mum so many times, but she just doesn't want to hear it. I'm truly sorry for misleading you and putting this all on you. I just know that I can't move on with my life until I find out the truth.'

She studies my face. 'Oh, honey. I can't imagine how it must have felt being in the dark all these years. Please come in – oh, and is this your friend?'

'Sorry, yes. Rani. She's here for moral support, and honestly, I don't think I could have got this far without her,' I say, releasing the tears I've been holding in, letting them flow freely. I'm getting tired of hiding who I am. I won't do it. Not any more.

Clarissa pulls a tissue from the deep pocket of her tunic and hands it to me. She places a comforting hand on my back as I blot the tears racing down my face. 'Can I get you something to drink? Lemonade, tea … or perhaps something stronger?'

We both nod emphatically. Stronger is good. Stronger is necessary.

'I've whipped up a sort of summer punch. My father was Jamaican, so we're never short of rum in this house. How does that sound?'

'Punch would be amazing,' Rani says, and I realise she's been silent this whole time, silent and watching. 'Thanks for inviting us.'

'Nonsense. It's nothing. Now that I'm retired, I struggle to find enough entertainment to occupy my days, so you are both very welcome here.'

She leads us down the hall into a living area and gestures to a plush velvet sofa before disappearing off into the kitchen. I feel relieved to have time to compose myself, thinking how mortified Mum would have been by my outburst.

Rani bounces closer to me on the sofa. 'How are you feeling?' But before I have a chance to answer her, she's rummaging in her handbag, distracted by her beeping phone. Strands of hair slip out of her ponytail, and I watch her tuck them behind her ears. 'Oh, it's from Robert … your dad. Sent a few hours ago, but it's only just come through. He says he's been trying to reach you. It sounds important …' She clocks my anxious expression. 'Shall we call him back later?'

I nod, and as she switches off her phone, Clarissa reappears in the doorway. 'Here we are, ladies, Leroy's signature rum punch,' she says proudly, lowering a tray onto the metallic coffee table in front of us.

After a sip of the sugary drink with a delectable kick, I feel my energy returning. My eyes wander around the room for the first time, noticing the bright orange curtains and gigantic tapestry rug. Eclectic ornaments and trinkets from around the globe. It's not a style I would have expected from the former headteacher of a village primary school. I smile to myself, thinking of snooty Mrs Springer positioned here on this sofa during a governors' meeting. Feeling completely out of place in her monochrome dress and tight bun.

'Lunch is ready and set up in the conservatory. But I thought we could chat in here first, if that's okay?' She lowers herself onto the rattan armchair opposite us and takes a long sip of her drink. Dutch courage?

'If I'm honest, I'm not sure where to begin. How about you tell me what you already know, and I'll do my best to fill in the gaps?'

'Yes, that makes sense. Thank you again for agreeing to speak to me. You don't know how much it means.'

She waves a hand in my direction. 'I'm honoured you came to me, really I am. You may not remember me too well. But let me tell you, from the moment you stood outside my classroom that day, with the face of an angel, I knew I would care for you like you were one of my own.' Her eyes droop with sadness. 'I wasn't blessed with children, Natalie. I would have loved to have been a mother one day, but it just didn't happen for me. It's why my first marriage broke down. But eventually I made my peace with it, and over the years, there were a few of you at the school who became my children.'

I feel awful. This woman is pouring her heart out, telling me how much she cared for me. Yet I feel nothing for her. Worse than nothing. I feel wary of her. A voice in my head is screaming at me to run far away from here. It sounds like my mother's voice. 'I had no idea,' I say. 'I'm sorry. I can't imagine what it must feel like to have a void inside you that no one else can fill.' But of course I can imagine. 'I wonder, do you think you could tell me what I was like as a child?'

'Gosh, honey, of course. Where to begin? You were that child every mother dreams of. In fact, what was it your mother used to call you? Yes, that's right. Her golden child.' I flinch at her words, feeling the weight of them. 'You were so polite and warm to everyone around you. Students as well as teachers. You never put a foot wrong. Never tested boundaries. Honestly, you were a dream to teach.' Her whole face seems to light up as she speaks about me. It reminds me of someone. 'And when we discovered you could dance!' She laughs. 'That was the icing on the cake. I was a dancer too, you see, in my youth.'

'I was a dancer? Really?' I shake my head in disbelief. People have always told me I have the physique of a ballerina – that is, until they notice my two left feet. Charles and I opted out of a first dance at our wedding for that reason. I didn't want to show him up in front of the guests.

'Yes, you were.' She nods. 'It was how your mother and I became friends. My heart went out to her. She was so brave, moving here as a single mother. And that dilapidated old cottage in the middle of nowhere … She did her best to make it a home, but really it was no place for a young family. So when we discovered your talent, I agreed to train you for free until you were ready to apply for a scholarship at the Royal Ballet School. We were waiting to hear back after your audition, and then, well … you left.'

'What? I don't understand … Did I get in?'

'Yes, Natalie, you did! But by then you were long gone. I did my best to track you down, but after a while, I realised that your mother must have been desperate for a fresh start after …' She stops abruptly, her mouth wrinkling up and her eyes filling with tears.

'What happened? Tell me, please. Whatever it is, I need to hear it.'

She takes a deep breath. 'Natalie … do you remember Niaomi?'

Her words slam into me. 'What? What's this got to with Niaomi? Who told you about her? She's not real.'

Clarissa's expression is pained, like it has been stretched with shock. She buries her face in her hands, and then slowly resumes her position. Upright. Facing me. Her eyes meeting mine.

'Natalie, no. Niaomi is … was real. She was your sister.'

Rani

Natalie stands over Clarissa, her face just inches away from the older woman's. And for a moment, I see fear splashed across Clarissa's face.

'No. You're lying. She can't be, she can't be,' Natalie cries out, her voice agitated. I lean forward and take her hand, trying to pull her back, but she shakes me away.

'Oh honey, I wish I was, I really do,' Clarissa whispers. Then, without saying another word, she stands up and folds her arms around Natalie's shaking body before edging her back down onto the sofa. Natalie flinches, closing her eyes. But then she snaps them open again, trying to stand up. 'Honey, I think it's better if you hear this sitting down. I've shocked you and I'm sorry. I'm so sorry. But if you want me to, I can continue.'

Natalie silently nods her head.

'When you first started at the school, all the teachers used to get the two of you confused. You looked more like twins than sisters. Those same dark brown eyes and long golden hair.' Her hands flutter in her lap like butterflies. She catches me staring at them and swoops them under her tunic. 'I never taught Niaomi, but I knew her well. No one went unnoticed in the village, and the beautiful single mother with her two young daughters in that ramshackle cottage were no exception. There go the three angels who live in hell, they used to say.'

I listen, frozen in disbelief. Yet deep down, a part of me is thrilled that the truth is finally out there in the open, and that I'm here to witness it. I glance over at Natalie. Her mouth is slack, but I can tell that she's fighting hard against her emotions. *How could she not remember she had a sister?* I picture her beautiful face in the café in Muswell Hill, the first time she mentioned her make-believe friend. Then I recall the conversation we had just yesterday. Dr Baldwin, her psychotherapist, reassuring her that Niaomi wasn't real, and the medication she took to numb the trauma of the past. She's been lied to her whole life. But why?

'For the first few weeks, you seemed inseparable,' Clarissa continues, 'the best of friends, but then something happened to Niaomi. It was like a switch went off in her head. At first I thought it was a loss of confidence. She had so much potential, even then, as a timid little girl, but she'd just sit there staring into space, a million miles away. She'd turn up at school looking like a wild animal, her hair tangled, her uniform covered in mud and leaves. It was like she'd been living outside.'

She pauses to check on Natalie. 'I remember she came to my office, just the one time. She was terrified, but I managed to get her to open up a little. She told me how much she hated herself for everything she had done, how she didn't deserve to live. I couldn't make sense of it. Your mum was so worried. She took her to see several doctors, but they all said the same thing. That Niaomi would grow out of it and eventually find her feet.'

I'm on the edge of my seat, hanging on her every word. My heart is racing, my palms starting to sweat. I know how this story ends. In the only way it can. Tragedy. But a small part of me clings to a glimmer of hope that Niaomi is alive right now, somewhere in this vast world. And feeling that same immeasurable void in her heart as her sister.

'And did she?' Natalie says, almost pleading.

'Natalie, I really wish I could tell you what you want to hear, but I can't lie to you. You've been lied to enough over the years.' Clarissa's hands start flapping in her lap again, but this time she can't stop them. 'I can't imagine what it must be like to lose a child. I don't want to defend your mother for what she did, but maybe she felt she had no option. Denial was the only way she could survive ... look after you without falling apart.'

'So, what ... Niaomi ... she died? When? How?'

Clarissa sighs deeply, as if reliving the moment. 'I remember that day like it was yesterday. The morning after your audition. Your mum and I were so happy. Happier than either of us had been in years. We knew this was your big break. Your chance for a better life. Your mum, she deserved this so much, after everything she'd been through with your father. Even Niaomi was excited for you. It was like we could finally see who she was under all that pain. But then the next morning, you found her ...'

'*I* found her? I don't understand. So ... she died in her sleep?'

'Well, that's what your mother thought. But the autopsy report revealed that she'd swallowed your mother's antidepressants, which caused her heart to stop beating.' She bends forward and takes Natalie's hand. 'It was ruled as an accidental death. She must have taken the tablets out of desperation, without any idea of the consequences. Natalie, I'm so, so sorry. God. I've been waiting over fifteen years to tell you that in person. You weren't at the funeral. Your mother sent you to stay with a family friend the same day you found Niaomi's body. I thought I'd never see you again.'

'No. No. I don't believe it!' Natalie stands up abruptly, raising her hands to her head. I can hear her breathing, loud and fast. 'There must be some mistake. You're talking about someone else … another girl. It doesn't make any sense.'

'No, honey, I'm sorry. I wish I was. The thing is, Niaomi was severely depressed. I doubt she was thinking straight. Maybe it was a cry for help, I don't know. But please, please don't blame your mother. Luella did all the right things. Talking to Niaomi's teachers. Consulting doctors. But no one officially diagnosed her. I could tell something was wrong. I suspected some sort of mental illness, but I had no idea how serious it was. I just assumed she would grow out of it. You have to understand, it was a different time back then. No one talked openly about depression, especially in relation to children. That was the world we lived in. Oh, honey. What can I do? Tell me what I can do.'

Natalie opens her mouth, her voice colourless. 'I need to see her. I need you to take me to her.'

Rani

We follow Clarissa's bright yellow Mini through winding country lanes. I'm in the driver's seat for the first time
in years. Natalie sits next to me, her shoulders hunched, her
face motionless. I've seen this side to her before. On the Tube
home after meeting Joanne. But this revelation is so much
worse. The girl she always thought was her imaginary friend
was real. The sister she'd forgotten has been dead for almost
twenty years. I know she must still be in shock. But my mind
has already jumped two steps ahead, fearing what might happen when she stops processing and starts feeling.

I push these thoughts away for now and force my mouth
tightly closed, concentrating hard on the road in front of me.
Now is not the time to mention that I'm breaking the law
driving Natalie's car. Now is not the time to mention that
I'm petrified.

Clarissa indicates left and parks up. Somehow I manage
to steer Natalie's car into the space behind her. And when
the engine stops, I realise that we're outside the entrance of
a church. 'Nat, I think this is it. Are you okay?' She doesn't
answer. 'Listen, it's totally fine if you're not feeling up to it
right now. It's a lot to take in. We could come back another day
maybe?' I gently squeeze her shoulder.

'What? No. I need to do this now. I have to see her.' She
snaps back to reality, her brain ticking away. 'This must be why

Robert wanted to see me. He must have found out about what happened to Niaomi. He's probably going crazy right now.' Panic flashes across her face. 'And what am I supposed to say to Mum?' Her breathing changes, heavy and fast. 'How can I face her, knowing she's been lying to me all these years? Oh God. I can't bear to even think about it.' She turns to look at me, patting down her face. 'Is it just me, or is it hot in here?'

'It's okay,' I say, taking her burning hand in mine. 'Deep breaths. Slowly. In and out. In and out.' I sit with her for a minute or so, until her breathing returns to normal. 'It's okay to take this one step at a time. You've only just found out yourself. Your father will understand.'

Clarissa peers in through the car window, causing Natalie to flinch. Her eyes are wet with overwhelming sadness. I feel it too. But for me, the sadness is diluted with something else that I'm ashamed to admit. Not quite satisfaction. But almost.

I reach over Natalie to open the passenger door. 'Here, let me get that for you. Can you manage to stand up?' She nods but says nothing, the calm before the storm. Clarissa looks at me, her eyes questioning. *Are we doing the right thing? Is she ready for this?* I respond with mine. *We have no choice. She needs this. She needs closure.*

She coaxes Natalie out of the seat and together they walk towards the church.

Watching them, I'm reminded of when I found her lying in the woods after her fall. It was only weeks ago, but already it feels like another lifetime. I can't believe how much has happened since then, how much her life has spun out of control. First Charles, and now Niaomi. Surely this is too much for one person to handle.

My heart swells with gratitude as I think of Joel and the girls. Unlike Natalie, I still have a home to go to. It may not be three storeys high and stuffed with expensive furniture, but it's safe and filled with love. Life is too damn short. I fumble in my handbag for my phone and quickly switch it on. I'll send him a message, I think. I'll tell him that I forgive him and want to make it work.

But suddenly the screen bursts to life with activity. Several missed calls from Joel and Jemima. A message from Robert. *Where are you? Is Natalie with you?* And another from Joel. *Call me back asap.* I quickly send Robert my drop pin location before selecting Joel's name and holding the phone up to my ear, waiting for it to ring. But there's just silence on the other end. The reception has dropped out again. 'Go ahead without me,' I shout to Clarissa and Natalie. 'I'll catch you up.'

Natalie turns around, squinting against the sun. Her expression is one of acceptance and understanding. But as the light drifts away from her face and her eyes open, I see something in them that burns me to my core. A sense that this is the end of the road for us. That our friendship has run its course, served its purpose. That there is nothing tying us together any more.

Turning my back on her, I notice what looks like a short-cut across a field towards the nearest village. I set off along it, glued to the screen, waiting impatiently for the bars to appear.

I'm about halfway to the village when the phone starts to vibrate in my hand, and I hold it to my ear. 'Joel! Joel. Can you hear me? I've been going insane trying to get reception here. Is everything okay? Is it the girls?'

'What? No, the girls are fine. We're all fine. That's not why I rang.'

'Oh.' I sigh with relief. 'You scared the hell out—'

'Rani, wait. Just listen to me. You need to come home right now. I think you might be in danger. Just get your things from the hotel and take the next train back.'

'What? What are you talking about? I'm fine, but you're not going to believe what we've just found out.'

'Yes. I know. I know everything. That's why I called you. Did Natalie tell you about her father?'

'Yes … but how do *you* know about him?'

'He showed up at her house. No one was home, so he tried Jemima's. She was really shaken up and called me. Anyway, I spoke to him. He wasn't making much sense, but he seemed to think that something terrible happened to Natalie when she was young, and when I told him where you were, he left straight away. I think he's going to look for her. He might even be there now.'

'What? I don't understand. He said that something happened to *Natalie* … are you sure he didn't say Niaomi?'

'What are you talking about? Who's Niaomi? Rani, listen to me. He kept saying, *She's in danger, she's in danger*, but I think he was talking about you. Oh God, I knew this was a bad idea. Rani, please, just get out of there.'

I hang up and turn round, sprinting as fast as my legs will carry me. Back to the church. Back to Natalie. There's a strong current around me that wasn't here before. It feels like an invisible force pushing hard against me. I run through it. My lungs start to close and my throat burns with acid, but somehow I keep going.

I thought we had all the answers, but the fear in Joel's voice made my heart stop. Should I be running away from Natalie, rather than towards her? I saw how the anger took over her at

Clarissa's, how she almost lost control. But then I remember the depth of pain in her eyes, and how the shock rippled through her body. Whatever happened, she is innocent. And if she's innocent, that can only mean one thing. She's in danger too.

Somewhere in the distance I make out the end of the footpath. I hear voices in the lane and chase the sound with my footsteps. Everything around me is a blur of greens and browns, and every step feels like I'm trekking through quicksand. My heart rumbles in my chest as if it's about to take off. But I don't have the words to calm myself down. I don't know whether I'll make it in time.

I stop abruptly and glance from left to right, deliberating what to do next, but that thought goes no further as something slams into the back of my head. I reach my hands out in front of me, desperately grasping at the air. I shout for help with all the strength I can muster. It sounds loud in my head but somehow gets lost in the atmosphere. A rush of sharp pain follows, like a bee sting but a million times worse. The sounds become fainter. The colours merge like a watercolour painting. And I feel myself falling, almost in slow motion, to the ground.

Natalie

I stare at the gravestone in front of me, identical to all the others around it. Like a village of broken dreams. Unwritten futures. It occurs to me that Niaomi has been here for longer than she was alive. I'm mourning a sister I can barely remember, while at the same time I can hardly believe she's gone.

And now I know for certain that I am alone in this world.

Niaomi Sabian
1997–2006
At peace at last

The words imprint on my mind as I try to make sense of them. Where are the phrases you usually see on gravestones? *Beloved daughter and sister. Gone too soon. Missed by all who knew her.* I see no clues here to the person she was. It's as if she was as anonymous in life as she is in death, and I shudder, thinking how familiar this all sounds. If I died today, who would mourn me? Who would visit my grave to lay fresh flowers? But this is it, proof. Proof that my nightmares were real. Memories. Niaomi's death elevated from a story to a fact.

Images of my sister float through my mind, wild and uninhibited. Running free. And I find myself unable to reconcile the memories I have with Clarissa's. The Niaomi I knew had a broken heart but a fighting spirit. I admired her. I wanted to be more like her. The Niaomi I knew would never have ended her life before it had even begun.

I hear Clarissa behind me. Rummaging around in her handbag for a tissue. Her knees clicking as she peels herself off the bench. I turn my head, watching her walk up to me, her printed tunic ballooning out in the wind.

'How are you doing, honey?' I feel her warm breath on my face, a strong scent of oranges and rum. 'Tell me what I can I do.' She hands me the tissue to dry my eyes and drapes an arm around my waist, pulling me closer. I feel the soft roundness of her belly. Her tenderness. And the hostility I initially felt towards her melts away. *She would have made a good mother,* I think. So different to the one I was born to. I wonder how my life would have turned out if she had been around more. To love me, nurture me. Niaomi's too.

'You don't know how much it hurts to be the person to tell you all this. Yes, I'd always hoped that one day I would see you again, but never like this.' She stands back to look at me, brushing my hair with her fingers. 'I still come here from time to time. More so since I retired. Occasionally I'll bring flowers to leave on her grave, but mostly I come to reflect. There's something strangely comforting about this place, having the space to process your thoughts without interruption. I think about Niaomi often. Whether there was more I could have done to save her. Whether there was something I missed.' Her eyes well up with tears. 'You know, I also had a sister. She died a while ago. Cancer. A merciless disease. I've never been the same since. Like a part of me will always be missing.'

'I'm so sorry,' I whisper. 'It must have been horrible to see her suffer. I know it's not the same, but even though I didn't know that Niaomi was real, I've always felt this deep sense of loss inside me. I just never knew why.'

'And what about now, Natalie? Now that you have all the answers. Do you feel any different?'

I think about what Mum convinced me of. Her and Dr Baldwin, drugging me for years, making me believe that Niaomi was all in my head. But why? To protect me? No. Guilt? It must have been that. She couldn't live with the guilt. She had to create her own reality.

'That's what worries me,' I say. 'I really believed that I would feel differently once I found out the truth. I've spent so many years chasing happiness, piecing together all the elements that I thought would make me feel complete. A high-flying career. A husband. A dream home. I had it all, but I still felt lost and alone. I still do.'

'I think it will take some time, honey. You've been through so much. But you're young. You have your whole life ahead of you. I know you'll find a way of putting this all behind you. And if it means starting again, wiping the slate clean, you'll do it. You're an incredible person. You always have been … don't ever forget that, honey.' She envelops me in a warm hug. 'So, what's next? What do you want to do?'

'I think I'm ready to leave. I mean, go home, back to London. Back to face reality and take things from there. My husband, he … Anyway, it's over between us now. I don't think it even really began. And I don't think we ever really knew each other. But I'm ready to start again. On my own.' My phone buzzes in my handbag. 'Speaking of home, that must be Rani calling me now.'

I slide my finger over the screen, answering the call before realising that it's from a number I don't recognise. My hands shake. It could be Luella or Charles. I'm not ready. But before I have a chance to end the call, a familiar male voice bellows up at me, loud and panicked. 'Natalie, is … you? Where's Rani? What … done with her?' It's an odd choice of words. 'If … do anything … hurt her, I'll … She doesn't deserve … Natalie … think of … girls. We'll keep … secret, whatever … is.'

The line is fuzzy. I can only make out every other word. 'Wait, I don't understand. I would never hurt her.' My voice curdles like gone-off milk. How can Joel think I would want to cause her harm after everything she's done for me?

'Please, Natalie, don't lie … me. I don't … time for this. I'm … way to you … Tell me where she … we'll forget this … happened.'

'Joel, I can't hear you that well. But you have to trust me. What reason would I have to hurt her? She's the only friend I have. She went to call you about an hour or so ago. I just assumed she'd taken a detour to the village to get a drink or something.'

'She … catching a train … London, but I haven't heard … her … her phone … switched off. Listen, I don't … time to explain … I spoke to … dad. He's coming to … you … he might even … there. He knows … Natalie. I couldn't get it … of him, but Rani … in danger. Natalie, are you there?'

My breath turns to ice, and I feel it again, fear penetrating all the way to my core.

Rani is in danger, and it's all my fault.

Rani

The first thing I notice is the smell. Damp and mouldy, like clothes that have been left in the wash for too long. And I think, *Am I home? Did I make it back?* But then I feel it, right there at the back of my head. Throbbing pain seeping into my skull. I open my eyes, but it's pitch black everywhere. I try to reach up, to find the source of the pain, but I can't move my hands. This is a nightmare of the worst kind. What else can it be?

I tell myself that it'll soon be over. That any moment now I'll wake up, sweating and shaking, but at least I'll be home. Safe and warm. The last thing I remember is running along a footpath in the middle of a field, trying to reach Natalie. To tell her something. Something huge. I can still hear Joel's voice in my ear, the sense of urgency and fear. Pleading with me to come home, warning me that my life was in danger. And I knew he was right. I had a feeling that something terrible was about to happen. But I couldn't leave. Not without her.

The space around me is ice cold. Dust collects in my lungs and panic rises in my chest, stifling every breath. If I stay here any longer, my airways will start to close. I picture my inhaler lying on the duvet at home. But it's no good to me there. How long do I have? An hour at the most, if I'm lucky. If I can visualise the oxygen entering my lungs. If I can control my breathing.

I wonder if this is what it feels like to be dying. Is this what Mum felt? The conflicting sensations of her body slowly freezing and the scorching heat of fear. My eyes well up and my heart aches for everything I'm about to lose. Sweet, wild Leela. Brave, confident Lydia. And Joel. The man who still has my heart.

'For God's sake, do something. Quickly, before she loses consciousness.' Someone comes up behind me. I feel hands grip the back of my head, holding it upright. A man's hands. Large and firm. Is it Charles? Was Natalie right all along?

But why me? What does he want?

I try to shake him off, swinging my body from side to side with all the energy I can muster. The hands slip away, footsteps hurrying off into the distance. There's a loud bang, like a door slamming. I hear muffled voices somewhere outside. Angry and aggressive.

Grunts, shrieks, screams follow. Each one causing me to flinch.

I hear a loud thud. A body hitting the floor.

And then silence.

I open my mouth to scream, but my voice feels suffocated. I can't see. I can't speak, and I'm running out of time.

Natalie

'I'm going as fast as I can!' Clarissa protests.

'Go faster. Please,' I beg.

'Natalie, are you sure you want to go to the cottage? I don't think Rani will be there. Maybe we should ring the police?'

'No. Not yet. Let's just take a look. You said it's not far from here.'

She pushes down hard on the accelerator, and we hurtle through the lanes. My heart is racing. I'm struggling to think straight. I've had no time to figure out a plan of action, no time to visit all the places they might be. But I have a feeling in my gut, and I have to follow it. Back to the beginning. Where it all started.

I take out my phone. There are several missed calls from Robert that I've only just seen. Messages too, partly visible on the screen.

Natalie, I'm outside your hotel. Where ar …

Please pick up. I think you might be in d …

I know where you are. I'll meet you ther …

Ignoring them, I hover my finger over the call button. My body trembles as I think of the last time I saw him.

'Who are you calling? The police?'

'No. Charles. My husband. I need to know if he's here; I need to know if he's behind this.' I hold the phone up to my ear, fear firing through my veins.

He picks up on the first ring. 'Natalie. Well, what a pleasant surprise. I knew you'd come crawling back eventually.'

'You're here, aren't you? Do you have Rani? Have you drugged her like you've been doing to me?'

He scoffs down the phone. 'What are you talking about? You sound deranged.'

'I mean it, Charles.'

'Why the hell would I drug you? You're already crazy enough as it is.' He sighs deeply. 'What are you doing in the New Forest, Natalie?'

'How do you—'

'Your car ... I have a tracker.'

His words brush over me. I'm too panicked to focus. 'Charles. Listen. I'm on the way to the cottage now. Please don't hurt her. None of this is her fault. You can take me instead, I swear to you.' I pause, suddenly confused. 'Wait, how do you know about the cottage? Did Luella tell you?'

'What cottage? God. Natalie. You really are crazy. Why would I waste my time chasing after that stupid woman?'

It's not him. He's not here. I take a deep breath and close my eyes. 'Goodbye, Charles,' I say, ever so calmly, and hang up before he has a chance to respond.

We approach a large expanse of water with a herd of cows grazing at the edge. I recognise it from the photograph. Glancing over at Clarissa, I ask, 'Is that Hatchet Pond?'

'Yes, honey. Do you remember? Is it coming back? Your mum used to take you both there for picnics after school.' I notice the woodlands behind the lake and feel a pang of loss for Niaomi. She must have loved it here.

I shake my head wistfully. 'No ... I don't.'

The country lane soon turns into a narrow, uneven track that looks like it hasn't been used for years. Civilisation is behind us, replaced by mile upon mile of green fields dotted with livestock. It's completely silent. Eerily so.

In the distance, I make out the shape of a small, derelict cottage. It's the only one for miles, and there's a vehicle parked in front of it. I recognise it immediately as Gerald's rusty old Jeep. Mum. What is she doing here? Is Rani here too?

'Clarissa, stop the car.'

'What?'

'Trust me. If we go any further, they'll hear us pulling up. Just park here and I'll get out and walk the rest of the way. It's not far.'

'No.' She shakes her head. 'Natalie, I can't just leave you. I'm worried. What if your mum …'

'Here, look, I've just sent you Joel's number. Can you text him the address of this place? And call the police if you want to, but I promise you, I'll be fine. It's probably just a misunderstanding.' I open the door and step outside.

'Natalie, wait. I really hope you're right, but please be careful. Don't do anything stupid.'

'I'll be fine,' I say again, with conviction. But my voice comes out croaky. 'I don't have time to explain, but it's my fault that Rani's here. I wanted so much to find out the truth.' I cover my face with my hands. 'If something happens to her, I'll never be able to live with myself.'

She nods.

I close the car door as quietly as possible and start walking in the direction of the cottage. Clarissa reverses. And when I hear the engine fading into the distance, I know that I'm on my own.

Rani

My head feels limp, like it could roll off my neck. A puppet dangling on a weak piece of string. I force it upright, thinking of how defenceless I am. How easily someone could end my life. If I'm to survive this, whatever *this* is, I need to gather my strength. Not just for me, but for my sweet girls. I cannot leave them without a mother.

Blinking my eyes open, I expect darkness. But I'm surprised to see shapes and colours emerging, blurry at first, but growing more pronounced as the room comes into focus. I scan my surroundings, looking for clues to my whereabouts. But it's like nothing I've ever seen before. Everything, from the discoloured rugs to the mouldy walls, is thick with layers and layers of dust. At one time this might have been someone's home, but now all I see are the years of neglect. And it makes me wonder what happened for it to end up like this. Left to endure a slow and painful death.

I hear voices in the next room. Low and muffled. The last thing I want to do is invite them in. But whoever they are, they could be my only chance of making it out of here alive. 'Hello. Is anyone there?' I call. Silence. 'There must be some mistake. I'm not really sure what I'm doing here. I'm supposed to be on a train back to London right now. My partner will be expecting me. He'll know I'm missing.' Silence.

Desperation creeps up on me. 'Please don't leave me here. This room. The dust. It's killing me. *Please*.'

There's a sudden movement somewhere in the shadows. The voices grow louder, and I see a figure emerging from the gloom, her golden hair catching the light. *Natalie? No. It can't be.*

'I'm sorry to disappoint you, Rani, but no one will find you here. No one remembers this place.'

'You. Where am I? What am I doing here?'

'I expected more from you, Rani. I thought you'd have it all figured out by now.' Luella lets out a sudden laugh that echoes around the room.

My heart jumps and the breath jolts in my chest. I suspected she was controlling, toxic, pushing Natalie to be perfect, never allowing her to be human. But I'd had no idea she was capable of this. 'How did you find me?'

'Oh, that was the easy part. I can always count on Charlie. He put a tracker on Natalie's car, of course. It's been there since he bought it for her, would you believe? I saw him checking it on his phone the other day and told him that I'd bring her home if he'd just tell me where she was.' She sighs, shaking her head. 'I expected more from Natalie. I taught her everything, Rani. A man like Charles would never have looked twice at her if it wasn't for me. But she failed me. And now he can see her for who she really is.'

'Luella, you can trust me,' I say calmly. Trying to keep her onside. 'I just want to go home and forget about everything. If you could untie—'

'I did try and warn you, Rani. I told you to stay away, to stop sniffing around her life. But no. You just had to stick your nose in, didn't you? And now … I'm sorry, Rani, but you know too much. I can't let you leave.'

I take a breath to steady myself. My lungs are ragged as I try to inhale, but I force oxygen in. I can still survive this. I know I can. Joel will soon realise that I'm missing, and he'll be looking for me. Natalie too. And this was her home. Clarissa knows she lived here. They will find me. I just need more time. 'You're right, Luella. You did warn me, and I was stupid not to listen. I know that now. I'm just amazed, really, how you've managed to keep everything a secret for so long.'

The corners of her mouth start to turn up. I have her attention. 'What do you take me for, Rani? I know what you're doing. If you think you're going to use flattery to get out of here, well, let me tell you—'

'No. No. I know I'm going to die here. I've made my peace with that. If you don't kill me, my asthma eventually will. No one will find me. You're all I have now. You're the last person I will ever see.'

'Yes, I suppose I am. Don't forget Gerald, too, though he's not much to look at.'

My throat rumbles like a cat purring. The wheezing has deepened. 'So … number 11 Priory Gardens. Natalie and Charles's house. Let's start there. You lived there, didn't you, when Natalie was young? Niaomi too.'

Her eyes darken, but then she nods. 'Yes. Their dad and I, we rented it when Natalie was a baby. Niaomi was born there.' She spits out Niaomi's name like it's covered in filth. 'But when their dad just upped and left us, I couldn't afford the rent on my own. I had nowhere to go, no one to turn to. Then I remembered this old cottage. I'd spent summer holidays here as a child, some of my fondest childhood memories, and it was cheap. I mean, look at it; of course it was cheap. It's practically uninhabitable. But I didn't have a choice.'

I nod my head. 'And Niaomi. What was she like?'

'Insufferable,' she growls. 'I can't bear to think of her. I had this feeling even when she was growing inside me that something wasn't right about her. The mood swings I used to have, and the constant sickness. It was like she was punishing me. She put a strain on our relationship even then. But when she came out of me, all red-faced and screeching at the top of her lungs, that's when I saw it. The child was pure evil.'

I watch her face contort, and my insides quiver. 'Did you talk to anyone about it?'

'What do you mean? Who could I have told? They would have said I was mad, locked me away. But I wasn't the crazy one, Rani. I don't know what I would have done if I hadn't had Natalie. My golden child. She was just perfect. But even *she* wasn't enough to make him stay.'

'You can't … surely you can't think he left because of Niaomi?'

'You have no idea. Robert was everything I had dreamed of since I was a young girl. So handsome, so talented. Just one of his paintings used to sell for thousands of pounds. We were the dream couple, Rani. The famous artist and his muse. Our future was bright … so bright.' She scowls at me. 'Until *she* came along, driving a wedge between us. He started painting less and less, and then stopped altogether. He'd spend all day at the pub, pissing our money down the drain. Stumbling in late at night stinking of booze. Cursing me. Screaming at me that it was all my fault. But it wasn't. It was all her. Niaomi.'

'How can you say that? She was just a child.' Even as I say the words, I want to take them back. Her face darkens, her fists clench. This is it. I can feel it. This tiny window of opportunity is about to close for ever. Unless … I hate myself for what I'm about to say. I don't believe a word of it, but I know I have to do something. Anything to save myself. 'No, wait! I understand. Believe me, I do. I understand what it's like to have the future you've always dreamed of ripped away from you. My girls. You've met them. They did that to me, too.'

She looks deep into my eyes, searching for the resentment and misery that mirrors hers. And when she sees it, she smiles. 'Ah, and there I was thinking you were just another boring housewife.'

'Tell me, Luella. Tell me what it felt like.'

'It felt like dying. But then having to live with your cold, dead heart, and spending every day caring for the person who murdered you.'

I hear her words and it brings me to tears. How broken she must be to think that Niaomi, an innocent child, was responsible for everything that happened. I know I've heard it somewhere before. This same nonsensical reasoning. The overwhelming guilt of someone who is clearly innocent. Natalie. How she blames herself for what Charles did to her, for their marriage falling apart. How terrified she is of letting her mother down. And a chilling thought unfolds in the back of my mind.

Natalie

I take a step back to observe my surroundings, working out my next move. Seeing the crumbling walls and cracked windows, it's hard to believe that someone once lived here. That *I* lived here. But I understand its desolation. In carrying the pain and torment of Niaomi's death, this is a home that doesn't hide from the truth. This is a home that openly mourns her.

Tiptoeing up to the front door, I press my ear against it. I hear the soft murmur of two familiar voices and can hardly believe that I made it here in time. Rani sounds exhausted, terrified, but on the surface she remains calm. Doing everything she can to placate my mother. To stop her emotions from spiking out of control. I've been there before. Many times. But not like this. Powerless. Rani must be riddled with nerves, yet somehow she's pushing through. Determined to fight. I squeeze my eyes shut, hoping she can read my thoughts. *Hang on, Rani. I'm on my way.*

'So tell me, how did it happen? Did she die here, in this house?' I tune in to her words, raspy and faint. A part of me wants to back away, to press my hands over my ears and hold them there for ever. But I know I need this. To hear my mother say it.

'Natalie found her one morning in her bed. She was stone cold. My empty bottle of antidepressants lying next to her. I have no idea how she got hold of them. I always kept them on the top shelf, out of reach. She must have been desperate, knowing how much pain she had caused our family. It

was the ultimate sacrifice. The only good thing she ever did.'
She says all this like she's talking about the weather. Not an
ounce of emotion in her cold, harsh tone.

'I … I just can't imagine how she must have felt, to end her
life like that. She was only a child.'

'Oh, don't go all soft on me, Rani. Like I said before, she
wasn't like the rest of us. She was barely human. But the people in the village … small-minded folk, you know the type …
they started gossiping pretty much as soon as we moved here,
saying she wasn't well. "Mental illness", they called it,' She
rattles on. 'It was that busybody Clarissa who came up with
that theory. A load of nonsense if you ask me. I told her I'd
taken Niaomi to the doctor so she'd stop hassling me. But
why would I waste a doctor's time? Not when I knew the truth
about her. A mother's instinct is never wrong, Rani. Never.
Anyway, she started to perk up around the time of Natalie's
audition … Natalie was going to ballet school in London, did
Clarissa tell you? I'm sure she did. Took all the credit, I bet.'

I'm getting flashes of memories. *Swan Lake* playing on the
record player. Floorboards trembling beneath my feet. Cream
rugs spotted with blood.

'Yes, she mentioned the audition. She said Natalie was
offered a place, but by then you had left and she was unable
to find you. Do you think it might have been something to do
with that? Why Niaomi … Maybe she was upset that her sister
was leaving? Oh, and what about Natalie? She must have been
devastated. Both her sister and her dreams gone in an instant.'

'Giving up ballet. Yes, that was painful. For both of us, mind
you. But Natalie understood why. I couldn't let her out of my
sight, not after what her sister did.' There's a pause. 'As for

Niaomi, Natalie couldn't stand her. You must understand, Rani, Niaomi wasn't like everyone else. People avoided her like the plague. That girl was always on her own somewhere. Hiding in cupboards, climbing trees. Sometimes she'd stay out all night ... filthy creature.'

Rani says nothing. But I know her. I know she must be thinking carefully about her next words. 'Luella,' she says finally, 'I feel like you're holding back. That there's something you're not telling me. Please, if you're going to leave me here to die, the very least you can do is tell me the tru—'

'I owe you *nothing*,' Luella shouts.

'But ... it doesn't make sense. Why you'd want to keep this from Natalie. Why you'd want to bury the past. I thought it might be the guilt and pain of losing a child, but you don't care about Niaomi at all.' I hear Rani cough, choking on her words. Then she takes a deep breath. 'Unless ... you do feel guilt, and pain, so much pain ... because you lost someone else that day, someone you loved – didn't you? '

My heart stops. What is she playing at? She was there when Clarissa told me what happened. I saw Niaomi's grave with my own eyes.

'What? What are you talking about, woman?' But Luella's voice is trembling, and for the first time, she sounds flustered. Rani has hit a nerve. I hear her stride away towards the back of the house, followed by rustling noises. Then Gerald's heavy footsteps and his pleading voice.

'Luella. You must stop this now. We already have blood on our hands. Think of your life. Our life. This woman, she's nothing. No one. She'll never be able to prove anything. No one will know what you did.'

'Shut up, shut up, *shut up*! Just give me a moment to think.'

My heart sinks. Time is running out. I need to get inside. I need to stop her before it's too late.

I tiptoe around the side of the cottage, clambering over a fence hidden beneath overgrown bushes. A loose nail catches my dress and rips right through it. I look down and see blood staining the cream silk. Blotting it furiously with my hands, I continue to the back, my breath quickening in anticipation.

There's a small wooden door. It stands ajar, and I hurry towards it. But as I start to squeeze myself through, I hear a pained groan coming from the bushes behind me. I jerk my head back. And that's when I see it. A large pool of blood on the ground and a muddy boot sticking out of the under-growth.

Robert's last text message plays in my mind. *I know where you are. I'll meet you ther …*

No. No. It can't be.

I run towards the bushes and crouch down. Craning my head inside, I see my father's limp body, sprawled like it's been left there in a hurry. Taking his hand, I quickly feel for a pulse. It's very faint, but he's alive.

Taking a deep breath, I try to drag him out of the bushes. He feels so heavy, I almost collapse under the weight of him. As I rest his head on my lap, his watery eyes open slowly.

'Niaomi … Niaomi …' he gasps.

'I know, Robert. She was my sister. I know what happened to her.'

He gestures with his head. 'You … you …'

'Yes. That's right. We used to live here. I can't believe you found this place.'

He hovers his limp hand in the direction of the cottage. I see rope discarded on the ground. Blood splattered around it. They must have found him nearby and tied him up. 'It's okay. Don't waste your energy. Listen, I have to leave you now. Rani is in danger. But someone is coming to help us. I promise you. You'll be okay.'

His head rolls on his neck. His eyes start to close. I think I'm losing him. But then he looks up at me again, and his hand moves towards mine, grasping at it like a baby. It feels ice cold.

'No. No. No,' I whisper. 'Wake up. Wake up.' Tears roll down my face. I pat his cheeks. They feel strange. Like rubber. I reach for his wrist, but this time I can't feel a pulse.

My body floods with red-hot fury. My ears are throbbing, my fists clenched tight. First Niaomi and now my father. Gone. Because of her. My mother. She did this. Nobody else.

I don't feel like myself any more. My emotions are taking hold of me, and I know I can't fight them much longer. Standing up, I move back towards the door and squeeze inside. I can hear Gerald's heavy footsteps, merging with my mother's rattled screams.

'Luella!' Rani shouts over the noise. 'Remember what I said. Your secret will die with me. This is your one chance to free yourself from the past. To live your life without carrying this darkness. Let me help you unburden yourself.'

'Just stop! Stop it! I can't hear myself think.'

'But I'm right, aren't I?' Rani says, her voice wound down to a low hush. I've never heard her so calm. So resigned.

My mother whispers something under her breath. I can't make it out.

Finding myself in the kitchen, I crouch down and peer through the hatch, my heart pounding out of my chest. My mother looks hysterical, clutching a hunting rifle close to her chest, while Gerald paces in circles around her, like he has no idea what to do next. And behind them sits Rani, tied to a wooden chair in the middle of the room.

My body trembles as I stare at her, willing her to notice me. Her lips are blue. Her eyes frantic. She's about to give up.

'Who died, Luella?' she pushes, struggling to breathe. 'Tell me.'

'Natalie! It was Natalie who died!' Luella screams. 'My baby. My precious baby.'

I watch, frozen, as she falls to the floor, gripping the rifle tightly in her hands. Her words ring in my ears. *It was Natalie who died*.

I'm Natalie.

Suddenly she sits up again, wiping the moisture from her face. I watch her smooth down her dress and get slowly to her feet, her face emotionless. 'You. You did this. You unleashed this. And now you have to pay.' She raises the gun, pointing it straight at Rani's head, and closes her eyes.

'Luella. Please. You don't have to …'

An invisible force propels me out of the kitchen, and I run as fast as I can towards them.

BANG.

I feel pain. Scorching pain. I hear Rani crying out, my mother's ear-piercing screams as she realises what she has done. Then it all comes flooding back. So clearly that it feels like I'm there in our bedroom. By her side.

And as the life drains out of me, I see it.

The moment Natalie took her final breath.

Six months later

I push open the front door and wander down the bright, airy hallway. It looks the same, but different. They've repainted all the walls a warm shade of cream, dressed the rooms to make it look like a young family live here. I see a luxurious doll's house in the corner. The kind that Lydia and Leela can only dream of owning. But the coldness remains, like it'll always be winter here.

Hearing my footsteps enter the kitchen, he turns. 'Hello! Lovely to meet … Oh, it's you. Mrs Rhodes, isn't it? Serena. You look … different.' Shit. I should have known it would be Paul managing the open house. He probably couldn't believe his luck, another 2.5 per cent commission in less than a year. Flicking through the iPad in his hands, he scratches his head. 'But I don't think you're on the list. Unless there's been a mistake. I can call the office if you like?'

'No,' I say quickly. 'I was just passing. Visiting a friend in the area and noticed that the house was back on the market … so soon?'

He nods, saying nothing, like he wants me to work for it. 'So …' he mumbles eventually, looking over my head, 'did you find somewhere else? I never did hear back from you.'

'Yes. Sorry.' His eyes flit to my left hand, searching for my sparkly wedding band. I catch them in the act, watching his pale cheeks flush pink. 'It's been a difficult few months,'

I explain. He nods, pressing his lips tightly together. 'So, the previous owners? Why are they moving?'

He observes me suspiciously before suddenly changing tactics and smiling. I remember that Cheshire-cat grin. 'You're a tough nut to crack, Mrs Rhodes. One day I'll sell you a house, I know it!' He lowers his voice. 'Between me and you, this is all fake. Our interior designers dressed it up for the open house. The owners moved out months ago. They were newly weds, seemed so in love. But looks can be deceptive, can't they?'

I nod, feeling self-conscious.

'I'm just dealing with the husband now, though. His wife was in hospital for months. You must have seen the case in the news. It was everywhere. Her mum and stepfather were arrested for trying to kill her!' His eyes widen with glee.

I suppress the urge to punch his smug, pasty face.

'Are you okay?' he asks.

'Yes, sorry. I wonder … would you mind if I looked around one last time?'

'Going somewhere?' He smirks.

'Yes, actually. We're emigrating to Australia,' I reply, brushing past him.

Wandering around the kitchen, I stroke my fingertips over the smooth, shiny surfaces. Gaze out into the garden from the spot where Natalie fainted. I'm staring at beauty. So much beauty. Yet I feel nothing.

He follows close behind me. 'Oh,' he says, forehead crinkling.

'My sister lives in Sydney, so we'll have help with the girls …' I stop myself.

'You have children? You didn't mention them before.'

'Didn't I? Look, I must go. So much packing to do!'

I head back down the hall, past the living room. The scene of the crime. I shudder, thinking of what Natalie must have gone through. Then, pausing at the front door, I turn my head. 'Thanks for this. I appreciate it. And by the way, my name isn't Serena. It's Rani. Rani Malhotra.' And I hurry out before he can follow me, almost colliding with a glamorous couple going in to view the house.

I can't bear to look at them.

When I'm a safe distance away, I glance at my phone. Five hours until we leave for the airport. Five hours until our adventure begins. I feel a burst of pure childish joy, followed by intense loss. I'm ready to leave. I'm ready to start again and give our family the future we deserve, but I know that a part of me will always remain here. With her. Wondering what happened, and if I should have looked harder for her.

Pulling my keys out of my coat pocket, I hear footsteps behind me and flinch, wondering if it's Paul come to demand answers. I turn swiftly. But it's not Paul. It's just someone out for a jog. A beanie hat covering their head, strands of reddish-brown hair escaping, and a woolly scarf around their neck and face to retain the heat. I don't recognise them. But something about them seems familiar.

I step out of the way to let them pass, but I'm not quick enough and our bodies brush up against each other, just for a second, before the jogger accelerates away. I notice something fall to the ground. It looks like an envelope. 'Wait!' I cry. 'I think you've dropped something.' But they're gone.

I bend down to pick it up, thinking it could be important. And my heart leaps as I see what is written on the front. *Serena*.

Suddenly I feel light-headed, my vision blurring. I stagger towards the steps to our front door and collapse onto them, the envelope heavy in my hands. My fingers shake as I break the seal and take out the piece of paper inside, unfolding it in my lap, flattening the creases with my knuckles so I can make out the contents.

It's a chilly autumn day, but I don't care. I cannot move until I have read every single word.

Serena, it's Niaomi. It feels weird seeing it written down like that. Niaomi. Weird, but at the same time more real than I've ever been. I don't really know where to begin, but I guess the most obvious place is with you, Rani. Thank you. Although thank you doesn't really cut it, does it? I still can't believe what you did, how you put yourself in danger for me. It's why I had to write you this letter before you left, so you understand that my disappearance is nothing to do with you. With us.

I have to start again, put it all behind me. To survive. You taught me that. Survival. That even when you've reached rock bottom, it's still possible to find a reason to live, a reason to keep going. But it's ironic, isn't it? How the closest person to me, the only person who will ever know the real me, can never see me again. It's better that way, Rani, I promise you. For both of us. You deserve a fresh start too, with Joel and your beautiful family. So please don't look for me, because you won't find me, and don't be sad. I don't deserve it.

You see, when I was lying in that hospital bed, I had nothing to do but reflect on the past. Every painful memory.

The many years of abuse. And I remember the night that Natalie died. I remember climbing into the cottage through the bedroom window. Seeing Luella's empty medicine bottle on Natalie's bed, and the remains of crushed white pills all over the bedside table. I remember hearing her gasping for breath, crying out for me to save her. *I don't want to die*, she said. *I … I just wanted her to stop … to leave me alone. I don't want to be perfect any more.* But I did nothing. I just sat there calmly, watching the life drain from her body.

I hated Natalie. To the outside world, she was pure and innocent, adored by everyone she met. But behind closed doors, she was a monster. She heard my mother's evil accusations, she saw the neglect, the brutality, but she did nothing. Worse than nothing. She enjoyed it. She grew stronger because of it, like the abuse was her superpower. So in that moment, I could see it all so clearly. This was my chance to save myself from a lifetime of abuse, and with Natalie gone, maybe my mother would finally love me in the way she had loved my sister. Her golden child.

If only I'd known then what it really meant to be loved by her. I bet you're wondering how she did it, how I became Natalie? Well, the details are a little hazy. But I remember how easy it was to believe in the story that she fed me, to be who she wanted me to be.

Natalie. An only child. My mother is my whole world. I don't need anyone else.

You see, while Luella needed Natalie, I needed to survive. And as Natalie, the world shone brighter, the possibilities seemed endless. I was adored and desired instead of abused and pitied. Then when Dr Baldwin came along, with his cocktail of drugs and psycho bullshit, every essence of Niaomi began to disappear, until I could no longer tell the difference between make-believe and reality.

So that's it. Everything. The whole truth. Now go live your life, my beautiful friend. Don't worry about Charles and Dr Baldwin. They'll get what's coming to them, I can promise you that. And don't ever worry about me. I'll be fine. Now that I know who I am. Now that I am finally free.

Yours,

Niaomi x

I reach the last word, gasping for breath; then, pushing the letter into my coat pocket, I jump to my feet, open the front door and sprint up the stairs to our top-floor flat. Joel is outside, arranging our suitcases. He turns to face me, and I dive into his arms, sobbing.

'Rani, what's wrong?' But he doesn't ask again, because he knows. He knows me.

I let him hold me for a few moments, comforted by the soft contours of his body, his natural warmth. Then I pull away and head down the empty hallway into the bathroom. I take the letter from my pocket, tearing it into hundreds of tiny pieces, until they look like flakes of confetti. Teardrops still cling to my lashes. Tears for her, for us and everything we could have been. Emitting a deep, hollow exhale, I gather together the fragments and drop them into the toilet bowl, pressing the flush button and watching them drown in a torrent of foamy water.

Thinking only of *her*. Natalie, Niaomi, or whoever she is now. Disappearing out of my life for ever.

Acknowledgements

Reader, you should know that I've failed at the task I rather naively set myself – to write my first ever set of acknowledgements with dry eyes. Let's just say, that if you were reading this in real time, there would be faded black splotches all over this page in place of words.

Now, where to begin! Well, of course, with the people without whom there would be no novel, who fell in love with Rani and Natalie's story from the very first page. First and foremost, my incredible agent Camilla Bolton. I don't have the words (funny that, being a writer) to describe how much I treasure you. From our very first meeting when you handed me six pages (double-sided) of brilliant notes on my novel with no guarantee of whether I would sign with you, I knew that I had won the agent lottery. Thank you for your unfailing faith in me, your words of wisdom, your astounding attention to detail and your tough love. Thank you for everything! And Jade Kavanagh, for your brilliant ideas and for scooping me out of Camilla's never-ending slush pile – it all began with you. Thanks also to the wider team at Darley Anderson. I may not have had the pleasure of meeting you all, but I have felt your support every step of the way.

A special thank you to my amazing team at Hodder! My incredible former editor, Sara Nisha Adams, you deserve a whole acknowledgements page of your own for the way you have transformed *Her* and my writing with your guidance and support. You are the editing Queen, and I'm so sad that we won't be working together anymore. My vibrant new editor, Lily Cooper, thank you for taking a chance on me, your enthusiasm for *Her* and for championing me through to publication and beyond! To Will Speed for designing the cover of my dreams, Bea Fitzgerald, my desk editor, Purvi Gadia, Ruchi Bhargava, my copy-editor, Jane Selley and my proofreader, Tara O'Sullivan, for all their brilliant editorial work, and to Katy Blott and Alainna Georgiou for their relentless support with marketing and publicity work. Thank you all for everything you have done for me and *Her* – I am beyond grateful.

My (super) early readers, you absolute gems. Dearest Georgina, who has read every iteration of *Her* from its amateur draft on the Curtis Brown Creative novel writing course. Thank you with all my heart for your faith in me and for being a pro bono extension of my editorial team! My sister Maya, my best friend Abi and my cousin Seema – your sheer elation (and surprise – let's be honest) upon reading what started off as a little lockdown project completely blew me away.

The wider writing community – writers, book bloggers, readers and other industry people. You have shown me such kindness, comradery and kinship ever since I dared to join Twitter in 2020. Social media can be a brutal place, but my little corner of the internet is only filled with joy. I would like to especially thank the pals who have shared their wisdom, listened to my relentless in-person/voice-note rants and made this somewhat-surreal-yet-challenging journey a million times more bearable – Liv (LV Matthews), Rebecca Ryan, Danielle

Owen-Jones, Stephanie Sowden, Sarah (SV Leonard), Lizzy Barber, Sally-Anne Martyn, Rebecca Lewis, Caroline Khoury, Paula Johnson, Amita Parikh, Jennie Godfrey and Sophie Flynn. Thank you also to super lovely writer pals, Neema Shah, Heather Darwent, Nicole Kennedy, Hannah King, Sarah Bonner, Sarah Clarke, Ronali Collings, Sophia Spiers, Emily Freud, Awais Khan, Helen Cooper, Vikki Patis and everyone from my amazing debut 23 group.

To the finest best friends a girl could ask for – Abi, Christine, Hetal, Karuna, Emma, Katie, Rami, Muds and Sophie – you've all saved me once or twice over the years and I'll always be grateful for our friendship.

Thank you to my wonderful family. My husband, Jon, the love of my life in every universe. You are a constant inspiration. You are home. My father, Raj – life hasn't always been kind to us, but we've come out the other side stronger than ever. Thank you for everything you have given me. Because of you, my life feels limitless. My (soul) sister Maya – the person without whom I would not have made it into adulthood, who stood by my side through tunnels of darkness. My brother-in-law Stevie for being a stable presence, offering up your very handy hands and completing our family. My furry children – Motsi, Jackson, Indie and Ava – your unconditional love is everything, even if it sometimes must be encouraged with treats!

Last, but always, always first, thank you to my darling mama, Veena, who this book is dedicated to. When you died, I lost my way. I was only young, and found myself on a path that felt wrong, chasing a dream that was not mine to chase, a dream that I thought you wanted for me. It turns out that no amount of money, prestige or 'success' could have made me happy. I think you knew that, though. I think that's what you tried to teach me in the short time we had together. Those weekly trips to the library, leaving with books piled high over my head, were some of the happiest moments of my life. I think you knew who I was before I even knew myself. Mama, you will never read this, but I hope you knew that you were and will always be my greatest inspiration.

And finally, you, the reader. If you have purchased this book, or picked it up in a library, THANK YOU. I hope you enjoyed it. Because of you, I can continue to do what I love.

Mira xx